THE
Christmas
TROLLEY

MARTA MAHONEY

Dedication

This book is dedicated to my son, John, who believes in
following your dreams.
And to my fellow author Diana Deverell, whose advice and encour-
agement helped me every step of the way.

With special thanks to John Carroll, Susan Carroll, Ann Grant,
Shannon O'Toole, Sarah Tauber, and Michelle Tuchman.

CHAPTER 1

October 12

"THE BOTTOM LINE IS ONE HUNDRED THOUSAND dollars."

Annie Mulvaney looked at each of her five board members in turn. The three of them who were physically present stared at her with open mouths. The two who were disembodied heads on laptops, attending via Skype, were still waiting for the transmission. A moment later, their mouths dropped open, too. Annie could see the shock on all five faces. She'd felt that way herself earlier that morning, when she'd looked at her three estimates.

It was mid-morning, and they were meeting in the conference room of the Macklin House, a historic Victorian mansion in the small town of Macklin, California. Six months ago, Annie had been hired as the executive director of the Macklin House Trust. It had been a major step up for a twenty-eight-year-old with a master's in arts management and a few years' experience as a junior curator at a small museum in

Ohio. She'd expected problems—any new job had them. But not this gaping hole in her budget. A big, red, one hundred thousand dollar hole. The end of the historic Macklin House, and the end of her dreams. Natalie Preston, the board's president, spoke first. Natalie was in her forties, dressed nicely but not expensively in tailored black slacks and a pink sweater. "It's one hundred thousand dollars to do—what?" Natalie was also the president of the Macklin Women's Club and the wife of Brent Preston, the mayor. They owned a car dealership, and by Macklin standards, were the richest people in town. In spite of that, Natalie and Brent were still down-to-earth people. Annie knew she'd need Natalie's support if they were ever going to find a way out of this crisis.

"The county building department did their annual inspection last month," Annie explained. "Their report says we need to fix all our deferred maintenance. I wasn't here last year, and I guess the inspectors used to overlook things if they weren't immediately life-threatening. But ever since that earthquake in January, they've become really strict." The board members nodded. The earthquake hadn't caused any damage in Macklin, but several buildings had collapsed in a nearby town.

"The Macklin House isn't up to code," Annie continued. "Even for a historic building. We've got dry rot everywhere. Mold in the bathrooms. Outdated wiring. Our ADA compliance is out of date. If we can't fix this, they're going to pull our operating permit. We'll have to close."

Annie might be young, but she was calm and confident at board meetings. No one would have suspected how dismayed she felt. Today, she'd worn her go-to board meeting outfit, gray pants with a white blouse and a dark blue jacket. She'd draped a floral silk scarf that picked up the jacket's color around her neck. With her blue eyes and light brown hair worn just below shoulder length, the effect was polished but not too formal. Her personal style ran more to jeans, hand-knit sweaters, and vintage jewelry. But if you had to deliver bad news, you wanted to look as professional as possible.

She handed out copies of the building department's notice and her three contractors' estimates. "I just emailed these to you," she told her

Skype attendees, holding up the papers. "Let me know when you've received them."

Sophie Macklin, one of the board members conferencing in remotely, said, "My great-great-great-great-grandfather Philip Macklin would never believe this. When he set up the trust and left the house to the city, it was supposed to go on forever." Sophie was the Macklin family's last surviving heir and had taken her trust fund and moved to Paris years ago. Annie knew Sophie was at least sixty, but she could have passed for someone ten years younger. She had perfectly coiffed silver-gray hair, and what they could see of her outfit on the screen was impeccably stylish.

Brad Lawrence, the other remote attendee, waved his hand onscreen. "If Philip hadn't insisted on putting his railroad line along the river instead of on the west side of town where it belonged, we'd have plenty of money. The town would have made a fortune when they built the highway." Brad was a history professor at UC Davis who specialized in the Victorian period, and he was taking a sabbatical year in England. Brad looked professorial in longish gray hair and black-rimmed glasses. Annie caught a glimpse of a book-lined study with mullioned windows behind him.

There was a three-second pause and then Sophie fired back. "And how was he supposed to know that? The state built the highway in 1956. He was *dead*."

Natalie picked up her gavel and banged it on the table. "Let's keep to the subject."

"Yes, please," said Allan Tolbert, the fourth board member. Allan was the pastor of the local Presbyterian Church. Today, he was wearing a blue dress shirt and navy sport jacket. He didn't know a lot about Victorian homes, but he was adept at keeping all the board members speaking to each other. Ron DeMarco, the last board member, said nothing but was carefully reading the estimates. He ran a real estate office in town and had a good idea of what building repairs cost. Ron had rolled up the sleeves of his striped shirt and loosened his polka-dotted tie in an attempt to be more comfortable. October was still warm in Macklin.

All of the board members were committed to the Macklin House, but from their aghast expressions, none of them had any idea of where to find one hundred thousand dollars. They turned their attention back to Annie.

"I had our attorney look into whether we could take the money from our endowment fund," Annie said. "Unfortunately, we can't. The rules of Philip Macklin's trust and the endowment bequest are really specific. We can only use the interest to cover operating costs. We can't touch the principal. And as you know, with interest rates what they are, we're barely making enough to cover our regular expenses."

"This is really bad news," said Ron. "We knew the place needed repairs but nothing like this."

"I know," said Annie. "I got three bids, and one hundred thousand dollars is the best one. It's from Ivan Renfro." The board members nodded. Ivan was a well-respected local contractor.

"The highest bid is almost two hundred thousand," Annie continued. All the board members groaned.

"I can't believe we'd have to close the Macklin House!" exclaimed Natalie.

"Annie, what do you recommend?" Allan asked.

"We're going to need a fund-raising campaign," Annie said. "Let's all think of ideas and present them at next month's board meeting. I'll work on a press release. We don't want someone to get hold of the building department's report and put it out before we do."

"I'll make some calls," said Natalie. "Even a few donations would help. I could put some flyers in our waiting room. You know, we've put in a refrigerator where our customers can help themselves to water and juice." The others listened amiably to this plug for the Prestons' car dealership. Natalie managed to throw at least one into every board meeting.

"Maybe there are some grants we could apply for," suggested Ron. "The state must have some money. I can look into that. But it's going to be a long shot."

He turned to Allan. "Are you going to pray?" They weren't exactly enemies, but Ron thought Allan lacked financial sense. Allan always graciously avoided mentioning that the church's budget was larger than Ron's business.

"It can't hurt," Allan replied. "But we'd probably have better luck with a social-media campaign. I'll talk to my niece. She's designed some websites. She could help us with one of those GoFundMe campaigns."

"Sophie? Brad?" Annie asked.

They were continuing their argument. "You think Philip was this enlightened philanthropist—" Brad complained. Annie waited for the Skype pause.

"You just want to tear down his reputation so you can write another book," Sophie countered.

Natalie banged her gavel. "Do either of you have any fund-raising ideas?"

"Oh. Not yet," Sophie answered.

"I'm in London," said Brad. "I can't do anything."

"You can think, can't you?" countered Sophie.

Natalie banged her gavel again. "The meeting is adjourned."

"Thanks, everyone," said Annie. "I'm sorry I had to deliver such bad news." She shook hands with Natalie, Allan, and Brad, and let them out the front door of the Macklin House. She gazed wistfully around the entrance lobby, which had been cobbled together from several smaller rooms when the stately mansion had been turned into a museum. Tears came to her eyes as she thought about having to close the Macklin House. And having to give up her dream job.

What Annie lacked in executive director experience, she made up for in desire. A native of Macklin, she passionately loved the Macklin House. She loved the imposing Victorian architecture, the turreted tower on the roof, the wraparound porch that supported a balcony in front. She could spend hours admiring the carved oak front door, with its curved fanlight above and stained glass side panels showing peacocks in full plumage. She loved the worn Oriental carpets, the fireplace screens and writing tables, the bell system in the kitchen that had once summoned the servants.

She'd dreamed of restoring the house to its original Victorian splendor, creating exhibits about the history of Macklin, turning the Macklin House into a center for community activities. She stared again at Ivan's estimate. The bottom line was still one hundred thousand dollars.

And Macklin was not a town where you could easily find one hundred thousand dollars. It was a small town in the middle of California, and the fact that it was in the middle of the state was the only thing anyone ever remembered about it. Attracted by cheap land and the river that ran through the south side of town, Philip Macklin had arrived in 1854 with three bags of gold. He proceeded to make his fortune in banking, real estate, and a small railroad. He'd laid out the street plan for the town center and built most of the historic civic buildings, including the Macklin House. In return, the town was renamed for him in 1915.

Try as he might, Philip had never been able to turn Macklin into a big city, or even a mid-sized city. It remained a small town too far from the mountains on one side, or the big cities of the coast on the other. But in Philip Macklin's day, it had been a thriving place. It had the railroad, a small steel mill, and a doorknob factory. Farms and orchards had surrounded the little town. Over the years, the factories had closed down, and farming was no longer profitable. Now, there were a lot of boarded-up storefronts and not many jobs. It was a nice place to live, but there weren't a lot of ways to make a living.

Annie suddenly realized that she was hungry. It was lunchtime, and she'd skipped breakfast while preparing for the board meeting. She waved at Danielle, the receptionist.

"I'm going to get some lunch," she explained, and stepped out onto the wide porch that surrounded the house. The Macklin House felt like home to her. It had felt like home since her first visit on an eighth grade field trip. Her brief thought of the field trip immediately triggered memories of her classmate, Ben Grover. She still couldn't think about that field trip, or Ben, without churning emotions.

The Macklin House and its grounds took up an entire block on Main Street directly across from the town square, a park-like area with a gazebo. The city hall, the police station, and the fire department occupied First Street, on the west side of the square. The town library and the courthouse were on Second Street, on the east side of the square. (Philip had not exactly been imaginative in naming his streets.) State Street, directly across the square from the Macklin House, was home to a number of shops and restaurants—among them Meyers' Hardware, the Never Too Late charity thrift shop, which was operated by the Macklin Women's Club, and the Macklin Café, one of Annie's favorite restaurants.

A few of the trees bordering the Macklin House had golden leaves, but most were the eternal green of Macklin's mild climate. Annie took in the fall flowers bordering the house, as she headed for a small cottage toward the rear of the grounds. In years past, it had been the living quarters for the head gardener. Now the tiny house came rent-free as a supplement to the executive director's salary. It had a sitting room, a small kitchen, one bedroom, and one bathroom. It would never have worked for a family, but it was perfect for Annie. She had reupholstered the comfortable sofa and chair in the sitting room, made curtains, and covered her bed with a vintage quilt (a souvenir of her days in Ohio). She'd refinished a table and four chairs she'd discovered at an estate sale on a nearby farm. She was hoping to find a set of antique china, but for the moment was making do with some plain white dishes she'd bought at the thrift shop.

As much as she loved her job, Annie was finding her life in Macklin a little lonely. She had to admit to herself that one reason she'd spent so much time redecorating her cottage was because she hadn't found a love interest in Macklin yet. She'd gone on a few dates since coming back to town, but there hadn't been any chemistry. Once you left college, it was hard to meet people.

She dropped the three estimates on her kitchen table. *I wish I had someone to talk to about this,* she thought. Her older sister Amber and her brother-in-law Tom were teachers in Palm Springs. A few years ago, their parents had happily moved into a retirement community nearby, so they could babysit their two grandchildren. They were close enough to visit on holidays and special occasions, but it wasn't the same as having your family in the same town. Or a serious boyfriend, who would listen to your problems and console you. *Although I may not be here much longer myself,* Annie thought.

Pushing aside these depressing thoughts, she fixed herself a sandwich and a glass of iced tea. She sat down with her laptop and the Macklin *Morning News,* which she never seemed to get around to reading until later in the day. Finally, looking for a distraction from the Macklin House's repairs, she clicked on eBay and started browsing through "antiques and collectibles." Annie loved to check out antique shops and yard sales, in person or online. She was scrolling idly through the listings when the headline on one ad stopped her cold.

"Need a way to make some money?" it asked in eighteen-point type. "Try a trolley!"

The photos showed a motorized trolley car with open-air wooden bench seats. The roof looked watertight and displayed fancy scrollwork on either side. The body of the trolley was decorated with large silver stars. The side walls were about waist-high and had a heavy metal railing along the top, to keep people from falling out.

"Straight from Hollywood! Antique trolley car used for tours of the Homes of the Stars. Street legal, GPS, new tires, engine has only fifty thousand miles. Great opportunity for tours, fairs, school events. Owners retiring, must sell, must sell, must sell! Only three thousand dollars!" There were no offers as yet.

A trolley, thought Annie, looking up from her computer screen. What could we do with a trolley? She glanced at the Macklin *Morning News,* lying open to an ad for Meyers' Hardware. "Holiday lights in stock now!" it proclaimed.

"A Christmas trolley!" Annie exclaimed. "A trolley tour of Christmas lights!"

Annie had been so busy since she returned to Macklin that she'd forgotten about Macklin's holiday lights. The citizens of Macklin may have lacked many things, but (according to the weather team at the local TV station), they had three hundred and fifty days a year of sunshine. And where there's sunshine, there's a solar power company. In 2005, a company called Sunshine Superman had shown up with a plan to take Macklin "off the grid." They promised to provide solar panels to every house in town and hook them up to Macklin's very own electrical plant. Homeowners would get free electricity, and Sunshine Superman would profit by selling the excess power. Things did not quite work out for Sunshine Superman, which went bankrupt in the recession of 2008. But the Macklin city council, with rare foresight, was able to buy the power plant at a big discount, giving the town some much-needed income and keeping electricity virtually free.

Since then, decorating with Christmas lights had become a Macklin tradition. Each year, the lights grew bigger and better. Seeing Meyers' ad, Annie remembered visits home from college. Her family would drive around town for hours, looking at the lights and ending up at the Macklin Café for hot chocolate. But there was no way to see the lights without driving in a car, and Macklin's streets weren't designed for a lot of traffic.

A trolley tour of Christmas lights to benefit the Macklin House! It was scenic. It was memorable. It was fun. And there was nothing like it in Macklin. Annie knew she'd found her fund-raiser.

CHAPTER 2

October 14

BEN GROVER SHIFTED IN THE ERGONOMIC CHAIR AT HIS workstation, gazing out the skyscraper window at San Francisco Bay. He was wearing a gray polo shirt with the logo of his employer, Jupiter Computer, some old jeans, and tennis shoes. Like many computer geeks, he looked a little scruffy. His dark brown hair could have used a trim, and his three-day growth of beard was sliding rapidly down the scale from fashionable to disreputable. Ben was a project leader at Jupiter, a firm that designed business software systems, and he'd been too busy the past few weeks to think about a haircut. After months of work, he'd just brought in a new client, Denton Consulting. Denton had offices all over the world, and Jupiter's software would streamline their operations. The contract was being finalized that week. Tonight, he planned to celebrate.

Ben continued fiddling with his chair. No one below the rank of vice president at Jupiter had an office, much less a cubicle. Employees were issued a laptop, and they plugged into the first open workstation they found when they came in. This assumed, of course, that they had gone home in the first place. Ben had become accustomed to adjusting a different chair every morning, along with carting his pens and paper clips home in his backpack every night.

He appeared to be admiring the view, but he was actually making plans for the evening. Should he try the new sushi restaurant that had a five-star rating on Yelp? Should he head to his neighborhood pub to meet up with some fellow tech workers? And then drop into a club for some music? What he *really* felt like doing was falling asleep in front of the TV. He couldn't remember when he'd last gone home before nine p.m. All his twelve-hour days had paid off, though. Denton was a major new client.

Ben glanced at his watch. He'd passed Ed Waters, Jupiter's sales director, in the hallway that morning. Ed was one of the few Black sales executives Ben had met in tech, and he was Ben's boss. Ben admired Ed's dedication to Jupiter and his strong work ethic. Ed had the rare ability to look at a software program and instantly tell which features would be truly valuable to their customers, a knack which had helped Ben immeasurably with Denton.

Ed had nodded at him. "Ben," he'd said, "I'd like to see you in my office at ten-thirty." That could only mean one thing. A promotion to vice president as a reward for his work on Denton. And this would come with a large raise. Ben visualized himself on a beach in Bali.

If my mom and dad could see me now, Ben thought. He had grown up in Macklin, always the smartest kid in the class except for Annie Mulvaney. *If only Annie could see me now*, he thought. He pushed aside his thoughts of Annie, and went on daydreaming about his promotion. When he'd left Macklin after high school with a scholarship to study computer engineering, he had never looked back. He had rarely *been* back. His father had died when he was in college, and his mother had passed away from cancer two years ago, leaving Ben the family home and their 1992 Dodge minivan. He'd tried sporadically to sell the house since then, but the real estate market in Macklin was slow, especially for a sixty-year-old house that needed a lot of work.

Ben checked his phone again. It was almost ten-thirty. Time to meet Ed. He went down the hall to Ed's office, which actually had a door and real chairs. Ed was staring at some spreadsheets on his desk, an unreadable expression on his face. Unlike most of the workers at Jupiter, Ed wore a jacket and a tie. He thought middle managers should look like middle managers, not teenagers in sweatshirts. He looked up as Ben rapped on the open door.

"Come on in," Ed said. "Close the door, would you?" Ben was surprised to see Sallie Harrison, the human resources director, sitting in Ed's office. *She must be here with some paperwork for my promotion,* he thought.

Ed sighed, glanced briefly at his spreadsheets again, and looked up at Ben. "Ben, I'm sorry to have to tell you this. Your position has been eliminated."

Ben was stunned. For a moment, he couldn't reply. "My position has been eliminated? I'm being laid off?"

"I'm afraid so. You did good work on Denton, but I talked with them yesterday. They don't want to finalize anything until the middle of next year. In the meantime, several other contracts are expiring, and the clients don't plan to renew." Ed stared at his spreadsheet again, then looked up at Ben. "We ran the numbers and we have to right-size our staff."

"Denton told me they wanted to sign the contract now," Ben answered. "I talked to them yesterday."

"You've been working with the operations manager," Ed said. "The CFO has the final say. And he says not until mid-year."

"You'll need to sign these termination papers," Sallie interjected smoothly.

"But I've been here for five years," Ben stammered. "I oversee twelve accounts. The clients like me. And Denton will be one of Jupiter's largest contracts."

"You'll have two weeks' severance pay," Sally added, as if she hadn't heard anything he said. "But of course, we can't release the check to you until you've signed everything."

"Two weeks?" said Ben, fighting panic. His rent was astronomical, even for San Francisco. He had student loans, balances on four credit cards, and a running bar bill at the pub down the street from his apartment building. He had about a thousand dollars in savings, but he owed his old college roommate Ryan, who worked at a venture capital fund, two hundred and fifty dollars of that from a spur-of-the-moment trip to Cabo San Lucas. He stared in horror at the stack of papers awaiting his signature.

He sat up straight in the chair and looked Ed in the eye. "I think I deserve at least one month of severance," he said. "Given my responsibilities here and the fact that I brought in Denton."

Ed smiled wryly. "You always were a good negotiator, but no. You're one of ten people we're having to let go. Frankly, you're lucky we're giving you two weeks." Ed hesitated. "Ben," he said, "this isn't personal. You've been a great employee. You're the kind of person we like to have on our team. I'll be glad to give you a reference. It's just—a numbers decision."

Don't burn any bridges, thought Ben. *Be professional. Be calm. You can scream later.*

"Thank you for my opportunities here," he said. "It was a good experience for me." He picked up a pen from the desk and began signing.

It was over in fifteen minutes. He turned in his company laptop and his ID badge. He didn't have a desk, so he had nothing to pack up. A security guard escorted him down to the ground floor.

Out on the street, Ben was too shocked to think. It was almost lunchtime, and people were starting to fill up the sidewalks, heading out for a quick meal or a walk down to the bay. Ben smelled pizza and Chinese takeout, but he realized he'd have to watch his budget. For the first time in his life, he felt alone and out of place. What was he going to do?

He headed slowly back to his apartment. Shutting the door behind him, he threw his backpack on the floor and sat down on the couch. He'd been proud of finding an apartment he could afford on his own, tiny as it was. The bedroom had been carved out of a walk-in closet, and he could only fit two chairs at his kitchen table. He had just enough space for some souvenirs from his travels, and his growing collection of single malt whiskies. And the apartment cost a fortune.

Ben opened one of the bottles in his collection, and dazedly poured himself a glass of whiskey. He reviewed his options. If he didn't find something within a month—make that three weeks for safety—what then?

CHAPTER 3

October 14

ANNIE WENT BACK TO HER OFFICE AND SCANNED THE budget for the Macklin House, wondering where she could pry out some money to buy the trolley. If there wasn't any extra money for repairs, there wasn't much extra in the budget, period. Annie looked over the budget line by line, trying to figure out something. She checked eBay every few minutes as the afternoon passed. No bids yet.

It was approaching five p.m. when she finally saw it. She had three thousand dollars set aside for an educational program in the spring.

"If we can't keep the Macklin House open," she said aloud, "we won't *be* here in the spring. I need to spend this money now. Desperate times call for desperate measures." It sounded nuts, even as she said it. A Christmas trolley? A tour of Christmas lights? But what did she have to lose?

Annie pulled out her laptop. Before she could change her mind, she typed in an offer of two thousand, five hundred dollars. "Come on, Christmas trolley!" she said. "The Macklin House needs you!" It was a nerve-wracking forty-eight hours until bids closed. Annie tried to keep calm by emailing the sellers with various questions. How many passengers could the trolley hold? (Fifty, more or less.) Did it have interior lighting? (Yes, and the sellers would throw in some extra bulbs.) Did it have seat cushions? (No, but those were easy enough to find.)

As the forty-eight hours ticked down, Annie sat in her cottage, trying to distract herself by watching the sunset. She was sure someone else would put in a higher offer. Finally, an email appeared in her inbox: Annie was the owner of the trolley!

"I did it!" she cried. "I bought the trolley!" Annie poured herself a glass of Chardonnay and read the email over and over. She suddenly wished she had someone to share the news. Not her parents or her sister—they'd immediately tell her to abandon the Macklin House and move to Palm Springs. Not the board—she couldn't let them see how unsure she really was about the trolley tours. Someone like—Ben Grover, back in the day, before they'd had their big fight.

That was over a long time ago, Annie told herself, sipping her wine. You bought the trolley! Think about what you need to do next!

The first step was to get the trolley to Macklin. The sellers were a married couple in their fifties, who explained that they were leaving Hollywood and relocating to Portland to start a yoga studio. They offered to tow the trolley to Macklin for free, since they'd be driving north anyway during the last week in October.

Meanwhile, Annie continued to research fund-raisers. Everything she came across seemed to be either too extravagant for Macklin, or too small to do any good. She was trying hard not to pin all her hopes on the trolley, but she knew she'd fallen in love with the idea. She could hardly wait to see it in person.

On October twenty-third, she found the email she'd been waiting for in her in box. "We're on our way!" The sellers, Sam and Julie Feldman, attached a photo of a large truck with a camper shell, pulling the trolley behind it. The trolley looked larger than the truck. It was hard to tell which vehicle was towing which.

The Feldmans had apparently upgraded Annie from "business associate" to "friend" and continued to send updates as they worked their way north. Some were typical travel reports: "Lunch in a beautiful vineyard in Paso Robles!" Some were ominous: "Only made ten miles today!" Some were helpful hints: "Never travel without a case of water!" They seemed in no hurry to get to Portland. Annie was getting impatient.

Finally, at the end of the week, just as Annie was sitting down in her office to go through the day's mail, her inbox pinged. "Just finished an amazing blueberry pancake breakfast. We're on our way to Macklin! Should arrive by noon!" Annie mentally prepared herself for a letdown all morning. It was one thing to order something on line, another thing to see it in person.

Just before noon, she heard the clanging of a trolley bell. Annie crossed her fingers as she rushed outside. She told herself to stay neutral, whatever happened.

But when she saw the trolley sitting in the Macklin House's parking lot, she knew instantly that she'd done the right thing! The trolley was just what she'd imagined. It looked like it had been parked next to the Macklin House all its life. Annie could already see it, decorated for Christmas and filled with happy, excited people.

The Feldmans climbed out of their truck and gazed appreciatively at the Macklin House. Julie and Sam were both wearing leather jackets and flowing scarves. They looked vaguely familiar, as though they might have been actors in some minor sitcom. "We love this trolley," said Julie. "We just hate to give it up. But it's hard to do tours of the homes of the stars any more. Traffic is terrible. And people can look at the homes of the stars on Google Earth. They don't need to take a tour in real life."

Sam showed Annie how to handle the microphone. "We put in a top-quality audio system. You don't want people complaining that they can't hear. The first-aid kit is under the driver's seat. And there's a big turbo diesel engine so it has a lot of power. It'll go up hills real easily."

He glanced around at the flat streets surrounding the Macklin House. "If you *have* any hills."

"We left you a couple of coolers, too," said Julie. "You'll need to give everybody drinks. Maybe not at Christmas time, but if you use it in the summer." They opened a storage compartment on one side, showing Annie two large coolers and a long length of thick chain. "What's that for?" Annie asked.

"Sometimes, it's hard to find a parking spot by the homes of the stars," explained Sam. "The stars are sort of possessive about their driveways." He reached behind the chain and pulled out two posts on rubber mats. Each had a hook at the top. He set them on the ground about forty feet away from each other, draped the chain between them, and slid the last link on either end over the hooks on the posts. An open padlock and a "Reserved Parking" sign hung from the chain, along with about fifty parking tickets. "If we couldn't find parking, we'd just set this up."

"It didn't seem to work," Annie said, pointing to the parking tickets.

"That's why we wanted to sell it to you. Nobody's going to follow up on them way out here," Sam said nonchalantly.

"And these are emergency supplies," Julie added, pointing to a large red leather backpack sitting next to the coolers. Annie unzipped it. The kit looked well-stocked. She saw screwdrivers, wrenches, flares, safety cones, and a crowbar. "It looks like you've thought of everything," she said.

She filled Sam and Julie's coffee mugs for them and gave them directions back to the interstate. "We'll keep you posted on our trip," Julie called as they drove away. "Come see us if you're ever in Portland!"

Annie waved until they were out of sight. Now to examine the trolley up close and personal.

She sat down in the driver's seat, feeling excited and nervous at the same time. She turned the key in the lock, and started to drive it very slowly around the parking lot. Once she got the side mirrors adjusted, it wasn't hard to maneuver. Passenger visibility was good. People would have fun riding in it.

It was just what she'd envisioned. Or, at least, it would be, once she made some repairs. Seen up close, it was definitely well used, even a little shabby. There were a few loose boards in the wooden seats, and the silver stars definitely had to go. But Annie had restored enough antiques to feel confident about taking this on.

I can fix it myself! Annie thought proudly. *Now, all I need to do is to convince the board to go along with my plan!*

CHAPTER 4

November 7

BEN SPRAWLED ON THE PLAID COUCH IN THE FAMILY room in his parents' old house in Macklin. Soda cans and a few empty pizza boxes littered the wooden coffee table. He was alternately dreaming regretfully of what he now thought of as his past life, and thinking gloomily about his future prospects. He'd gotten a haircut, dug out his interview wardrobe, and updated his resume. But two weeks of job searching in San Francisco had produced exactly one lead, and that was a phone interview for the help line at a twenty-four-hour call center. The minute Ben had mentioned his prior employment with Jupiter, the recruiter had pronounced him "overqualified," and hung up. All the tech companies he contacted told him they wouldn't be hiring until after the first of the year, and probably not until the second quarter.

As much as Ben hated to admit it, it had made sense to move back to Macklin temporarily. Unemployment went a lot further in a small town than it did in San Francisco. He'd boxed up everything in his apartment, and returned to Macklin two days ago. He was a little upset that no one seemed particularly sad to see him go. Life in San Francisco moved too fast for deep relationships. His landlady was thrilled. (Now she could raise the rent!) His work colleagues made brief sympathetic comments, and said to email when he landed somewhere. His pub buddies just wanted to know when he was going to settle up. Only his old college roommate, Ryan, tried to be encouraging. "You've been working eighteen-hour days. It'll be a good break for you," Ryan told him. "Keep in touch. Send me a weekly update."

He really didn't want to leave the house, but he was starting to feel hungry, and he was tired of ordering pizza. A trip to the store was inevitable. Sighing, Ben got off the couch and hunted out the keys to the minivan. Backing out of the driveway, he remembered learning to drive in the van, and smiled for the first time all day. He'd hit the mailbox the first time he tried backing up. The minivan still had a small dent in the rear bumper. His parents had left it unrepaired as a reminder to him to drive safely.

In the parking lot at the Supersaver Market strip mall, he noticed that many of the small shops were vacant. Some of his favorites were gone—the video-game rental place, a sandwich shop, the comic book store. The Supersaver Market, however, was going strong. Ben grabbed a cart and made his way through the bakery, the produce section, and household cleaners. He ended up in the pasta aisle, looking for the cheapest thing he could find.

"Benjy Grover!" said an unmistakable voice. "Is that you?"

As always, when he heard that voice, his first thought was, *what have I done now?* He turned around. "Hi, Mrs. Martinez," he said. One of the drawbacks of living in a town as small as Macklin was that you could run into your middle school principal in the grocery store.

"Benjy!" she exclaimed, throwing her arms around him. "Look at you! What are you doing back in town?"

Mrs. Martinez was a little grayer and a little heavier than when Ben had last seen her. She was wearing a Macklin Middle School sweatshirt and pushing a cart optimistically filled with vegetables. She examined

Ben critically. He decided just to come out with the truth. This had always been the best strategy in dealing with her.

"I got laid off," he said. "Nobody's hiring until after the first of the year, so I decided to come home and wait it out."

"Oh, Benjy," she said, hugging him. "You're so bright, you'll find something soon. It's good to have you back. And guess who else is here in Macklin! Your adorable little girlfriend, Annie Mulvaney."

Ben started to say, "She wasn't my girlfriend," but stopped himself just in time. Mrs. Martinez didn't need to know about what had happened between him and Annie.

"Annie's the executive director of the Macklin House now," Mrs. Martinez continued. "She's doing a great job, too. She has so many ideas for revitalizing that old mansion. Believe me, this town needs someone with that kind of energy and vision. You should stop in at the Macklin House and say hello."

"I should do that," Ben agreed. In his heart, he knew he'd never do it. He was glad Annie had a job she loved. But he couldn't bear for her to see him at this low point, jobless and practically broke.

"And come over to the school and visit us," she added. "I'd love to have you talk to our eighth graders. Maybe after winter break?"

No student who passed through Macklin Middle School regarded a suggestion from Mrs. Martinez as anything less than a command. Ben was no exception. He nodded. "I'll do that," he promised. "It's good to see you, Mrs. Martinez."

"Stay in touch, Benjy," she said, as she headed off to the deli counter. "We've missed you here in Macklin."

Ben felt a lump in his throat. It was nice to know that *someone* missed him.

CHAPTER 5

November 9

ONCE AGAIN, ANNIE SAT AT THE HEAD OF THE LONG mahogany Victorian table in the Macklin House's conference room, ready to meet her board. To put them in the holiday spirit, she'd decorated the room with poinsettias and baked some cinnamon cookies. She'd discarded her formal business wardrobe for some fashionable jeans and one of her many Christmas sweaters. This one had a green background with Santa and Mrs. Claus in front of an igloo on the back. Annie had added a necklace of candy canes. She figured you could never have too much Christmas décor when you were trying to sell your board on a Christmas trolley tour.

Natalie rapped her gavel. Neither Sophie nor Brad had been available, so only Natalie, Ron, and Allan were present. Allan was writing a memo titled "Thanksgiving Food Drive" on a legal-sized yellow notepad, while Ron was swiping through photos of an older but well-kept farmhouse on his iPad. Both of them flipped to blank pages as Natalie called the meeting to order. "Do you have some ideas for us, Annie?" "I do," Annie answered. "But first, let's talk about what the three of you came up with."

Ron hit a key on his iPad and consulted a page of notes. "I spoke to Gabrielle Gordon, our state senator. The good news is there are a couple of programs in Sacramento for historic preservation. The bad news is they've already committed all their funding for the next five years. I told you this was going to be a long shot."

"Thanks, Ron," said Natalie. "I guess we can't count on any help there. I found ten members of the Macklin Women's Club who've agreed to donate one thousand dollars each to the Macklin House. Preston Automotive will donate five thousand dollars. That's fifteen thousand in pledges. And the Women's Club will donate one week's worth of sales from the Never Too Late thrift store. That's probably another two thousand." Natalie looked distressed. "We just aren't the kind of town where a lot of people can afford to donate thousands of dollars."

"Natalie, that's impressive!" Annie exclaimed. "Seventeen thousand dollars is a great start. Allan?"

"My niece is going to set up a GoFundMe account and a Facebook page. She says this is how you reach people now. They should be ready next week," He sighed. "I mentioned the Macklin House in my sermon last Sunday, too. People came up afterward and asked what they could do. We've got a lot of support from the community. Unfortunately, this isn't the kind of thing that the church could help directly."

"That's great!" Annie said enthusiastically. "It's nice to know that people are behind us."

"Now, what are your ideas, Annie?" Natalie asked. "And why do we have a trolley car out in the parking lot?"

"And where did it come from?" asked Ron.

"That's my idea!" Annie said happily. "We're going to have a fundraiser. You know how everyone loves the Macklin holiday lights. The trolley in the parking lot is the key. We'll have trolley tours of the lights during December to benefit the Macklin House!"

THE CHRISTMAS TROLLEY

Natalie nodded enthusiastically. "I went on a trolley tour in San Francisco once!" she said. "It was a lot of fun. You got to see all the sights and you didn't have to drive. Of course, people in Macklin don't mind driving," she added. "Especially if they've got one of the new models with all the latest electronics. They're absolutely amazing! They practically drive themselves!"

"You're right," Annie assured Natalie. "People in Macklin love to drive down the street and see the lights. But if they're riding the trolley, they can sit back and really take in the lights. They'll be able to see all the details. And it could be like a party. Invite your friends and buy a bunch of tickets."

Allan said, "How often will the tours run?" Annie noted the word "will." *I've got one of them on my side*, she thought.

"Two tours a night," she answered. "One at six-thirty p.m. and the second one at eight o'clock. The tour should last about an hour, with a couple of photo stops along the way. We'll have tours on Tuesday through Saturday."

"We need more details. How is this going to work?" asked Ron. "You'll collect the tickets and then you'll drive them around?"

"It's going to be much bigger than that!" Annie assured him. She handed each of them a packet of papers. The top sheet was a map of the town square.

Pointing at the map, she explained, "I want to put the trolley stop, where everybody boards and exits, here on Main Street. It'll be right at the end of the walkway leading up to the Macklin House. I think we need a staging area where we set up some folding chairs for people waiting to board. And we'll want entertainment to keep the crowd occupied. We'll put a small stage over here on the lawn. I'm sure we can find plenty of people who would love to sing or play the guitar or whatever. Someone could lead Christmas carols. That type of thing." Annie pointed to another spot on the map. "Over here, still on the lawn, I want to have Santa Claus for the little kids. We'll get someone to play Santa. Maybe a craft table, where the kids could color or make ornaments. And here's where we'll have a refreshment booth. Coffee, hot chocolate, cookies. Picture all this with lights and decorations and Christmas music!" Annie hoped her excitement was spreading to the others.

"It would be a place where the whole town could come together," said Allan.

"Exactly!" Annie beamed. "That's what I want the Macklin House to be!" Of course, she didn't add, "If we raise enough money."

"I don't know," said Ron. "I'm not convinced. It would be fun, but it'll never raise a hundred thousand dollars."

"But if we could raise something, we might be able to make a start on the work. That would show the county we're trying. If they know we're making an effort to do the repairs, they might not shut us down."

"Annie, it's a cute idea," Ron answered. "But it's not a serious long-term solution. And you didn't answer my question. How did we get this trolley?"

The moment of truth, Annie thought. "We bought it," she said.

"We bought it?" Ron said incredulously. Natalie and Allan looked confused, but not angry.

"The director has discretionary spending authority up to five thousand dollars annually," Annie said. "It's in the trust. I spent twenty-five hundred. I know it's a gamble, but if we don't try something unique for a fund-raiser, we'll have to close down anyway."

"I like it," said Allan.

"So do I," said Natalie. "Shall we vote? All in favor of a Christmas trolley tour to benefit the Macklin House?"

"Aye!" said Allan.

"Aye!" from Natalie.

"No," Ron grumbled.

"Two to one. It's approved," Natalie said.

"Welcome to the Macklin House First Annual Christmas Trolley Tour of Lights!" Annie exclaimed.

CHAPTER 6

November 10

HOW HARD CAN IT BE TO REPLACE A KITCHEN FAUCET? BEN thought. He could do pretty much anything with electronics, but he had no experience with home repairs. And his parents' old house needed a *lot* of repairs.

Two sleepless nights of listening to the dripping kitchen faucet had driven him to a YouTube tutorial on plumbing. It hadn't looked that difficult on his phone. Now he was headed for Meyers' Hardware, a fixture on State Street for generations. Dave Meyers had come home from Vietnam and gone to work for his father, who had inherited the store from *his* father. Meyers' had started out selling feed and agricultural supplies to the local farmers. Now it took up three storefronts along State Street. A green-and-white striped awning shaded the large front windows. The sidewalk outside the store was cluttered with colorful seasonal flags and animated holiday lawn figures covered in lights. Ben noted a waving snowman, a bobbing reindeer, and a set of carolers whose heads turned from side to side. An American flag flew prominently over the main entrance.

He smelled fresh coffee as he approached the door. What room was left on the sidewalk was taken up by a collection of patio furniture, ranging from cushioned outdoor love seats that would have been at home on a deck in Malibu, to 1950s-style metal chairs with plastic tubular seats. A cluster of senior citizens had decamped from the senior center two blocks away and was cheerfully lounging on the furniture, sipping takeout coffee from the Macklin Café down the street. Two of the men were eating slices of pie, although it was only nine o' clock in the morning.

Ben eyed the pie. Seeing his questioning look, one man raised his fork and said, "Banana cream. It's good for you." The other man added, "Lots of bananas. Lots of potassium." They clinked their forks together in satisfaction, and went back to eating.

The whole group was collectively trying to finish the daily crossword in the Macklin *Morning News*. A man in a bright yellow shirt waved at Ben. "Hey! Computer guy!" Ben looked around but didn't see anyone else. He pointed questioningly at the Jupiter Computer logo on his shirt. The man nodded. "What's a seven-letter word for search engine?"

"Browser," said Ben.

A woman in a pink hat waved at him. "Founder of Microsoft. Five letters. Gates doesn't work."

Another woman said dubiously, "Steve?"

"Wrong company," three people said in unison.

"Allen," Ben contributed. "Paul Allen."

"What's a twelve-letter word for—" Ben held up his hand and sidestepped toward the door. "Have to go," he said. A distressed "Ohhh," came from the group. "Have to shop," he implored, waving good-bye at them as he entered the store.

An ice-cream freezer and a selection of soft drinks sat to his left, along with a rack of greeting cards. The checkout counter stood across from them on the right. Ben remembered buying ice cream at Meyers' as a kid. He glanced at the ice cream freezer. Prices seemed to have gone up considerably since then.

He started looking for the plumbing section, and was amazed by the sheer variety of items crammed into the store. Along with hundreds of holiday light displays, Ben ticked off paint, cleaning supplies, nuts and bolts, kitchen appliances, barbecue grills, window blinds, camping equipment, a whole aisle of light bulbs, and power tools. Each section was neatly organized, but nothing seemed to be stocked in any logical relation to anything else. Ben counted twelve different kinds of hammers and mallets, and thirty-six types of wrenches. At the far end of the store, he found a huge selection of drawer pulls, door hinges, and cabinet knobs. Lest Meyers' forget its humble beginnings, the area next to the loading dock was stocked with chicken feed and fertilizer.

Ben finally located the plumbing department, which contained a bewildering collection of kitchen faucets. They seemed to come in all sizes, shapes, and colors. Several linked to a sensor that would track your daily water consumption or show you a picture of the inside of the pipes. Nothing faintly resembled the plain stainless steel faucet he'd removed.

Unable to decide on a faucet, he wandered into the electrical aisle, where he found two kids, a boy and a girl who looked to be about twelve or thirteen. They were playing with the controls on a giant holographic light display. "If you program it this way," said the girl, "it makes whirly circles." Ben watched the whirly circles for a minute as they rapidly expanded and contracted. He was starting to feel a little dizzy when the boy said urgently, "Turn it down! Turn it down! I'm going to throw up!" The girl rolled her eyes, but changed the display to a soothing glide through the color spectrum. The boy glared at her.

"Are you supposed to be doing that?" Ben asked them. "Why aren't you kids in school?"

"It's a late-start day," said the boy, who was wearing a San Francisco 49ers t-shirt and had curly brown hair. "Who are you?"

"Ben Grover. I used to—I live here. Who are *you*?"

"Jackson," said the boy. "We live here, too."

"Emma," said the girl. She had straight dark hair in a long ponytail, and she was wearing a pink t-shirt decorated with multicolored glitter. "We go to Macklin Middle School. We're in seventh grade."

"Why are you hanging around the hardware store on your late-start day?" Ben asked.

"Our moms work at the Macklin Café," answered Emma. "Mr. Meyers lets us use his computer to do our homework. We come over here after school on regular days, too."

"Why aren't *you* at work?" asked Jackson. He pointed at the circular Jupiter Computer logo on Ben's gray polo shirt. Ben glanced involuntarily at the logo, since he'd now been identified by it twice in the last thirty minutes. The words "Jupiter Computer," in red script, wrapped around the outer edges of the circle. Inside was a stylized picture of the planet, showing brown and cream stripes. Jupiter's famous "red spot" was centered under the "p" in "Jupiter." He suspected that the red spot was in the wrong place, planetary wise, but it looked artistic. Ben hated wearing a dress shirt and tie. His logo polo shirts had been his standard business attire.

"I'm trying to buy a faucet," he replied, sidestepping the question. "Help me pick one out." They followed him back to the plumbing section. As they went around the corner into the next aisle, Ben caught sight of a young woman at the cash register, buying some cans of paint. She's cute, Ben thought. About my age, pretty hair, looks sort of outdoorsy, a really nice smile that reminds me of—Annie Mulvaney?

"So—here we are… faucets," Jackson was tugging on his arm.

"Yeah. For a kitchen. Nothing too expensive," Ben replied.

"Do you want the one that you can turn on with an app on your phone?" asked Jackson.

"Nothing that fancy." Ben turned around to look at the woman again, but she was gone.

"That one," Emma pointed. "And you can get a matching towel rack."

"I don't need a towel rack in the kitchen."

"Of course you do," Emma said. "You change your towels with the holidays. Right now, you put out Christmas towels." She pointed to a display of holiday dishtowels, artfully arranged on a sample kitchen counter. "The ones with the pine trees would look nice in your kitchen."

"You don't know what my kitchen looks like," Ben answered.

"If you're buying a new faucet, it's probably old," Emma said. "The pine trees will go with an old kitchen." Both of the kids nodded in satisfaction at this decorating tip.

Carrying the faucet, the towel rack, and two pine tree towels, Ben made his way to the counter. Dave Meyers was scowling at the cash register. Ben mentally calculated that Dave must be nearing or past retirement age. He was wearing a blue Meyers' Hardware logo shirt, and distractedly running his hands through his once-black hair, now a thinning salt-and-pepper gray. Ben remembered Dave helping him find materials for his Eagle Scout project back in high school.

"I can't ring you up right now," Dave said. "The register's computer system just went down again."

"Don't pull on your hair, Mr. Meyers," said Emma. "It'll make you go bald."

"I'm already going bald," said Dave. He continued to punch buttons on the register.

"Maybe you should put your glasses on, Mr. Meyers," said Jackson. "You should keep them at the cash register instead of in the drawer in your desk." Dave scowled at him.

"Um," said Ben, "I work with computer programs. Maybe I could help."

Dave looked at him for a moment, and then his face lit up. "Ben Grover!" he exclaimed. "I haven't seen you since you went off to college. What are you doing back in town?"

"It's a long story," Ben said, hoping to avoid the details.

"You got laid off? I'm so sorry."

I might as well have a sign on my forehead that says, "Unemployed," Ben thought. "It's given me a chance to come back to Macklin and see how the old town's doing," he replied diplomatically.

"It's been tough here," Dave admitted. "I'm trying to keep up, but the margins keep getting thinner and thinner. I used to have three sales clerks but I had to let them go." Ben grimaced, feeling a lot of sympathy for those sales clerks. "It's just me right now. I can barely afford to pay minimum wage, and the teenagers can get a job at a fast-food place for more than that. At least I own the building."

"How many items do you carry here?" asked Ben, looking around at the maze of products.

"To be honest, I don't really know any more," Dave admitted.

"You don't know?" Ben said. His brain instantly snapped into consultant mode. "You need an inventory management system."

"Right now, I just need the cash register to work," Dave said glumly.

Ben pushed a few buttons on the back of the machine and it rebooted. The screen came to life.

"You—just made it do that?" asked Dave.

Ben nodded. "And I can install an inventory system for you, too." Dave held up his hand. "I know you can't pay me," Ben added. "But it would be a good project for me. To take my mind off things."

Like how I might run into that girl I just saw, he thought.

"You really think this would help me?"

"Dave, you're handling this whole store by yourself!" Ben said. He thought back. "Don't you have a son?"

Dave nodded. "Adam. I guess he'd be enough older than you that the two of you were never in school together. He's thirty-six."

"Does he live in Macklin?" Ben asked.

"No," said Dave. "Adam was always musical, really talented. He can play practically any instrument. He taught himself to play the piano when he was three years old! He majored in music in college. That's where he met his wife, Stacey. She's a singer." Dave sighed. "I always hoped he'd want to take over the store, but he was so talented, it obviously wasn't going to happen. So, to answer your question, right now, it's just me."

"Dave, if you can't afford to hire someone to do the work physically, you've got to automate. Trust me. It'll increase your profit." Ben suddenly felt more cheerful than he'd felt in weeks. A business project!

And a girl who might turn out to be Annie Mulvaney! Not that Annie Mulvaney would be likely to speak to him, but still.

Dave thought. "Okay," he said finally. "Come back on Monday. We open at nine."

CHAPTER 7

November 10

ANNIE WAS AT HER DESK EARLY, TRYING TO CATCH UP ON her regular work. She paid some bills, ordered supplies, and scheduled a training session for her new docents. But her mind was really on the trolley. Finally, around nine a.m., she gave up. "I'm taking a break," she told Danielle. "I'm going over to Meyers' Hardware."

She headed across the square to Meyers'. As advertised, the store was filled with displays of holiday lights. With the store already bursting at the seams, Christmas lights were stocked in every available inch of space. Where there weren't Christmas lights, there were pine cones, Hanukkah décor, and ornaments painted with snowy New England vistas that no one in Macklin had ever seen in real life.

Annie found Dave Meyers on a ladder, hanging a large flashing reindeer on the back wall. "Hi, Dave," she said. "You sure have a lot of holiday stuff. Where did you put the paint?"

THE CHRISTMAS TROLLEY

Dave climbed down from the ladder and surveyed the reindeer, which was squeezed between two life-sized Santa Claus figures covered in red and white lights. "You know Macklin," he said. "People love their holiday lights. The paint's been moved to Aisle Four. Let me show you."

As she followed Dave back through the store, Annie caught sight of a man about her age looking confusedly at faucets in the plumbing section. *That guy's cute*, she thought. Dark brown hair, works out but not too much, some kind of logo on his polo shirt, and his ears remind me of—Ben Grover? It *surely* wasn't Ben Grover. *Ben Grover*, Annie told herself, *would not be caught dead within the Macklin city limits*.

"Here we are," said Dave, breaking her train of thought. "What kind of paint do you need? What's it for?"

Annie explained about the trolley. Dave enthusiastically helped her select primer and paint, and when they walked past the plumbing department again on their way to the cash register, the cute guy was gone.

Annie spent every spare moment over the next few days working on the trolley. The silver stars turned out to be paste-on stickers that refused to peel off. It took her two days to remove them, and another two days to sand and paint. She dripped red paint on one of her favorite t-shirts, and her nails were a mess. "I hope Philip Macklin appreciates this," she muttered as she touched up her work.

She couldn't stop thinking about the guy in the hardware store. It *couldn't* be Ben Grover. Ben Grover would never come back to Macklin. That was how the whole thing had started.

Every year the eighth graders at Macklin Middle School had a field trip in social studies class to visit the Macklin House. Up until that field trip, she and Ben had been best friends all through school. They ate lunch together. They rode all over town on their bikes. He admired her attempts at poetry. She praised him when he won a statewide math competition in fifth grade. Secretly, she had a crush on him.

The day of the field trip, they'd been partners, as usual. None of their class had ever been to the Macklin House before, and they had no idea what to expect. When they passed through the elaborate Victorian doors and stood beneath the gleaming crystal chandelier, Annie was transfixed. It was as if she could feel the old mansion in her soul. This is what I want to do, she thought. I want to work at a historic house like this. I want to work at *this* historic house.

They went from room to room, while Annie grew steadily more entranced. She went on and on about the stained glass windows, the furniture, the woodwork on the stairway. Ben didn't say much. Finally, they found themselves alone outside on the wraparound porch. "I love this house!" Annie said. "I want to live in Macklin forever, and come here every day!"

Ben had looked astounded. "Why do you want to live in Macklin? It's boring!"

Annie had been completely shocked. "You—you don't want to live in Macklin?" It was her first inkling that she and Ben might not want the same things out of life.

"No! I'm going to be a computer scientist and move to San Francisco!" he'd replied.

"But Macklin is nice. We've got the Macklin House."

"Let's not talk about this dumb old house," he'd said. "I really like you, Annie. Will you be my girlfriend? Can I kiss you?"

Annie was overwhelmed. Ben liked her? But he didn't like the Macklin House? How could he like her, and not like the same things she liked? To her eighth grade mind, that wasn't possible.

"How can you like me and not like the Macklin House?" she'd said. "It's the same thing."

"Annie, that's stupid," he'd said. "This old house? It's—it's nothing but a piece of junk!"

"Ben Grover!" she'd exclaimed. "It is *not* a piece of junk! And I'll never kiss you until"—she tried to think of the most improbable thing she could—"until snow falls in Macklin!"

Annie and Ben had many good qualities, but forgiving and forgetting were not among them. Snow was never going to fall in Macklin, and they were never going to kiss. They remained casual, no longer inseparable, friends all through high school. She won the history awards.

He won the math and science awards. She went to prom with Jeremy Corcoran. He went to prom with Shelby Longaberger. They went off to college. They went to grad school. They got jobs that weren't in Macklin.

But Annie was still wondering, as she carefully applied another coat of red paint over a spot where she'd removed a silver star. *Could* that have been Ben Grover in Meyers' Hardware?

Am I wondering, she thought, *or am I hoping?*

CHAPTER 8

November 11

AFTER SOME TRIAL-AND-ERROR, BEN MANAGED TO install the faucet. Proud of his success, he tried the towel bar next. He successfully drilled the required holes in the wall, but the screws that had come with the package didn't seem to fit. After trying them in several combinations, he sat down at the kitchen table for a break.

He'd been working all day, and it was almost three o'clock. *Maybe I need to make another trip to the hardware store*, he thought. Dave said Monday, but if I show up this afternoon, he'll be impressed.

And if I'm at the hardware store, maybe I'll see that girl again.

The girl who looked like Annie Mulvaney. Who probably *was* Annie Mulvaney, according to Mrs. Martinez.

Ben had been away from Macklin for ten years, and he'd managed to push Annie way down into his subconscious. But now that he was back, everything seemed to remind him of her. He'd driven past Macklin

Middle School that afternoon. If it hadn't been for that eighth grade field trip ...

He'd had a crush on Annie as long as he could remember. He hadn't thought of it as a crush until eighth grade, when suddenly romance burst out among their classmates. He knew Annie thought of him as her best friend. That had been fine in seventh grade, but now he knew better. He wanted Annie to be his girlfriend.

He'd fantasized constantly about holding her hand or hopefully, kissing her. He knew there were boys in their class who were better looking or more athletic than he was. Annie might be thinking of one of them. But he had a plan. He'd become a famous computer scientist and whisk Annie away to San Francisco. Ben's parents had taken him to San Francisco on a family vacation the year before. He'd instantly fallen in love with the city. He couldn't imagine a more magical place to take Annie when they grew up.

He remembered their tour guide at the Macklin House leading them through room after room. Ben had only half-listened to the guide. He thought the building looked old. He was horrified to learn that it had been built without electricity. It wasn't his kind of house at all.

But he could tell Annie was thrilled. She lagged further and further behind the group, reluctant to leave one room for the next. He began lagging behind, too. Finally, they ended up alone together on the wide porch. The rest of their class was heading out to the front lawn, where they'd be served Victorian-style tea sandwiches before getting back on the bus.

"I love this house!" Annie had said. "I want to live in Macklin forever, and come here every day!"

Ben had tried to impress her with his plan. "I don't want to live in Macklin. I'm going to live in San Francisco."

It hadn't worked. She'd been completely shocked. "You—you don't want to live in Macklin?"

"No. I want to be a computer scientist and live in San Francisco."

"How can you say that? Macklin is nice. We've got the Macklin House."

"Let's not talk about this dumb old house," he'd said. "I really like you, Annie. Will you be my girlfriend? Can I kiss you?"

"How can you like me and not like the Macklin House?" she'd said.

"It's the same thing."

"Annie, that's stupid," he'd said. She wasn't listening to him. He tried to think of something that would absolutely, completely get her attention. "This old house? It's—it's nothing but a piece of junk!" As soon as he'd said it, he'd known it was a mistake.

"Ben Grover!" she'd exclaimed. "It is not a piece of junk! It's a beautiful piece of history!" Annie had paused dramatically, as only thirteen-year-old girls can do. "And I'll never kiss you—until snow falls in Macklin!"

So here he was, back in Macklin and thinking again of Annie Mulvaney. Mrs. Martinez hadn't mentioned a boyfriend. Or a husband.

He looked at the towel bar. It wasn't like he had anything else to do. Why not make a run to the store? He could start work on Dave's inventory management system. It was a good excuse to hang around. Maybe the girl—okay, Annie—would show up again. Running into her accidentally wouldn't be the same as seeking her out. They could talk casually. He wouldn't have to explain the truth about why he was back in Macklin.

Ben didn't have to think twice. He reached for the car keys.

He found Meyers' Hardware full of customers, all browsing through the Christmas lights. Dave's cash register still seemed to be functioning. Ben mentally patted himself on the back and began methodically working his way through the store, looking for replacement screws. Suddenly, he heard an electronic voice. "Help me! I'm being held prisoner!"

He turned around to find a large mounted deer head sitting on top of a turkey smoker. He realized he was in the Outdoor Living section. People in Macklin could grill outside all year long, and the store always carried a large selection of barbecues and accessories.

The deer had a red rubber ball taped over its nose and a sign that read "Rudolph" hanging around its neck. Rudolph was a three-point buck with glassy green eyes and a sales tag dangling from one of his antlers. Ben recognized a motion-activated voice recorder next to Rudolph's somewhat moth-eaten neck.

"Help me! I'm being held prisoner in Meyers' Hardware! Help me escape! Contribute to my escape fund!" A large Mason jar with a label reading "Rudolph's Escape Fund," sat on the shelf next to the smoker. The jar held some coins and bills. Ben stifled a laugh. He had a pretty good idea of who was trying to finance Rudolph's escape.

"Young man! Do you know where the bird feeders are?" Ben turned around and saw an older woman wearing a green t-shirt and black yoga pants. She was carrying a small brown basket that held a tawny-colored Yorkshire terrier. The dog peered over the edge of the basket and looked around uncertainly.

"Sit down, Peanut," cooed the woman. Suddenly the dog spied Rudolph. With a louder squeal than Ben would have thought possible for a dog that size, he stood up in the basket and clawed his way frantically over the edge. He landed on the floor with a loud thump, all four legs sprawled out. Then, he shook himself and stood up. Howling and snarling, he clattered down the aisle toward Rudolph.

His owner screamed, "My baby! My baby!" just as the dog reached the deer head and leaped at Rudolph, ready to fight. He landed on the floor again, but he'd tripped the motion detector. "Help me! I'm being held prisoner!" the deer intoned.

Startled, the dog stood up on his hind legs and howled in terror. Then, he whirled around and raced off into the store.

The woman pulled on Ben's arm. "He ran away!" she cried. "Find him! Find him!" Ben pried her fingers loose. "I'll look for him," he promised, "Ms.—uh—"

"I'm Angie Morgan," the woman said. "Please, you've got to catch him before he runs into the street!"

Ben quickly canvassed the area nearest to the barbecue equipment. No luck, but he could hear barking. He zigzagged through the store. The dog was so small he could hide under anything. Ben couldn't remember the dog's name, except that it began with a P. "Here Pokey ... Pesky ... Poopie ... Peanut!" he cried triumphantly.

He skidded around a corner and finally saw the dog trying to climb up a shelf of screws and bolts. Peanut lost his footing. Several boxes of screws fell to the floor and burst open, as Peanut scrambled to stay upright. He howled again, and raced madly down the aisle, scattering screws in his path. He ran under a large white, oval plastic object.

Ben tapped on it. "Peanut, come out!" he coaxed. There was no more barking, but he could hear the dog moving around underneath. Ben went to find Dave.

Dave was ringing up lights and looked harried. "You're back again?" he asked. "What was all that noise?"

"Angie Morgan—" Ben started.

"Did she bring that comfort food dog in here again?"

"I think that's a comfort dog," said Ben. "Or an emotional support dog." Dave glared at him, not pleased with the dog under any name.

"Whatever. Where is it?" he asked.

"He ran under this big white thing in the middle of Aisle Twelve, and he won't come out."

"Oh, that's the igloo kit," said Dave.

"The igloo kit? What happened to global warming?"

"It's a playhouse, except it's shaped like an igloo," Dave explained. "It comes with two stuffed polar bears and a bag of dried fish. There's a latch on the back. You can lift the top off."

Ben dutifully trudged back to Aisle Twelve. Now he heard growls as he approached the igloo. He found the latch, removed the top, and unearthed Peanut, happily snarling at the remains of one of the polar bears. The fish packet lay next to it, a shredded mass of paper with no fish left. Freed from his basket, Peanut had heard the call of the wild.

Ben reached down and tried to pick up the dog. Peanut barked and sank his tiny teeth into Ben's thumb. Muttering curses under his breath, Ben wrapped both hands around the squirming dog's middle, and hauled him out.

Angie ran up, sobbing. "You saved my baby! Thank you! Whoever you are!"

"Ben Grover," Ben said. At last, someone who didn't remember him as a ten-year-old. Dave came up to check the damage.

"You should give this young man a job," Angie told him. She put Peanut back in the basket. Peanut didn't look too happy about it.

"I'd love to give him a job," said Dave, "except I don't have any money. What started all this?"

"Rudolph," said Ben. He led Dave back to the barbecue section and showed him the deer head.

"Well, I can guess where this came from," said Dave. "EMMA! JACKSON! COME TO THE OUTDOOR LIVING DEPARTMENT RIGHT NOW!"

A few minutes later, the kids sauntered over. Ben was fingering the price tag hanging from Rudolph's right antler. He looked at it more closely. It read, "Twenty dollars." He turned around and stared sternly at Emma and Jackson.

"Did you steal this deer from the thrift shop?" he demanded.

"We would NEVER do that," said Emma. She looked insulted.

Ben focused his stare on Jackson, who he figured was more likely to confess. He was right. Jackson's bottom lip trembled. After a few moments, the words came out. "We told them we wanted to borrow it for a school play," he mumbled.

"So you tricked those kind-hearted, unsuspecting women at the thrift shop into letting you have their deer head?" Ben was having trouble keeping a straight face. In his heart, he was admiring their ingenuity. Where the Women's Club was concerned, "school" was the magic word.

"We *said* we'd bring it back," Emma retorted.

"Wait until they find out about this. They're going to put your photos up on the wall, like a 'Wanted' poster. 'Do Not Lend Anything to these Kids.'"

Dave was examining the recorder. "Where'd this come from?"

"It was in your office," said Jackson. "Remember? It goes to that home security system the Johnsons returned last week. You were going to send it back to the manufacturer." He gave Dave a look that said, *if you left it out, it's your own fault.*

Dave pointed to Rudolph. "Clean up the mess in Aisle Twelve and return Rudolph to the thrift shop RIGHT NOW." He turned to Ben. "Could you help me up front? I've got a bunch of people asking about Christmas lights!"

"Sure," Ben answered cheerfully. *Because if that girl—Annie—comes in,* he thought, *I'll have a much better chance of seeing her if I'm at the cash register.*

CHAPTER 9

November 12–15

ANNIE NEEDED A TROLLEY DRIVER. SHE COULD SELL TICK-ets, oversee the food and entertainment, and generally run the event every night. But she couldn't do that and drive the trolley, too. She needed someone who was available every night from Thanksgiving to Christmas. Someone who could handle a crowd of passengers, make comments about the lights, and show the right holiday spirit. And most importantly, someone who would do it for free.

She thought about her docents at the Macklin House, but none of them seemed right. "Time to advertise," she said, and pulled up Craigslist. "All I need is one person."

By the next day, Annie's ad for a trolley driver had actually yielded three applicants. She decided to interview all of them on the same afternoon. Wanting to put them in the Christmas spirit, she dressed in another one of her Christmas sweaters. It had tiny green Christmas trees on a white background. She wore a necklace made from large Christmas tree light bulbs, with matching earrings. She thought of this as a test. If her interviewees admired her sweater or her jewelry, that would be a sign that they'd enjoy driving the trolley. If they didn't react, they might be too Scroogey to make a good driver.

Her first appointment was an elderly gentleman named Ted Worley. Ted had a pleasant face and neatly combed gray hair. He seemed quite friendly, but walked stiffly with the help of a cane. Annie reminded herself that the driver didn't have to walk, just sit.

"Nice Christmas sweater," he said. Annie gave him points for that. He sat down carefully, favoring his left knee, and smiled at Annie.

"First of all," Annie began, "you understand this is a volunteer job. I can't afford to pay anything."

"No problem," Ted answered. "I'm retired. I don't need any extra money."

This sounded promising. "Why are you interested in driving the trolley?" Annie asked.

"I know a lot about Macklin. I've lived here all my life. It's a great little town. And I love to drive. You know I've driven across the country five times?"

"That must have been a lot of fun," Annie responded. "Have you had any experience driving something other than a car?"

"Trucks, boats, you name it, I can drive it. I love to drive! I used to have a Corvette. I had to give it up, got too old to climb in and out of it." Ted frowned and shifted around in his chair. "Sorry. I've had all my joints replaced. Some of them twice. Ever since the last operation, I just can't seem to get comfortable. But I can still drive!"

"Let's run through some questions," Annie said. "What would you do if a passenger started to act belligerent?"

"I'd try to calm him down. Defuse the situation. Put him off the trolley if things got too bad."

"What would you do if a passenger got hurt?" Annie asked next.

"I'm sure you'd have a first-aid kit, if it was just a minor accident. If someone was really sick, I'd stop the tour and phone for help."

"What would you do if the trolley broke down?"

"I'm pretty mechanical. I can usually keep things running long enough to get home," he replied.

All this sounded positive. Then Annie remembered. "Ted, can I see your driver's license?"

Ted rooted around in his pockets and came up with a folded piece of paper. He opened it up, and handed it to Annie. It was a photocopy of his license.

She thought, *this is strange. Why doesn't he have his actual license?* It seemed to be a photocopy of a photocopy. She peered more closely at the expiration date.

"Ted. This is an expired license," she said.

Ted squirmed. "No, it's not," he protested.

"Yes, it is," Annie replied. "You copied the license and then you altered the date. Then you copied it again so it wouldn't be so obvious."

"I can drive," he said. "I just couldn't pass the written test at the DMV."

"Why not?"

"It's rigged against us. They ask about all these things you'll never need to know. What to do if your car hits a piece of black ice. There's no ice here. There isn't even any *water* here, ten months out of the year. If you move to California, how soon do you have to apply for a California driver's license? I'm already here! I've been here for seventy-five years! And they ask how fast you can legally go on an electric scooter. I'm never going to ride an electric scooter! Why do I have to know that?"

"Oh, Ted," Annie said. "I know you'd love to be our driver. And you'd probably be a good one. But I'm afraid our insurance company won't let us consider anyone who doesn't have a driver's license. You understand. It's completely out of my hands."

She had learned, in her few years in museum work, that it was always good to have an excuse. And blaming the insurance company was a fail-safe excuse for everything from no-gum-chewing-in-the-museum to no-hot-air-balloons-at-the-annual-gala.

Ted looked downcast. "I really wanted to drive the trolley," he said bitterly.

"I could give you something else to do," Annie offered. "You could be a greeter."

"No, thanks," Ted replied. "If I can't be the driver, I don't want to be involved." He got up hesitantly from his chair and walked out slowly. Annie heard him muttering about the "damned DMV."

The second applicant was a young guy named Zach Curtis. He was wearing a black t-shirt and black jeans, and his dark hair was cut in a creative mix of triangular shapes. Annie thought he looked barely old enough to drive, but his driver's license said he was nineteen. And it was a valid license.

"Why do you want to drive the trolley?" Annie asked. She was wondering why he wasn't looking for a paying job.

"It's the perfect setup," Zack said excitedly. "Here's our trolley full of happy, laughing people. People from all walks of life. Completely innocent. They have no idea what's going to happen."

"They're going to ... see Christmas lights?" said Annie.

Zach became even more animated. "They see Christmas lights! And then—the lights get dimmer and dimmer. Now they're going down a dark street." He waved his arms to illustrate his story. "And then—someone's trying to climb onto the trolley! The driver can barely hold on! Screams! More screams! Someone comes up the aisle. He falls at the driver's feet! There's blood everywhere! It's—it's a headless Santa Claus!"

"Zach!" Annie exclaimed. "Why do you want such a horrible thing to happen on our trolley tour?"

"Because it'll make a great movie. For my capstone project. I'm in the film studies program at Macklin Community College," he explained. "And this year for our capstone project, we have to make a short film about something to do with Macklin. The trolley's new. No one else will think of it." He looked at Annie eagerly.

"Zach! I need a driver, not a director!"

"I can do both. We build a platform on the front of the trolley to hold the camera, and it films as I drive."

THE CHRISTMAS TROLLEY

"Oh, Zach," Annie said. "Our insurance company won't let us consider anything like that. It's too risky for the passengers. You understand. It's completely out of my hands."

He looked crestfallen. "But," she added, "I have another project you could work on. NO BLOOD," she added, as he started to look excited again. "Could you make a short video that would tell about the trolley tour, and how it's raising money for the Macklin House? Something we could put on the website, or send out to local TV stations? It wouldn't work for your capstone project, but it'd be a good resume-builder."

"That would be easy," Zach assured her. "I'd be glad to do that. But what if it wasn't a headless Santa on the trolley? Could it be a cyborg Santa?"

"No, Zach," Annie said firmly. "No headless Santas, zombie Santas, cyborg Santas, or mutant Santas. I'll be in touch about the video."

The third applicant was a woman in her fifties. She had silver hair streaked with purple, and was wearing a flowered tunic over a pair of leggings. "Mimi Cloverley," she said, introducing herself. "I really want to drive this trolley! I love holiday lights! I'm completely into holiday lights! And I love your necklace! I want one!"

She was definitely enthusiastic. And her driver's license checked out. Annie felt hopeful.

"Have you had any experience working with the public?"

"I was a tour guide at Yosemite for three summers while I was in college. Then I was a barista at the coffee kiosk at the Supersaver Market. And now, I run a dance studio over on Fifth Street. I teach all kinds of dance, plus Pilates." Mimi looked at Annie expectantly.

"You sound like you could be a great fit," Annie said.

"There's just one thing," Mimi added. "I need to bring my reindeer."

"Your reindeer?" said Annie. She'd never heard of reindeer in Macklin.

"My grandchildren. And their friends. I run a home daycare in the evening. You might have heard of it. It's called Night-Time Day Care?"

"I haven't heard of it," said Annie. "I don't have any kids yet."

"It's five p.m. to midnight, and I have nine kids, counting Justin and Sara, who just stay through dinner, so that's enough for Santa's reindeer plus Rudolph." Annie looked confused. "They tap dance," Mimi explained. "They have little reindeer antler hats and they tap dance. So I thought, they could tap dance in the aisles of the trolley, and I could get out of the house."

Annie didn't have to think twice. "Oh, Mimi," she sighed, "they sound so cute. But we only have one aisle on the trolley, and our insurance company insists that we keep it clear at all times, in case there's an emergency. You understand. It's completely out of my hands."

She let Mimi Cloverley out the front door, went back to her office, and sat down with her head in her hands. There *had* to be a trolley driver somewhere in Macklin.

It was almost six o'clock, and the streetlights had come on in the town square. Annie suddenly remembered that she'd meant to stop by the hardware store and buy more red paint. She felt mentally exhausted as she locked up and walked across the square to Meyers'. As always, Dave was happy to see her.

"How's your trolley coming?" he asked as he rang up her purchase. "Did you get the stars off? Did that primer work?"

"It's turning out to be a bigger project than I expected," she admitted. "Dave, you don't know of anyone who'd like to drive the trolley, do you?"

"I'll think about it," he said as he handed her the paint. "Heading home?"

"You know, I think I'm going to dinner at the café tonight," Annie answered. "It's been a long day. I really don't feel like cooking."

Dave ushered her out of the store and went back to closing up. He heard a lot of electronic beeps from his office. Ben came out, carrying a laptop.

"I set you up on the cloud," he said. "You need to back up your sales figures and your inventory every day. I'll fix you up tomorrow with a program that'll upload them automatically." He could tell Dave had no idea what he was talking about.

"That sounds pretty impressive," said Dave, as he set the alarm system. "You've been a big help with all this tech support. You're over here working on it all the time." He thought for a moment. Then a smile played around his lips. "Any hot dates tonight?"

"I'm cooking ramen noodles."

"Ramen noodles? Are you still in college?" Ben turned red. "I'm not really used to cooking. In San Francisco, I ate out all the time. But there don't seem to be a lot of restaurants around here."

Dave opened the cash register and handed Ben a twenty-dollar bill. "The Macklin Café is right down the block. Great food. A good place to meet people. A *really* good place to meet people. It's sort of the local hot spot. You've helped me out a lot with the computer. Go treat yourself!"

CHAPTER 10

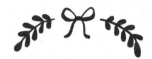

November 15

THE MACKLIN CAFÉ LOOKED WARM AND INVITING AS BEN opened the door. Red leatherette booths lined two walls, and a fireplace about halfway down one wall had cozy armchairs on each side. Tables dotted the center section. Ben could smell fresh apple pie as he stepped up to the hostess station next to the cash register. The hostess looked about his age. She had curly blond hair and a tattoo of a monarch butterfly on her left forearm.

"Ben!" she exclaimed. "Ben Grover!" Seeing that Ben was struggling to remember who she was, she added, "I'm Cammie Johnson. Well, Cammie Warner now. I was two years ahead of you in high school. You're back in Macklin?"

"For a few weeks. So, you work here?"

Cammie nodded. "I was going to go to art school, but things came up. I'm a single mom now. You may see my son, Jackson, around here. He's supposed to be doing his homework in the back."

"I think I met him at Meyers' Hardware," said Ben. "Seems like a smart kid."

"He is!" Cammie said proudly. "But he's a handful. Seventh grade, you know."

"Hey, it's good to see you," Ben said. "Can I just sit anywhere?"

"Oh, sure," said Cammie, handing him a menu. Ben turned around and scanned the restaurant. He saw a cute brown-haired woman sitting alone in a booth near the fireplace. It was the girl from the hardware store. She looked up, staring at the fireplace. Ben's heart stopped. It was her! Annie Mulvaney!

Annie, meanwhile, had been deep in thought for the past half hour. She was drinking a cup of coffee and trying to think of ways to publicize her trolley tours. A Facebook page, Instagram, maybe the trolley could have its own Twitter account. And if Zack could make a video for local TV …

I guess I'd better order, she thought, and looked around for Paula, the other waitress on duty that evening. Instead of Paula, her gaze locked on a guy standing by the hostess stand. The guy from the hardware store. Who was, she saw now, unmistakably Ben Grover. And he was looking straight at her.

Annie felt her heart pounding, and she blushed. The guy—Ben—looked equally stunned. Then he waved at Cammie, gestured in the general direction of Annie's booth, and came down the aisle.

"Annie Mulvaney!" he exclaimed. "I thought I saw you in Meyers' Hardware the other morning!" He seemed at a loss as to what to say next, but added, "Are you alone?"

Annie slid out of the booth and hugged him, then pointed to the other side of her booth. They were old friends, after all, and there was no reason they shouldn't have dinner together.

"Ben Grover! I thought you were in San Francisco. What are you doing back in Macklin?" They sat down across from each other.

"I—sort of parted ways with my last employer. I'm taking some time to look at my options."

"You got laid off? That's awful. I'm so sorry," she said.

She looks truly upset, Ben thought. *And she hasn't even seen me in ten years*. "Nobody's hiring at this time of year. I thought I might as well come back here for a while until things pick up. It's not San Francisco, but I'm living in my parents' old house, and it's free rent."

"What did you do in San Francisco?" Annie asked.

"I worked for Jupiter Computer," he said, indicating the logo on his polo shirt. "I designed and sold business software. I had an apartment downtown. It was great to live in the city! Restaurants, concerts, always something happening." He realized he was trying to impress her. She seemed interested, but not impressed. "But enough about me. I heard you're running the Macklin House museum now." Annie looked at him in surprise.

"I ran into Mrs. Martinez at the Supersaver Market," Ben explained. "She filled me in."

Annie rolled her eyes. "Mrs. Martinez knows everything about every person who went to Macklin Middle School. What they did then, what they're doing now, and everything in between."

"She missed her calling," Ben agreed. "She should be working for the FBI. Tell me about your job."

"I've been the director of the Macklin House Trust for about six months," Annie said. "The previous director retired and moved to Hawaii. I was working at a small museum in Ohio, and I heard about the opening. I applied and I got the job! You know how I've always loved the Macklin House."

"Ever since our eighth grade field trip," Ben said. There was an uncomfortable moment for both of them, but Annie forged ahead.

"I have so many ideas for it," she continued. "It's such an important historic building and it's so underused. We could have living history tours for the kids and make the exhibits more interactive. The lobby could be a concert space for small musical groups. We could turn some of the unused rooms on the second floor into meeting rooms—book clubs, discussion groups, you know ... I met a film student from MCC today. We could host an annual film festival of student films. Art shows. Photography exhibits. If we put up a tent on the back lawn we could serve high tea in the summer." She couldn't believe she was rambling on like this. She'd mentioned a few ideas to her board, before the dismal news about the repairs. But she'd never told anyone about all the things she hoped to do.

"When is this going to happen?" asked Ben.

"It's not going to happen," Annie said sadly. "The county building department sent out an inspector last month. The building needs to be brought up to code if we want to continue operating. It's going to cost a hundred thousand dollars for the repairs. We don't have that much money. We, basically, don't have *any* money for repairs. There's a small endowment fund, but we can't touch the principal. And the interest really only covers our operating expenses."

"That's terrible," said Ben. "You have all these brilliant ideas. There must be some way to get the money." The conversation was actually cheering him up. It was nice to focus on someone else's job problems.

"Well, I do have an idea. You'll probably think it's silly. Oh, I guess we should order." Paula was standing at their booth, pointedly glancing at her watch. She was tall and willowy, with long, straight dark hair. "I want the chicken Caesar salad," Annie said.

Ben was having trouble distracting himself from looking at Annie long enough to read the menu. "A cheeseburger," he threw out. Any restaurant in Macklin would be serving cheeseburgers.

"How's Emma?" Annie asked Paula.

"She's having trouble with her history assignment," said Paula. "Could you look at it after you're done?" Paula sighed. "I think she just glanced at it and went back to this book about computers she's reading. That's all she's interested in. She and Jackson want to take this after-school class. 'How to build your own computer,' or something like that."

"I'd be glad to help," Annie said. "After all, history's my thing. I'll stop by the break room when we're finished."

Ben watched Paula head back to the kitchen with their orders. "Do you know her?" he asked.

"We both know her. Paula Stanley." Ben looked confused. "She was a senior when we were freshmen. She was a song leader?" Ben shook his head, the name still not registering. "She was dating Bill Andrews?" "Basketball player," Ben remembered. "Bill joined the Marines right after graduation. When he came home from basic, he and Paula got married. Then they went to Camp Pendleton for a couple of years. That's where Emma was born. So Bill did his six-year enlistment, and then he decided he got married too young. He divorced Paula and moved to Florida. She's raising Emma by herself."

"Emma from Meyers' Hardware!" Ben exclaimed. The pieces were starting to fit together. He could see the resemblance to Paula. "She helped me pick out a faucet! And Cammie—Warner—is the other waitress, and she's Jackson's mom."

Annie nodded. "Paula and Cammie work the evening shift here from five o'clock to ten because the tips are better. Dave lets the kids hang out at his store after school, and they come over here when their moms go on shift. That way, they don't have to pay for child care."

Ben thought back to his own childhood. His dad had been an engineer at the electrical plant. His mother had worked part-time as a bookkeeper for several local businesses. An only child, he'd never had to worry about one or the other of his parents always being available.

"What's Cammie's story?" he asked. Annie shrugged helplessly. "I'm not really sure. She went to MCC and studied art for a while, and I've heard her refer to her 'no-good ex,' but I don't know any details."

"I guess I'll be a little more understanding the next time I run into those kids in Meyers," he said. Just then, Paula appeared with their food. "Paula, I'm Ben Grover, remember me? I met your daughter Emma this morning at the hardware store. She helped me find a faucet. She was really nice."

"That's so sweet!" Paula looked gratified.

"So here we are, ten years after high school graduation," Ben said between mouthfuls of hamburger. He was trying to think of a tactful way to ask Annie if she was still single. "Do you have, um, any kids?"

Annie shook her head. "No husbands, no kids. I dated a boy all through junior year of college, but then I found him kissing another girl at a fraternity party, and that was that. Then I met this guy, Nolan, in grad school. I thought things were getting serious. When we finished the program, I got my job in Ohio, and I thought he was planning to move to Ohio with me." Annie grimaced at the memory. "Then Nolan told me he was going backpacking in Europe for a year! To 'study art in its original environment.' He asked me to go with him, but I could tell he didn't really mean it. And I'd already accepted the job, and I just couldn't drop everything and go off for six months. It wasn't meant to be." Annie felt a little unsettled, telling all this to Ben, and yet it seemed perfectly normal. She took a drink of water and tried to refocus the conversation. "How about you? Are you married?"

Ben shook his head. "It's different in the city. You meet a lot of people, but you just know them on the surface. Everybody works ten or twelve hours a day. It's very competitive. Even when you go out socially, it's all about where you're going, not who you are. I dated a girl I met at Jupiter for a while, but eventually we broke up. She wanted somebody who worked at a more prestigious tech company." He played with his fork for a moment. "I can't believe we're both back in Macklin. Tell me about your idea." Inwardly he thought, *was this meant to be?*

"I bought a trolley car," said Annie.

Ben looked stupefied. "You bought a *what?*"

"A motorized trolley car. I told you, you'd think it was silly. I bought it on eBay." Ben looked even more stupefied. "I'm going to start a trolley tour of Christmas lights to raise money for the Macklin House."

"Christmas lights? Macklin's famous Christmas lights?" he echoed.

"I think they're only famous in Macklin," said Annie, "But if we could get everybody in Macklin to take the tour, it would bring in some money. And if I proved we could do fund-raising, I might be able to get some grants."

"That's a perfect idea, Annie," Ben said. "When are the tours going to start?"

"I was thinking December first. Tuesday through Saturday. Two tours a night. One at six-thirty, and one at eight p.m. I'm trying to work out the logistics."

"People *love* tours. There were tons of them in San Francisco, but I was always so busy working, I never had time to take one. And now that I'm not working, here I am in Macklin."

Annie was secretly thrilled by his enthusiastic reaction. He liked her idea! He didn't think it was silly! In fact, he thought it was a great plan! Then, she eyed Ben. She was getting an idea.

"So besides looking at your options, what do you do all day?" she asked him.

"I'm helping Dave Meyers at the hardware store," he answered. "His cash register is programmable and he doesn't really understand how to do it. And his business systems really need updating. Then I'm trying to clean out our old house. I think my mom kept every piece of paper she ever got."

"It sounds like you have a lot of free time," Annie said.

Ben sighed. "I look for job openings, but nothing's clicked yet."

"It's really hard to find the right thing," Annie said sympathetically. "And it's hard to find the right person. For instance—I need a trolley driver. I interviewed three people today and none of them was right. The driver has to be good with the public. And I can't pay anything." She paused. "Is there any chance that—you could help me out?"

"Drive the Christmas trolley?" said Ben. Annie nodded. "Oh, no way. I'm not a Christmas guy. I hate holidays."

"You hate holidays?" Annie was shocked. "What did you do for Christmas last year?"

"I worked," Ben said, as if it were the natural thing to do. Seeing Annie's expression, he added, "A bunch of my friends went to Switzerland on a ski trip, except for Ryan who went home to his parents' in Buffalo. He invited me to come with him, but I really didn't want to go to Buffalo in December. I had this project, and I was behind, and Christmas is a good day to work. Everybody's gone, so no one calls you."

THE CHRISTMAS TROLLEY

"That's the most depressing story I've ever heard," Annie said. "I can understand working ten-hour days, but on Christmas? Ben Grover, I am going to give you some holiday spirit if it's the last thing I ever do." She tried again. "You'd be a *perfect* trolley driver. You're businesslike, you're cute" (Ben perked up, even though he knew it was a sales pitch), "and you're nice to people." She left out, *and I'd like to see you again. I'd really, really like to see you again.*

"I'm nice to people?" asked Ben. He knew he was fishing, but being laid off had been a blow.

"Sure. You're helping out Dave. You complimented Emma and made Paula happy. You can't make any money right now, or you'll lose your unemployment, and I can't afford to pay anything. You're perfect. Please, Ben?"

Ben opened his mouth to say no. But somehow, he couldn't. Annie's blue eyes were pleading with him. How could he turn her down?

"I could give it a try," he conceded.

CHAPTER 11

November 17

NEEDING AN AFTERNOON BREAK, ANNIE HEADED OVER to Meyers' Hardware. She found Ben and Dave in a heated stand-off with Jackson and Emma. Rudolph was back in the Outdoor Living department.

"We told you to return that deer to the thrift shop!" Ben was yelling as she walked up.

"We did," Jackson said defensively. "The lady at the thrift shop told us to take it back."

"She said they'd had it for sale for six months and nobody wanted it, and maybe someone would buy it if it was over here," Emma explained. "She said we can have a ten percent commission if we sell it."

"Don't they teach multiplication in school these days? That's two dollars," Ben grumbled. "It's not worth it."

"We could buy an ice cream bar for two dollars," Jackson pointed out. Ben paused. Jackson was right. Two dollars, an amount he would have scorned a few weeks ago, could buy a lot of things.

"Hi!" Annie said cheerfully, intervening. "How would all of you like to take a look at the trolley?" That got their attention. Rudolph was forgotten as they trotted eagerly across the street.

Now the five of them were in the visitors' parking lot at the Macklin House, going over the trolley inch by inch. Annie's new paint job had transformed it. The roof was a deep forest green, and the body was a rich crimson color. She'd enlisted Cammie from the café to paint a border of Christmas balls and holly leaves around the base. Strings of battery-operated Christmas lights hung from the roof.

Jackson and Emma stared at it in astonishment. "It looks completely different!" Jackson exclaimed.

"It looks like Christmas!" Emma added, proudly tracing part of Cammie's border. "Now it's really—a Christmas trolley!"

"The paint job looks great, Annie," Dave told her. "I couldn't have done a better job if I'd done it myself."

"It's easy to drive," Annie said. "For a trolley." She had practiced driving it for a few blocks along the potential route. "It's a little wide on the turns, but you won't be going very fast."

Ben was impressed. "You fixed these seats yourself?" he said. After trying to install his towel bar, he had a newfound respect for repair work.

"Annie does lots of things," Jackson informed him. "She put a new cover on her couch. She made new curtains. Then she gave my mom the old curtains for my bedroom."

Emma started playing with the GPS. "Look at these prepro-grammed addresses! Beyoncé's house! Arianna Grande's house! All the Kardashians' houses!"

"Those can't really be their addresses," said Annie.

Now Jackson was fiddling with it. "LeBron James' house!"

"I think they just drive by a house and make something up," said Ben.

"Ronald Reagan's house!" exclaimed Dave, who was helping Emma scroll through the names.

"Well, that one's probably accurate," Annie said. "Here, try the microphone." She handed it to Ben.

"Welcome to the first annual Macklin House Christmas Trolley Tour!" he said into the mic. Nothing happened. Dave leaned over and flipped some switches. Ben tried again. "WELCOME TO THE FIRST ANNUAL MACKLIN HOUSE CHRISTMAS TROLLEY TOUR!" This time his words boomed across the town square and ended with an ear-splitting metallic screech.

"That needs some work," said Dave.

Ben walked slowly around the trolley, inspecting it from every angle. He pictured himself in the driver's seat. Suddenly he could see it, just the way Annie had described it. The trolley, the excited riders, the Christmas lights. He hadn't really believed it until now.

"What are you going to say on the tour, Ben?" asked Emma.

"I'm going to tell jokes," he answered. They all stared at him. "Tour guides always tell jokes."

"What kind of jokes?" Annie said.

"Christmas jokes! What do elves learn in school?"

"I don't know."

"The elfa-bet!" Ben said triumphantly. "Why is Santa so good at karate?"

"Uh ..."

"Because he has a black belt! How much did Santa pay for his sleigh?"

"I give up," said Annie.

"Nothing! It was on the house!" Everyone groaned.

Ben looked like he was ready to go on from there, but Dave held up his hand. "I'll just take the mic back to the store and see if I can fix it," he said. "Kids, I think you have homework." They complained but followed him back across the street. Ben continued to gaze at the trolley.

"What do you think?" Annie finally asked.

"I think—it just might work!" Ben answered. He was rewarded with a giant smile from Annie.

"And I think," she replied, "that you're going to be a *fantastic* trolley driver!"

CHAPTER 12

November 18

ANNIE HAD DECIDED THE TROLLEY TOURS WOULD START on December first, a Thursday night, and finish on Saturday, the twenty-fourth. With less than two weeks to go until the first tour, she still had a million things to work out. Her ideas were multiplying.

She wanted to talk to Emma's mom, Paula, and Darlene Ridgeway, the café's owner, about one of them. Paula would be working her usual evening shift, and Darlene normally arrived at the café around five o'clock. Looking at her watch, Annie realized it was almost five. Perfect timing for her to approach Darlene and Paula before the dinner rush. And she needed to see Cammie, too.

Annie locked up the Macklin House, and hurried across the town square. The gazebo in the center of the square, and the trees scattered around it, were lit with twinkling white lights. Annie always thought it looked like a fairyland. They'd be adding colored lights to the town square and decorating the Macklin House, inside and out, in a few days.

THE CHRISTMAS TROLLEY

Annie made a quick detour into the Never Too Late thrift shop, which was next door to the café. Once upon a time, it had been a true antique store, with heirloom jewelry and rooms of vintage furniture and china. The owner had eventually died and left the city with ten years' worth of unpaid property taxes. The city had sold the building to the Macklin Women's Club for a dollar, and they'd turned it into a not-for-profit thrift store. The store now funded a scholarship each year for the most outstanding girl and boy in the graduating class at Macklin High. Back in the day, Annie remembered, she and Ben had been the winners their senior year.

Annie liked to browse the thrift shop for items relating to Macklin's history. She never knew when she might come across some old photographs or documents that would help build her archive at the Macklin House. Tonight, she didn't find anything of historical interest, but she did buy a dark blue Christmas sweater with a pattern of silver stars. One more sweater to add to her collection, which already took up way too much room in her closet. But with a trolley tour almost every night in December, she reminded herself, she was going to have to dress appropriately.

Leaving the thrift shop, Annie could hear laughter coming from the alley that ran between the café and the store. Curious, she walked around the corner of the shop into the alley. Emma and Jackson were standing by the café's delivery entrance. They were giggling at something on a cell phone. Annie knew they were supposed to be doing homework in the café's tiny break room. Whatever they were looking at, it definitely didn't sound like homework.

"Hi, Emma, hi, Jackson," she said calmly. "You must be looking at something really funny. Can I see it, too?"

They both looked startled to see her, and very guilty. She could see Jackson click a button on the phone as he slid it into his pocket.

"It's nothing," said Emma.

"You wouldn't be interested," said Jackson.

"We were just—goofing around," said Emma. "We should go back to our homework."

"That's an excellent idea," said Annie. "I was just going in to see Darlene. I'll come with you."

They all walked in the side entrance that opened to the alley. Annie found Darlene in the kitchen, making chili. "You'll have to talk to me while I work," she told Annie. Just then, Paula came in. "Oh, good," said Annie. "I can talk to you both at once." Jackson and Emma crept past them on the way to the break room, but neither made eye contact. More proof that something was going on, Annie thought. Usually, they would have barged into the kitchen to talk.

"We're going to need refreshments for the trolley tours," Annie said. "Paula, when my sister Amber was a song leader with you, you made those delicious cookies that you brought to all the practices. Could you bake twelve dozen cookies a night? And run a coffee and cocoa stand?"

"I'd love to do that!" Paula exclaimed. "You know, when I was a little girl, I always wanted to open a tea shop. Tea, scones, little sandwiches." She looked wistful. "What kind of cookies?"

"I'm thinking plain sugar cookies," Annie replied. "We give everyone on the trolley tour a free cookie, and we sell the rest. I'm just estimating twelve dozen to start. Darlene, if Paula could do the baking, could she use the café's kitchen?"

"We could handle that easily," said Darlene. "You'll have to pay for the ingredients, but we can provide the labor."

"You sound like you're used to cooking for a crowd," Annie commented. Darlene smiled. "I've had a lot of experience," she said. "Years ago, my ex-husband and I owned the restaurant over at Macklin Lake. The Blue Heron Grill. We'd serve five hundred dinners a night."

Annie was impressed. The Grill had been the best restaurant in Macklin. "It was a special occasion place," Annie remembered. "We went there once to celebrate my mom's birthday. It was just beautiful, looking out over the lake. What happened?"

Darlene sighed. "I got the house and he got the restaurant when we divorced. He ran it into the ground in three years and closed it up. The last I heard, he was working at a McDonald's in Fresno. Meanwhile, I had to support myself, so I bought the café. And here we are. Baking cookies for the multitudes."

"And serving the best food in town!" Annie exclaimed. "It's a deal! And we'll put up a big sign saying that the refreshments came from the Macklin Café, with cookies by Paula Andrews. It'll be great advertising for you. Now, I need to talk to Cammie."

Cammie was at the hostess station. Business was slow, and she was reading a romance novel in between customers. Something about "Love on the Rocks in the Rockies." Annie caught a glimpse of a cover scene with a mountain cabin next to a waterfall. A muscular cowboy with his shirt open gazed into the distance, where a wild horse perched on the edge of a cliff. Cammie guiltily dropped the book into a pocket in her apron. "Is this about Jackson?" she asked.

"Cammie! Not everything is about Jackson! This is about you! I love the decorations you painted on the trolley. Could you design a logo for the trolley tour? Something with a picture of the Macklin House in it?"

Cammie was instantly on board. "Oh, that would be awesome!" she said. "Of course you need a logo. It's the First Annual Macklin House Christmas Trolley Tour."

"Thanks for the vote of confidence," Annie replied. "I *hope* it turns out to be the First Annual Macklin House Christmas Trolley Tour."

"It will! Darlene says Dave says it's going to be fantastic."

Annie had trouble following this train of thought for a minute. "Darlene and Dave Meyers are talking about the trolley?"

Cammie looked around to make sure no one was listening, and then whispered, "Darlene goes over to the hardware store every morning and takes Dave muffins."

Annie looked inquisitively at Cammie.

"Well? Don't you think that means something?"

"Darlene's getting rid of her extra muffins?"

"No!" Cammie said. She was clearly hoping for more drama. "Do you think they're secretly dating?"

"Cammie. This is Macklin. Everybody knows everything. You *can't* secretly date someone."

"I guess you're right," Cammie admitted. "But wouldn't it be perfect if they fell in love?"

Annie thought this over. "It could happen. They're about the same age. They're both divorced. As far as we know, neither of them is seeing anyone else."

"See! It would be perfect!"

It would be perfect if Ben and I fell in love, Annie thought. Then, sanity returned. *Ben isn't interested in me. He has his life, and I have mine. He's only driving the trolley because he doesn't have anything else to do.*

"We need to find out what Dave thinks," Cammie added. She looked expectantly at Annie.

"About what?"

"About Darlene!"

"Well, he's helping us get the trolley in shape," Annie said. "If he says anything about Darlene, I'll let you know."

"Yes!" Cammie said happily. Two customers came in the door. "Back to work," she said reluctantly. "I'll have a sample of that logo for you in a day or two."

Annie decided to leave the way she'd come in, through the side door. As she passed the break room, she saw Jackson and Emma, studiously doing math worksheets. Neither of them looked up. The cell phone was nowhere in sight.

CHAPTER 13

November 20

"ELVES?" BEN SPUTTERED. *"ELVES?"* HE SPILLED HIS COFFEE all over his polo shirt. He and Annie were sharing a breakfast burrito at the café. She'd sent him a text the previous night, saying they needed to meet. This morning, she was wearing a purple sweater with an ice-skating reindeer on it.

"I want Emma and Jackson to be elves on the Christmas trolley," Annie said, handing him a napkin. She watched as he dabbed at his shirt. "They can take tickets and give out cookies."

"I'm not a Christmas guy. I hate elves."

"Ben," Annie said. "How can you hate elves?"

"They speak this weird language and shoot bows and arrows," he explained.

"Those are 'Lord of the Rings' elves," Annie replied. "Ours are regular elves."

"There's more than one kind?"

"Ben, seriously," said Annie. "Emma and Jackson need something to do. They're smart kids and they're bored."

"I thought they were going to take a computer class," Ben said, puzzled.

"That would be great, but their moms can't afford after-school activities. They were out in the alley last night hiding something on a cell phone from me. They're going to get into trouble."

"You're right," Ben agreed. "They're driving us nuts over at Dave's. You remember I told you about Peanut and the deer."

"What now?" Annie asked.

"You know that big fiberglass snowman Dave had out in front of the store?" he continued. Annie nodded.

"It has an opening in the back where you can put in a CD of Christmas songs. You push on the top of its hat to turn it on and off. Yesterday afternoon, Dave had put in a CD of instrumental holiday music. I was working at the cash register, and Jackson and Emma were fooling around with the snowman, and all of a sudden it was playing Hanukkah songs at full volume. It had on a big blue scarf and was holding a dreidel."

"Well, Dave's Jewish," Annie said judiciously. "That shouldn't bother him. At least they're being ecumenical."

"Then, they put in a Halloween haunted house CD, where ghosts scream every two minutes. And they put a skull mask on it and a hatchet in its hand. So, we had to bring it inside and change it back to a Christmas CD. We set it by the cash register where we could keep an eye on it. And we put all the hatchets in our locked glass case." Ben sighed.

"And?" Annie prompted. She could tell there was more to this story.

"The top of the hat is level with the counter, and people kept putting their stuff on the hat, and then it would turn on. Elaine Gilpin came in. You know Elaine?"

Annie nodded. Elaine worked for Ron DeMarco's real estate office and was president of the Macklin House docents. Elaine was known for her upscale wardrobe. Even her casual clothes were perfectly coordinated three-piece ensembles. She dressed like a woman who had never touched a hammer in her life. In reality, Elaine was constantly remodeling her house, and showed up at Meyers' several times a week. "She came in to get her knives sharpened because she's cooking this gigantic turkey for Thanksgiving dinner. Her purse must weigh twenty pounds, and she set it on the hat, and the snowman started playing 'Jingle Bells.' She was so startled she dropped a knife and stabbed herself in the foot."

"So much drama at the hardware store," said Annie. "Who knew?"

"Dave's afraid if he puts it back outside, the kids will switch the CD again," Ben said.

"See, if we make them elves, it's a win-win for everybody." Annie had sat through enough board meetings to be able to reel off business jargon.

"But I'm not a Christmas guy! I don't want to be an elf babysitter!"

"You won't be an elf babysitter," Annie said cheerfully. "You'll be …" Annie searched for a word Ben would feel comfortable with. "An elf mentor!"

"Oh, *that'll* look good on my LinkedIn profile," Ben grumbled.

"I think it'd get a *lot* of attention on your LinkedIn profile," Annie retorted. "People will interview you just to see what an elf mentor does."

"What does an elf mentor do?"

"Your first job—uh, goal—is to make sure they show up on time. The trolley tour starts at six-thirty, so they'll have to be in costume and ready to go by six." Annie held up two small green jerkins with bells for buttons.

"Did you make those?" Ben asked.

"I did," she replied proudly. She shook them up and down so that the bells jingled. "That means they have to finish their homework by five-thirty. If their homework isn't done, they can't go. Neither one will want to get left behind, so they won't mess around. They'll go in the office and work. Dave can put the snowman back on the street." She jingled the costumes again.

"They have to eat," said Ben. "The second tour doesn't get back until nine."

"They can grab sandwiches from the café on their way over to the trolley," said Annie. "Then you, elf mentor, take over. Think of me as your CEO. I'm giving you two assistants. Train them."

First a Christmas trolley driver, now an elf mentor, Ben thought. For a guy who didn't like Christmas, he suddenly seemed to have a lot of Christmas responsibilities. He had a fleeting idea that maybe Annie thought he needed more things to do, too. But it all made sense.

"An elf mentor?" he said again, in resignation. He pointed at the green jerkins. "I have to admit these are cute, but I don't have to wear one, do I?"

"Oh, no," said Annie. "You're going to look very professional. We'll make sure you have a *great* picture to add to your LinkedIn profile."

CHAPTER 14

November 21–22

THEY MET FOR BREAKFAST AT THE CAFÉ AGAIN THE NEXT morning. Dave had promoted Ben to the sales floor. With the trolley tour only two weeks away, people were buying more holiday lights than ever, and Dave needed the help. Ben still wasn't being paid, but Dave had given him fifty dollars' worth of coupons at the café. He and Annie were splurging. They'd each ordered one of the more expensive breakfast specials instead of their usual shared breakfast burrito.

"What's left to do on our tour?" Ben asked over his bacon and eggs. Annie pulled out a notebook from her purse.

"We need a stage," she said, reading from her list as she poured maple syrup on her French toast. "Nothing elaborate. Just a small stage by the trolley stop where we can have entertainment."

She'd convinced Mike Newton, the chief of police, to let her park the trolley in the middle of the block, in front of the Macklin House. It would be their dedicated parking spot for the whole month. Passengers could board and exit the trolley from the sidewalk in front of the Macklin House lawn.

"Dave could build something. He'd love an excuse to get out of the store. We have so many customers the cash register is freezing up again."

"Can't you fix it?" Annie asked.

Ben shook his head. "Dave needs an internet upgrade, but he won't buy it."

"Let's talk to him as soon as he opens this morning," Annie said. She went on down the list. "Then we need a Santa Claus. And entertainment." Her list was still several pages long. "I've got some ideas. But we need that stage first."

They found Dave unlocking the store and staring unhappily at the musical snowman, who had somehow returned to the sidewalk. The snowman was wearing wraparound green sunglasses and holding a giant inflatable shark. Hawaiian music blared from his hidden CD player.

"Dave," Annie said as Ben carried the snowman back inside, "I need a favor. I want to put a stage on the Macklin House lawn near the trolley stop. Ben said you could build one for me. Of course, you'd have to let Ben run the store for a couple of afternoons while you put it together."

Dave started pushing the cash register buttons as he listened to her. "It won't start up," he muttered.

Annie looked sympathetic. "I bet you need an internet upgrade," she said. "My computer did that, and after I got the upgrade it was fine. It made all the difference." Channeling Natalie Preston, she continued. "Everything downloaded *so much faster*. And you're so lucky! If you bought the upgrade, Ben could install it for you! I had to do it myself, and it took *hours*."

"Oh, for God's sake," said Dave. "Buy the upgrade, Ben. Annie, show me what kind of stage you have in mind."

Dave quickly designed a low platform stage with a back wall where they could put up backdrops or hang lights. He went off to find the lumber. With Ben happily installing his upgrade, Annie continued down her list. Her next stop was Macklin High School. The three-story building brought back memories as she parked and walked to the office. The high school had been built in 1925 and had pillars on either side of an imposing front entrance. "Learning is Light" was chiseled over the lintel. The classrooms were small, there was no air conditioning, and Annie knew the structure was only marginally earthquake safe. But generations of Macklin teenagers had graduated from the high school, and no one would dream of suggesting the city should replace it.

The main office was just as Annie remembered. Trophy cases lined one wall, and college pennants lined another. She checked in at the office and explained that she wanted to see Rick Jordan, the football coach. The receptionist called over to the gym, where Rick was teaching a physical fitness class, and told Annie to meet him there.

The gym was a separate building behind the school. The smell of floor wax and gym shoes brought back more memories. In middle school, Annie had spent hours on the bleachers watching Amber perfect her song-leading routines. In high school, she'd played volleyball, although she'd never been tall enough or athletic enough to really do well. Coach Rick was sitting at one end of a row of bleachers, watching a group of students jog around the perimeter of the gym. He was happy to see her, but puzzled.

"How've you been, Annie?" he asked. "Are you married? Any kids?" He was always on the lookout for future athletes.

Annie was hoping that Rick hadn't changed since she'd last seen him at high school graduation, and he hadn't. He was six feet tall and probably weighed two hundred fifty pounds. He was wearing a warmup jacket that read "Coach," across the back, and still looked fit. But after thirty years of coaching high school football, his blond hair had turned almost completely white.

"You know we're going to have a holiday lights tour for the Macklin House?" she asked. She'd sent the press release announcing the trolley tours to all the teachers in town, but wasn't sure how many of them might have actually read it. Rick nodded, however, giving Annie hope. "Can my players help? They always need community service hours."

"No, but you can. I want you to play Santa Claus."

"Annie," Rick sputtered. "I'm the football coach. I can't be Santa. I'm the hard-nosed guy who makes them do wall squats if they're late to practice." He demonstrated a wall squat, and continued to hold the position as their conversation continued. "What would this do to my reputation?"

"You've been the football coach forever," Annie reminded him. "Your reputation is safe. Your reputation is *enshrined*. You'll be a model for your players doing community service hours. Besides, I heard you have two grandchildren under the age of five. You'll be able to handle anything." She gazed at him hopefully. Part of the reason she wanted Rick was that his mere presence, even in a Santa suit, would keep any unruly teenagers in line.

"Think of the publicity," she coaxed. "Think of all the future players you're going to meet. And," she threw in her final pitch, "the Macklin Café is going to provide cookies baked by Paula Andrews. You remember Paula."

Rick nodded. "Song leader. Used to be Paula Stanley. Married that guy on the basketball team who couldn't make free throws." Since this comment perennially applied to most players on the Macklin High basketball team, Annie ignored it. "Works at the Macklin Café now."

"All the free cookies you want," Annie said persuasively.

"Well, when you put it that way ..."

Annie happily crossed "Santa Claus" off the list. Now, to line up the entertainment. She found Mimi Cloverley in her dance studio, trying to instill a sense of rhythm in a group of preschool children. The studio was on the ground floor of an old brick building a few blocks from the Macklin House. Three walls were covered with floor-to-ceiling mirrors, with a ballet barre running horizontally on each wall. The polished wood floor was covered with rubberized mats at the moment.

The toddlers were playing xylophones and banging drums, but seemed to be barely walking, let alone dancing. Mimi greeted her warmly. "Annie! You came to visit my studio! Want some coffee? Is that a Christmas sweater?" No one else had yet commented on her sweater today. It was pink, with white bunny rabbits holding baskets all around the bottom. Instead of Easter eggs, the baskets held Christmas presents and small American flags.

"It's sort of a multi-season sweater," Annie explained, accepting a cup of coffee from Mimi. "I came about your tap-dancing reindeer."

"That's my four o'clock class," Mimi said. "These are my beginners." The kids seemed to be having fun, even if they weren't actually dancing.

"Here's my idea," Annie explained, trying to talk over the noise. "We need something to entertain the trolley customers while they're waiting. Dave Meyers is building a small stage. We'll set it up by the trolley boarding area. Your reindeer can't dance on the trolley, but I think they'd be perfect on our stage."

"They'd love it!" exclaimed Mimi. "Their parents could all come to watch. How often could you use them?"

Annie thought. "If we put them on first—because they're toddlers and they'll need to go to bed early—every third night?"

Mimi was ecstatic. "Will you have a videographer?"

"We will now," Annie said, adding "videographer" to her list. Another job for Zach!

There seemed to be no shortage of talent in Macklin eager to appear on the trolley's stage, even after Annie eliminated all the twelve-year-old girls who wanted to sing Broadway hits. The high school had a choir. The community college had a string quartet. The Rotary Club had a banjo group. Ron DeMarco could recite "The Night Before Christmas" by heart. Annie was beginning to wonder if she could fit everybody in.

"It really shows how valuable the Macklin House could be as a place for community productions," she told Ben. They were back at the café for breakfast yet again, working their way through Ben's coupons. This morning they were both eating pecan-crusted waffles.

"It means you're on the right track," said Ben. "With your ideas. Historical lectures, art shows, tea on the lawn. People in Macklin are looking for things to do."

Annie's eyes widened. "I just remembered! Paula told me she always wanted to open a tea shop! She could cater our afternoon tea!"

"One thing at a time," Ben cautioned. "How's that list coming?"

Annie pulled it out. "Update Facebook page. Send video out to TV stations. Find a red and green afghan."

"What's that for?" Ben asked.

"Santa's chair," Annie explained. "The thrift shop donated an armchair for him to sit in, but it's covered in fabric with bright yellow daisies. We need to cover up the daisies. And last but not the least, a trial run with the trolley."

Ben pulled out his phone and looked at the calendar. "Are you spending Thanksgiving weekend with your parents?" he asked.

Annie nodded. "I'm driving down tomorrow. Coming back on Sunday."

"Monday's the twenty-eighth, and we start tours on December first. Can we do a trial run on Monday after I finish at the store?" Ben asked.

"That's a good plan," Annie said. "Everybody's lights will be up after Thanksgiving weekend. We'll finalize the route."

"The First Annual Macklin House Tour of Holiday Lights!" said Ben. They clinked their coffee cups together.

I hope it's not the *last* Macklin House Tour of Holiday Lights, thought Annie. But it was too late now to have any second thoughts.

CHAPTER 15

November 23–27

ANNIE ALWAYS SPENT THE THANKSGIVING HOLIDAYS WITH her parents in Palm Springs. She enjoyed visiting them and catching up with her older sister, Amber, and her brother-in-law Tom. Their son, Scott, was in second grade, and his little sister Savannah had just started kindergarten. Between the kids and their teaching jobs, Amber and Tom were always busy, but they'd still volunteered to cook Thanksgiving dinner.

Annie found herself thinking constantly about Ben as she drove from Macklin to Palm Springs. She was finding that she relied more and more on Ben as a sounding board for her ideas. They'd started meeting for breakfast every morning at the café. He'd approved her plan to put up space heaters in the seating area, while rejecting any refreshments other than the cookies as too complicated. He always had another funny story about the hardware store. She cheered him up when yet another job lead fell through. Annie had to admit to herself she was hoping a job *wouldn't* come through. At least for a while.

All the way to Palm Springs, she wondered if she was feeling more than friendship for Ben. She remembered her fleeting thought when she and Cammie had discussed Darlene and Dave. *It would be perfect if Ben and I fell in love.* Why would that come to mind if she didn't feel something more than friendship? And could Ben be feeling more than friendship toward her? The long drive gave her plenty of time to analyze and re-analyze every conversation she'd had with him. She realized, ironically, that these were the same confused feelings she'd had when she'd had a crush on Ben in eighth grade. Well, sort of. There were a lot of feelings now that she hadn't been aware of in eighth grade. It was a relief when she finally turned into her parents' driveway and could focus on her family instead.

Annie's dad opened the front door, and lifted her off the ground in a huge hug. He was wearing a t-shirt that read "Old Guys Rule" and a pair of khaki hiking shorts. His blue eyes matched Annie's, and his hair had once matched, too. But Annie had inherited her mother's height, and her father was a good six inches taller.

"Annie's here!" he called out, setting her carefully back down on the doorstep. He insisted on carrying Annie's suitcase inside, even though she could have managed it easily. Annie followed him into the guest bedroom, where the bedspread and curtains had a brown and green pattern of geckos and roadrunners. Sand-colored pottery was displayed on a rustic wood bookcase, and a painting of a desert sunset hung over the bed.

"We're so glad you're here," her father said, squeezing her hand. "Scott and Savannah are really looking forward to your visit!" She knew this was code for, "Your mother and I are really looking forward to your visit."

Her parents had bought a one-story house in Palm Springs with an open floor plan. Their home in Macklin had been very formal, with lots of antique furniture and crystal. In retirement, they'd shifted into a more relaxed lifestyle. The great room had a wall of glass sliding doors that opened onto a patio and a lap pool. Cozy leather recliners faced a flat-screen television hung over the fireplace. The tile floors throughout the house were covered by Southwestern-patterned area rugs. It suited her parents perfectly at this stage, but Annie sometimes felt a pang of longing for their old house. She missed the Lenox china and Waterford crystal, which were packed away in the garage. On moving, her mother had announced that she was never again going to use a dish that couldn't go in the dishwasher. Now her parents ate at their clubhouse three nights a week, and seemed to spend the other nights using Happy Hour coupons with their neighbors. Amber had inherited the role of holiday dinner hostess.

Annie's mother came in from the patio and happily shouted, "Annie! You made it!" Her astonished tone implied that Annie had made the trek from Macklin in a covered wagon. Her t-shirt read, "Ask me about my grandchildren," superimposed over a photo of Scott and Savannah. Her gray hair was short and curly, and her brown eyes peered out from behind large silver-framed glasses. After a hug, she said eagerly, "I've got something for you!"

Annie took this in stride. Like Annie, her mom was constantly doing something. Her mother *always* had something for her. This time, it was a large, gift-wrapped box, with candy canes tied to a white bow.

"It's an early Christmas present," her mom explained, unnecessarily. Annie opened it, and found a Christmas sweater. It was a red cardigan with a huge Christmas tree covering most of the back. One of the presents under the tree had a gift tag that read "Annie."

"I joined the knitting club here," her mother explained. "Everyone else was doing iPad covers, but I wanted to knit you a special sweater!"

"I love it!" Annie exclaimed. "It'll be perfect for the Christmas trolley." She poured out the whole story of the Macklin House's finances, the need to raise one hundred thousand dollars, and the trolley tour. Her parents hung on every word. "You put this whole thing together?" her father asked. "They're not paying you enough! You could make a fortune if you came down here. I know you love Macklin, but with your brains and your ideas ..."

"How's your golf game, Dad?" Annie asked, changing the subject. They had this conversation every time they got together. Her parents not-very-secretly wanted both their daughters close by. It was sweetly endearing when it wasn't totally frustrating.

Annie's dad always organized an early morning family activity on holidays. This year he'd planned a hike in a nearby state park.

"We're going to Bobcat Canyon," he said happily. "Lots of rock formations and desert flowers."

"You want to take your grandchildren hiking in a place called *Bobcat Canyon*?" Annie said.

"There aren't any bobcats," her mother explained. "The state park used to be a ranch owned by a couple named Bob and Catherine Parker. They named the canyon after themselves." Her mother had also joined the Desert History club.

Annie hadn't done much hiking since returning to Macklin, but her father assured her she'd be able to keep up. She fell asleep wondering about this, since her dad was used to hiking with Amber and Tom, both athletic people who'd met on a coed softball team. She reminded herself that Scott and Savannah would keep things from getting too challenging. The last thing she needed was to break a leg climbing out of a slot canyon!

But as promised, the hike turned out to be an easy loop where they saw jackrabbits, and some hawks gliding overhead, but no bobcats. Scott and Savannah babbled endlessly to their grandmother, who told them the names of all the flowers and pointed out tiny lizards under the rocks. Annie's dad discussed basketball with Tom, who coached middle school kids in an after-school program.

As they continued down the trail, Annie and Amber fell back behind the others. Amber was tall, like their father, and today wore her long, sun-streaked hair pulled back in a ponytail under a Los Angeles Dodgers' baseball cap. In spite of the six years between them and their different personalities, the sisters had always been close. Annie couldn't wait to fill Amber in on the story of the trolley.

"For once I agree with dad," Amber said when Annie had finished. "You should move to Palm Springs and work for one of the museums here. Or become an event planner. You're wasting your potential!"

"But I love the Macklin House. This is my dream job!" Annie responded.

"I *know* it's your dream job. But is it your dream life? Do you have any friends in Macklin?" Amber was tactful enough not to say "boyfriends."

"Not really," Annie admitted. "I've been too busy with work to socialize. But guess who's back in town, at least temporarily? Ben Grover."

"Ben Grover?" Amber replied. "The cute little nerdy guy who dumped you in eighth grade? I thought he was in San Francisco starting the next Facebook or something. What's he doing in Macklin?"

"He got laid off from his job in San Francisco, so he's moved back home while he looks for work. He's living in his parents' old house."

Amber cut to the chase. "Is he single?"

"Well, he's not married, and he hasn't mentioned any girlfriends. He's going to drive the Christmas trolley for me."

"Do you think he wants to go out with you?" Amber asked.

Annie considered this, not wanting to admit that she was hoping Ben *did* want to go out. "Maybe. He seems happy to see me at breakfast ..."

Amber stopped in her tracks. "Oh my God!" she said breathlessly. "Tell me everything!"

"No, no, no," Annie said, to Amber's obvious disappointment. "It's not like that. We meet at the Macklin Café and talk about the trolley."

"How often?" asked Amber.

Annie thought. "Every day this week."

"Either he likes you or he can't cook. Why did you guys break up, anyway? You were so close all through elementary school. Personally, I always thought the two of you would end up married."

Annie groaned. "It's a long story."

Amber waved her hand at the surrounding rocks. "We've got another two miles of this," she said.

"It—it happened on the eighth grade field trip," Annie began. "The one everybody takes to see the Macklin House." Amber nodded. "I had a crush on Ben. We'd always been best friends. And I thought he liked me, too. So, we got to the Macklin House. I'd never been there before. We all went in, and it was like—it was like my whole life changed. You could just feel the history. I never wanted to leave!"

"And then ..." Amber prodded.

"We ended up alone together on the porch, and I said something like, 'This is the most interesting old house in the world, I never want to leave it,' and Ben said, 'That's so dumb, I can't wait to leave Macklin. I'm going to study computer science and move to San Francisco.' And I said, 'Don't you care about history? Don't you care about the past?'"

Annie swallowed. "And he said, 'No! I don't care about the Macklin House. I'm thinking about the future.'" She hesitated. It was painful to explain all this to Amber. "And then he said, 'I really like you, would you be my girlfriend? Can I kiss you?'"

"And ..." Amber prodded again.

"I was so stunned that he didn't like the Macklin House that the part about being his girlfriend didn't register. I couldn't believe anyone wouldn't like it, especially Ben. We'd always liked the same things! And I said, 'You really don't care about the Macklin House?' and he said, 'It's a piece of junk!'"

"And then," Annie added, "I said, 'Ben Grover, I'll never kiss you until snow falls in Macklin!'"

They walked a few steps in silence.

"Annie," said Amber. "Here's your problem. You think too much about the past. You *love* the past. But sometimes, you have to let the past go. Forget what happened back then. Ben Grover, your childhood sweetheart, is sitting right there under your nose. Think about the future for once!"

Annie sighed. She could tell Amber was already visualizing Annie and Ben married and living in a house down the street.

But Amber was usually perceptive about things. Grudgingly, Annie admitted, there might be some truth in her advice. And if she and Ben were only friends, why had she just spent a five-hour car ride thinking about him?

CHAPTER 16

November 24

BEN HAD INTENDED TO SPEND THANKSGIVING FOLLOW-
ing up on his job applications and cleaning out more of his mother's
cupboards. (As much as he had loved her, he really couldn't understand
why she'd needed seventeen pieces of Tupperware.) His plans changed
after a call from Mrs. Martinez, inviting him to Thanksgiving dinner. A
call from Mrs. Martinez was an offer he couldn't refuse. Substituting a
blue button-down shirt for his usual Jupiter polo, and carrying a bottle
of Chardonnay, he knocked on the Martinez' door at three o'clock.

Mrs. Martinez opened the door, beaming at him. "Ben!" she
exclaimed. He could tell she was trying very hard not to call him "Benjy."
She led him into the kitchen, handed him a beer, and sent him into the
family room to watch football with her husband, Ray. "Hi Ben," Ray
said, shaking hands. Everyone in Macklin knew Ray, who had spent
twenty years as a detective in the Macklin police department before

blowing out a knee while chasing a suspect down a flight of stairs. Now he taught criminal justice at Macklin Community College.

Ben had never been to the Martinez' house. He'd always pictured it as a forbidding fortress—the principal's house! He was surprised to find it looked pretty much like his parents', down to the collection of Tupperware and the kitchen magnets with inspirational sayings. One wall was hung with portraits of their three grown kids, a boy and two girls who were a little younger than Ben. The boy was in the Air Force, stationed in Alaska. The two girls were in college in Boston and would be home at Christmas.

Another wall was filled with photos of every Macklin Middle School graduating class for the past twenty years. "There you are, Ben!" Mrs. Martinez said proudly, somehow picking him out from a sea of eighth graders. "And there's your friend Annie. I can't wait for that trolley tour!"

"I'm driving the trolley," Ben volunteered. Mrs. Martinez obviously thought the trolley was the best idea in the history of Macklin. He wanted to get some credit, too.

"Oh, that's wonderful," she said. "You know, I always thought you and Annie would end up getting married."

"Um ..." Ben said. Not only were the furnishings like his parents' house, the conversations were too. He could remember his mother asking about various girls he'd mentioned, subtly trying to find out if he was seeing anyone.

"Ignore that, Ben," Ray contributed from the family room. "She wants everyone to get married. She asks our son Nick every week. Like he's going to meet any girls on that Air Force base!"

"It could happen," said Ben, glad to shift the conversation to Nick's marital prospects from his own. "Women are in the military. Just wait, one of these days you'll get an email. Don't worry, Mrs. Martinez," he added, seeing her dark look, "he wouldn't dare get married without inviting you to the wedding!"

"That goes for you, too, Ben," she retorted. "You'd better send us an invitation. Whoever she is!" Not one to beat around the bush, she inquired, "Did you leave anyone special in San Francisco?"

"Not really," Ben admitted. "There were a couple of women in my office that I went out with a few times, but it's hard to date someone from work. All we'd talk about was office gossip and whether we were going to get stock options."

Mrs. Martinez' look clearly implied that these topics lacked romantic potential. "Tell me about driving the Christmas trolley."

"Oh, it's going to be great!" he said enthusiastically. "Annie and I have a route in mind. We're going on a test drive on Monday. She made elf costumes for Jackson and Emma. They're going to be my helpers. She has different entertainment lined up for every night." He went on and on about the trolley tour. If Mrs. Martinez noticed that he mentioned Annie in every other sentence, she was smart enough not to say anything.

They had a long discussion about Macklin Middle School over dinner. Ben found it interesting to hear things from Mrs. Martinez' perspective. The kids were different, older in some ways and younger in others. Social media was a problem. The textbooks were outdated. The school was always short of money.

"We do okay with the ones that are like you and Annie, who are smart and self-motivated," she explained. "It's all the others that are a challenge. They don't see any future in Macklin. A lot of them don't see any future, period. I need more after-school programs. I need more in-school programs that will keep them involved."

"Annie has a lot of ideas for using the Macklin House," Ben offered. "You should talk to her. I'll bet she could adapt some of them for the middle school."

"I just hope she can keep the Macklin House going," Ray said.

"So do I," Ben said. "But we all know Annie. She'll do everything she can to make it work out."

Mrs. Martinez insisted on sending him home with leftovers (more Tupperware, Ben thought). As he started to leave, she suddenly stopped him.

"I'm glad you're back in Macklin, Ben," she said. "You know, you were always the boy thinking about the future. Even in middle school, you knew what you wanted to do and where you wanted to go. But you can't just forget about the past. Get to know Macklin again as an adult. I'm so glad you and Annie are working together on that trolley tour. It's good to reconnect with your old friends."

Driving home, Ben thought of last year's Thanksgiving. He'd spent the entire day working on a PowerPoint presentation. He couldn't even remember now what it had been about. By the time he'd finished, it had been too late to go out for dinner. He'd heated up some leftovers and watched the sports recap on TV.

Thanksgiving this year had been so much nicer. He suddenly wished Annie had been there to share it. She'd be gone all weekend, but they'd be together on Monday night for the trial run.

It suddenly came to him that he'd forgotten the elves. Annie was counting on him to teach those kids to help with the trolley tours. She'd never forgive him if something went wrong.

If Annie wanted him to be an elf mentor, he'd be an elf mentor! The next evening, Ben spent an hour on the internet, reading articles on mentoring. None of them seemed to address what he thought of as his main challenge, making sure the elves went to the bathroom before they got on the trolley. He started thinking of things to discuss with Emma and Jackson. Then, he realized he had a bigger problem.

The tour would last about an hour, including two photo stops. He was the tour guide. And he was going to have to fill a lot of time with something besides Santa jokes.

You could only talk about Christmas lights for so long. Ben needed filler. The trolley route wound through Macklin, and the tour was to help the Macklin House. He could talk about the history of Macklin, and how the Macklin House was built. Annie would have all this information at her fingertips, Ben realized. He knew he could call her, and she would gladly answer his questions, even write a whole script for him. But she had a hundred other things to do. And, Ben admitted, he wanted to impress her. With a little research, he'd be able to spout facts about the Macklin House, too.

Wikipedia was just a click away, and soon he was engrossed in the story of his hometown.

CHAPTER 17

November 28

ANNIE DROVE BACK TO MACKLIN THE SUNDAY AFTER Thanksgiving, mentally running through last-minute details of the trolley tour the whole way. Periodically, she thought about her conversation with Amber. She felt uncertain about seeing Ben. Was Amber right? Should she forget that moment on the field trip that had changed everything between them? Could she? Could Ben?

"This isn't getting anywhere," she eventually told herself. "I'll see him tomorrow night for the test run. Maybe that will give me a clue." She wondered, briefly, if she could bring herself to apologize for their fight on the field trip. *Except*, she thought, *why should I apologize?* She put the whole thing out of her mind again as she came to the Macklin turnoff from the interstate. She loved going to Palm Springs to see her family, but she loved coming home to Macklin just as much. She always felt happy when she came to the Macklin exit.

Annie still had all her regular duties at the Macklin House, and she spent Monday handling a clogged sink, fixing a misprint in a brochure, and preparing some reports for the board. She had just enough time to run over to her cottage for a quick bite to eat before meeting Ben at the trolley after work. She changed her old t-shirt for her mother's new Christmas sweater, and carefully fixed her hair.

This is pointless, Annie thought. My hair will just blow all over the place on the trolley ride. But she did it anyway. Okay, she was taking Amber's advice. It wasn't really a date, but ... there wasn't any harm in trying to look extra-special.

Holiday lights had gone up all around town over the Thanksgiving weekend. The Macklin House itself was decorated with white lights along the porch rail and the roofline. Two large Christmas trees covered with rows of colored lights flanked the front walkway. A third tree was visible in the foyer through the glass door panels. Red poinsettias lined the porch.

The trolley was parked in front of the Macklin House, in its designated "passenger loading" spot. Annie thought the trolley looked more festive than ever. Dave and Ben had strung small red lights along the roof and all the outside corners. The lights reflected off Annie's holiday paint job. It no longer looked like a worn-out, well-used trolley from "Homes of the Stars." It looked like something from a Christmas storybook.

Ben was standing next to the trolley, swinging the keys back and forth. At the sight of him, Annie felt her heart lurch. He was wearing a red down vest over a green pullover. "You look so Christmassy!" Annie told him. She wanted to say, "And handsome," but couldn't quite do it. "And the trolley looks spectacular! *Anyone* would want to take a ride on this trolley!"

Ben managed to say, "Let's start on Main Street." He felt a rush of happiness at seeing Annie again. She was wearing a new Christmas sweater he hadn't seen before, her hair was different somehow, and his brain was suddenly plotting ways to make this trolley tour last a lot longer than one hour.

From Main, they turned left on Second Street, and then left again. State Street was busy. If people weren't shopping, they were certainly browsing. All the stores were decorated with lights. Lights twinkled in the trees and bushes. Shoppers waved at the trolley as they drove by. Ben rang the trolley's bell, and he and Annie waved back.

Now was the time to impress Annie with his Macklin history. "Did you know that Philip Macklin made the land the Macklin House is built on three feet higher than the surrounding lots, so the house would be taller than any other buildings around?" Ben asked.

"I did," Annie replied. They turned down Bluebird Avenue. Now the lights were getting more elaborate. Lights on houses, lights on mailboxes, lights wrapped around the trunks of palm trees. The lights came in every size and color.

"Did you know that, during the gold rush, so many miners were coming to town every Saturday with their gold that it took four armed men to keep order in the bank? And there were twenty-one saloons in town?" Ben continued.

"I did," said Annie. They turned right, and came to a street lined with candy canes. Giant lit-up figures of Santa and his sleigh stood on the roof of the first house on their left. A reindeer stood on the roof of each house going down the block. Their legs moved up and down as "Rudolph, the Red-Nosed Reindeer" blasted from a boom box in someone's yard.

"Did you know that the day after Pearl Harbor, forty percent of the able-bodied men in Macklin went down to the train depot to enlist?" Ben went on.

"I did *not* know that," Annie replied. "Although I know there's a memorial plaque in city hall to honor all our veterans. You've been studying Macklin's history!" Ben was secretly thrilled. He could tell she was pleased.

The next street had a train theme. Each yard had a different light display of a train car filled with presents. The middle house on the block had a child-sized model train set up in the front yard. Lights covered the engine, two cars with seats, and a caboose. A giant teddy bear wearing an engineer's cap sat in the engine cab, and a stuffed polar bear rode in the caboose. The other two cars held some delighted toddlers. More were lining up, waiting for rides. The street was having a block party. Ben clanged the trolley bell and all the kids waved.

"We need a photo op," said Annie. "Somewhere about half-way through, where people can get off and stretch their legs, and take pictures!"

"Columbus Street," Ben answered promptly. "We're selling tons of lights to that neighborhood. Even some special orders." He turned left and Annie was floored. This was it, the street that everyone would want to see!

Each house had a different display. Each was trying to outdo the other. There was Santa's workshop. There was a winter fantasy filled with snowflakes and silver fairies. A two-story Eiffel Tower with a wreath on top. A miniature mountain with animated sleds going up and down. A Ferris wheel. A candy land, with lollipops, candy canes, and every possible kind of holiday cookie.

"This is our photo op!" Annie exclaimed. "You stop here, you take a ten-minute break, and then you start back."

"Do you know why this street is called 'Columbus Street'?"

"No," Annie admitted.

"The first person to build a house on the street was a carpenter named Jacob Miller. He was from Columbus, Ohio! So he named the street after his home town."

"I always thought it was named for Christopher Columbus. Are you studying up for a Macklin trivia contest?" Annie joked.

"I'm taking notes for my tour guide speech," Ben said proudly. "And you know what? I'm learning a lot about Macklin. There's a lot of history here. I hope the trolley riders will remember some of it."

Annie felt a lump in her throat. Maybe Ben was starting to see her side of things.

"And the Macklin House," he continued to her surprise, "is a great example of Victorian architecture."

Annie's mouth fell open. Fortunately, it was dark, and Ben didn't notice.

"Of course it is!" she exclaimed enthusiastically.

"It's the most important Victorian building in the county. So this trolley tour has got to be good!"

"Ben, your tour guide speech is going to be perfect," Annie said. "It's going to make the tour!" She was having a wonderful ride. Alone with Ben, seeing the beautiful lights, sharing their plans for the tour—it was very romantic.

"We'll have the best Christmas Trolley tour ever!" he agreed, delighted by her praise.

"Where are we going after Columbus Street?" Annie asked. The lights were starting to dwindle. Ben, meanwhile, was trying to think of some romantic spot where he could end the drive. Nothing came to mind. None of the romantic spots where he'd taken girls in high school seemed romantic enough. If they'd been in San Francisco, it would have been a different story. But Macklin?

"What's this street up ahead?" Annie asked. It looked like a wide street with large brick houses on both sides.

"Oakmont Avenue!" Ben exclaimed. "This is a great street!" He was still thinking. They could always go to the café for dessert. Unlike most of the women he'd met in the city, Annie still believed in eating dessert.

"This is a *perfect* street to end the tour!" Annie said enthusiastically. Most of the homes had their front drapes open to showcase huge Christmas trees. Suddenly, Ben pointed at one of the houses. It was smaller than the others on the block, and it was the only one without any holiday lights. Amid the dazzling lights surrounding it, the house looked forlorn and lonely. "I wonder what's going on with that one?" he said.

They pulled up closer. Annie could see that the lawn needed mowing, and some of the roof shingles were missing. A light inside shone through the drapes across the living-room windows. They could just make out the house number from a dim bulb next to the front door.

"We're on Oakmont Avenue, right?" Annie asked suddenly. Ben nodded. "That house is 83 Oakmont."

"Ben, pull over," Annie said urgently. "That's Grace Iwamoto's house."

"Who's Grace Iwamoto?" Ben asked, as he parked the trolley.

"She's one of my docents," explained Annie. "She lives alone and uses a walker. I hope nothing's wrong."

They rang the doorbell.

A quavering voice called, "Who is it?" They could see someone looking at them through the peephole, and then a small elderly woman opened the door. Annie hugged her.

"Grace, we were driving down the street and saw your house," she said. "You haven't been in for a while. Is everything okay?" Then she added, "Oh, this is Ben Grover. Ben, Grace is our expert on the antique china and porcelain at the Macklin House."

"I've had that flu that's going around," Grace said, and immediately started to cough. Annie and Ben exchanged glances. Grace sounded terrible. "Have you been to see the doctor?" Annie asked, steering Grace and her walker back toward the couch. "Can we fix you some tea? Or some soup?"

"Tea would be nice. I haven't been to the doctor," Grace confessed. "I feel so weak. I couldn't get my walker in the car by myself."

"We could help with that," Annie volunteered, as she opened a cupboard looking for the tea. "I can drive you to the clinic in the morning." Grace started to shake her head, but Annie persevered. "You need to see the doctor. We don't want you to catch pneumonia. We can pick up some groceries, too."

Ben settled Grace on the couch as Annie heated a steaming mug of tea. Grace sipped it gratefully. "Why were you driving down my street?" she asked Annie.

"You remember? I talked about the Christmas trolley tours at the last docent meeting. It's a way to raise money for the Macklin House. If you're going to fund-raise, you need something that will get people's attention."

"Annie's good at marketing," Ben interjected. Annie turned pink.

"Ben's going to drive the trolley," she said. "We're planning our route, so we were driving around tonight looking at the lights. Your street definitely made the cut!"

"I wish I could put up Christmas lights again," Grace said sadly. "My husband used to do it, but after he passed away, I just couldn't manage it. The man next door came over last week and told me my house was a disgrace because I didn't have any lights."

"He said *what?*" Ben was indignant. "Which neighbor?"

"The one with the crisscrossing lights on his roof. He always puts up a fancy light display. He hires someone to do it. Last year, he had a bungee-jumping Santa."

"I'll put up some lights for you," Ben offered. "And I can fix your shingles and mow your lawn. We'll show this guy."

"Oh, my goodness," said Grace. "You'd do that for me? But I don't have any Christmas lights. I gave them all away."

"I've got that covered," Ben assured her. "I'm living in my parents' old house and we've got lots of boxes of lights in the garage. I've got plenty of lights to spare."

Annie and Ben quickly realized that Grace needed more than just a cup of tea. They fixed soup and toast, made sure Grace had taken all her pills, and put her to bed. Annie did a load of laundry while Ben cleaned up the kitchen. By the time they were ready to leave, it was too late for either of them to think of anything except getting home.

Most of the houses had turned their Christmas lights off, and the streets were dark as Ben slowly drove the trolley back to the Macklin House. I *did* get to spend more time with Annie tonight, he reflected. Just not in the way I imagined it. That was what happened in real life. Grace had needed their help. What if he'd missed her little house among all the glittering lights on her street?

"It was lucky that we were driving by on our trial run," Ben said. "Grace needs to see a doctor. It was really nice of you to offer to take her to the clinic tomorrow."

Since he was driving, Annie hugged his arm. She thought of kissing him on the check for an instant, but instead she said, "That was really nice of *you* to offer to cut her grass and put up her Christmas lights. Are you *sure* you're not a Christmas guy?"

CHAPTER 18

November 29

BEN FOUND SEVERAL STRINGS OF MULTICOLORED LIGHTS in his garage the next morning that he could use on Grace Iwamoto's house. He wanted something extra, though. Nothing fancy, just something special to make her house stand out. Off he went to Meyers'.

He was looking through the holiday lights when he happened to wander into the back section by the loading dock where Dave kept the farm supplies. To his astonishment, this area was crammed with large light displays. Why weren't these out on the main sales floor? Looking at them more closely, Ben realized all of them were damaged in some way. Dave couldn't sell them. But maybe he would let Ben have a few.

"What are you going to do with those damaged lights in the back?" Ben asked him.

"Throw them out," Dave answered. "It's not worth my cost to ship them back."

Ben was elated. "Could I have some of them? And could I borrow one of your long contractor's ladders?"

"Take whatever you want," Dave replied. "In fact, take them all and drop off the ones you don't use at the dump."

Ben bought a heavy-duty extension cord with a lot of outlets and a roll of duct tape. There were some angels and Santas, but most of the damaged lights seemed to be Christmas packages made of colored plastic panels lit up from behind. Many of the corners had cracked, and one was missing its bow. Ben found the bow on top of a bag of fertilizer. He could easily put it back in place with duct tape.

He met Annie at Grace's house around noon. Annie had taken Grace to the clinic that morning.

"Grace doesn't have pneumonia, but they prescribed an antibiotic," Annie reported. "I'm fixing her lunch, and then I'm going to the grocery store." She looked in the back of Ben's minivan. "Are you going to put all those lights on her roof?"

"Probably not, but Dave wanted to get rid of them." He was busy duct-taping the bow back in place. "That works!" Annie said approvingly. "You'll never notice the tape once it's on the roof."

Annie made grilled cheese sandwiches and tomato soup for lunch. Grace was thrilled with the idea of lights on her house. "You two are such a nice young couple!" she said happily, if somewhat inaccurately. Neither of them said anything to correct her.

"I can't wait to see how the lights turn out!" Grace added. "I'm going to fit right in with all the neighbors!" She looked better already.

After lunch, Grace went to take a nap. Annie and Ben put the strings of colored lights around the edge of the roof. This part was easy. Mr. Iwamoto had taken a lot of pride in his holiday lights. There were already nails in place where they could attach them.

"Do you really think it needs more?" Annie said when they had finished. The large, old-fashioned light bulbs Ben had found in his garage seemed to match the style of Grace's small ranch-style house. All it needed was Bing Crosby singing "White Christmas."

"Of course it needs more!" Ben answered. "Lots more!"

"Well, you're the one who's going to put the stuff on the roof," Annie said, seeing she wasn't going to change his mind. "I'm off to Supersaver." As soon as she drove away, Ben set up his ladder and got to work. He took out the panel that was the package with the patched bow, and carried it up to the roof. He was fixing it in place when he noticed an older, heavyset man in a brown t-shirt and jeans standing in front of the house next door, watching him. The man looked irritated. *This must be the disgruntled neighbor,* Ben thought.

"Hi," he said. "You're putting a Christmas package on that roof?"

"Right," Ben said.

"Humph," the man muttered. He disappeared into his garage. A moment later, he came out with a ladder of his own.

Ben climbed down to get a better look at the Christmas present on Grace Iwamoto's roof. When he looked at the house next door again, the man was on his own roof, busily putting up a Christmas present of his own. It was smaller in size than Ben's, but had more colors. Now, he was putting up a second present. Still on the roof, he turned around and looked challengingly at Ben. "I've got more presents than you have!" he yelled.

"We'll see about that!" Ben shouted back. He ran to his van and pulled out two more of the Christmas package lights. He climbed up his ladder as fast as he could, and fixed them in place. The neighbor sat down on his own roof and watched.

"There!" Ben yelled at him. "Now *I've* got more."

The man promptly climbed down, went into his garage, and came out with more lights. Ben sat on Grace's roof and watched him install two more Christmas box lights. Now, he had four.

"See if you can beat that!" the neighbor yelled. Then, he started to lose his balance. Ben watched as he slid down to the edge of his roof, teetered for a horrible moment, and then caught himself. The man ended up sitting unsteadily on the edge with his legs hanging down, but he was ten feet away from his ladder.

"Are you okay?" Ben called.

The neighbor ignored Ben. He tried tentatively to push himself up enough to get his legs back on the roof, but teetered again and almost fell off.

Just then, two cars drove up. One was Annie, back from the grocery store. The other car pulled into the neighbor's driveway. A woman got out, and ran up to the house. "Charlie!" she yelled accusingly. "What are you doing? You know you shouldn't be on the roof. That's why we pay your nephew to put the lights up." She tried to pick up their ladder to move it closer to her husband, but it was too heavy for her.

"Don't move!" she yelled at him. "I'm going to call the fire department!"

Ben sighed. "No, wait!" he yelled in return, and climbed down to the ground. He went to the house next door, picked up the ladder, and moved it next to Charlie. He held it in place as Charlie managed to pull himself onto the ladder and climb down. They glared at each other.

Charlie's wife said, "I'm Chrissy Belmont. This is my idiot husband, Charlie. *What were you thinking?*"

Annie had put the groceries away, and came over. Chrissy's eyes widened. "You're Annie Mulvaney!" she said. "From the Macklin House! I took my mother on the tour last month. I saw you in the lobby."

"This is Ben Grover, who's going to drive the trolley on our holiday lights tour. He's putting lights on Grace's Iwamoto's house," Annie explained.

Chrissy eyed Ben and Charlie. "And you guys turned this into a contest?"

Charlie pointed at Ben. "He started it!"

Ben pointed back. "What, by putting up a Christmas package?"

"I have more presents than you," Charlie said.

"Mine are bigger!" Ben retorted.

"STOP THAT!" Annie yelled. Both of them fell silent.

"The holiday season is *not* about who has the most presents or the biggest present or who has the best Christmas lights. It's about good cheer and—sharing with your friends and—remembering the people you love," Annie said fiercely.

"And having enough sense not to climb on a roof when you're sixty-two years old," Chrissy added.

Ben and Charlie kept quiet. Chrissy whispered something to Annie. They nodded in agreement.

"Where's the property line?" Annie asked. None of the front yards in Macklin were fenced. The lawns just ran into each other.

Charlie pointed at a spot between the two houses.

"Here's what we're going to do," said Annie. "Ben, take ALL those Christmas boxes down. Including Charlie's. He shouldn't be up on the roof."

"What about Grace Iwamoto?" Ben said in an aggrieved tone. "She's losing out. They've got two blow-up Santas and a blow-up Christmas tree on their porch."

Annie pointed to the minivan. "You can find something else for Grace. ONE thing."

"And then," Chrissy added, "you, Charlie, are going to set up ALL the Christmas presents right here in the middle." She gestured at the invisible property line. "TOGETHER."

"As a show of Christmas spirit," said Annie.

The two women folded their arms and stared at Ben and Charlie, daring them to say anything. Ben and Charlie looked at each other. They knew when they were beaten.

"Get to work, guys," said Chrissy.

CHAPTER 19

December 1

"IT'S SHOWTIME!" ANNIE EXCLAIMED.

The first trolley tour was ready to start. The weather couldn't have been better. Cool but not too chilly for an open-air ride, with a big moon glowing overhead and lots of stars. Riders had been gathering on the Macklin House lawn for the past hour, drinking coffee and hot chocolate while they waited for the tour to begin.

Ben had spent the past hour reviewing the finer points of elf etiquette with Jackson and Emma. He was determined that nothing was going to go wrong with this first trolley tour. It would set the bar for all the other tours. If it went well, word would spread and people would be lining up to buy tickets. If it didn't, word would spread and they'd be doomed.

He had made the kids put their costumes on to get into character. Emma had accessorized hers with a necklace of tiny silver stars. Jackson had brought along a bow and arrow, which Ben promptly confiscated.

"I need that!" he protested. "I'm Legolas, the archer …"

"No, you're not," Ben retorted. "You're Santa's helper. Now pretend I'm a customer getting on the trolley. What do you do?"

Jackson drew himself up, held out his hand, and said, "Welcome to the trolley tour." Ben shook his hand.

"That was great," he told Jackson. "You looked me in the eye and had a good, firm handshake." He turned to Emma. "Now what do you do next?"

"I show them to their seats." She posed and recited dramatically. "Ladies and gentlemen! Down this aisle to your seats for this spectacular trolley tour! There's nothing like it in Macklin! You'll remember this night for the rest of your lives!"

"That's good," Ben said, "but, uh, could you leave out that last part. We may not *want* them to remember it."

"Well, *we* want to remember it," Jackson countered. "We've never *been* on a trolley tour."

"And neither have I," Ben said. Just like Emma and Jackson, he was dressed for the occasion. True to her word, Annie had made him look professional. She'd found him two dress shirts at the thrift shop, one red and one green, so he could alternate colors.

Satisfied that the elves were ready, Ben led them over to the trolley. Annie was waiting for them. She handed him a small bag. "I made you a Christmas tie."

"I'm not really a tie guy," he protested. "Do I *have* to wear it?"

Annie produced the tie. It had a pattern of Santa popping out toy trains from a 3-D printer. Ben's eyes lit up.

"I love it!" he said.

Annie was wearing one of the Christmas trolley tour souvenir t-shirts. She loved Cammie's logo. It had everything—the trolley, the Macklin House, Christmas lights, and the words "First Annual Macklin House Trolley Tour." She'd talked the Prestons into putting their five-thousand dollar donation toward purchasing the shirts. They would sell them for fifteen dollars each. That would be pure profit.

Zach and some other film students had set up the sound system and lights on the little stage. "Testing," Annie said over the mic. "Testing." The trolley was going to get an official send-off from the mayor, and she wanted to be sure the sound was working. Satisfied, she ran over to the trolley for a last word with Ben.

"Are you ready?" she asked nervously. "Got everything? First aid kit? Cookies?"

"We're all set," Ben said confidently. He was secretly afraid that he was going to forget every word of his tour guide script, but he wasn't about to let Annie know how nervous he felt. They clasped hands, and Annie thought for a moment that he was going to hug her. She thought of saying, "Here's a kiss for luck." Even if it wasn't snowing. But Emma interrupted. "Mayor Preston's here."

Brent was up on the stage, waving to the crowd. Everyone liked Brent. He'd grown up on a farm outside town, and still wore cowboy boots most of the time. He drove around town in a fully restored cherry-red 1967 Mustang GT, and consequently fixed any potholes immediately. Annie gazed at the trolley, now filled with excited, happy people eager to see the Christmas lights of Macklin. It was now or never. She handed the microphone to Brent.

"Good evening, Macklin!" Brent announced enthusiastically. "Are we ready for some fun?" The crowd roared back. "Are we ready for some Christmas lights?" The crowd roared again. "Are we ready for a trolley ride?" They roared even louder. "Then, I want to turn this over to the woman who put this all together for us tonight. Our very own Annie Mulvaney!"

He handed the mic back to Annie. The crowd cheered again. "Welcome, everyone!" she said. "Welcome to the first annual Macklin House Christmas Trolley Tour! Our driver and guide, Ben Grover, and his invaluable elf assistants, Emma and Jackson, are going to take you through a winter wonderland. You'll be amazed by the creativity and holiday spirit right here in Macklin. And remember, this tour is a benefit for the Macklin House. So if you'd like to make an extra contribution at the end, we'll be happy and grateful. But first, some entertainment! Let's all welcome Mimi Cloverley and her dancing reindeer!"

Mimi climbed on to the stage, followed by nine small children wearing deer costumes with antler headbands. One of the girls, slightly taller than the others, wore a round red nose. Mimi tapped her phone screen and "Rudolph, the Red-Nosed Reindeer" began to play. The toddlers lined up, four on each side of "Rudolph," and started to do a rudimentary tap dance routine. Only "Rudolph" was remotely in time with the music, but none of the kids seemed to care. When the song finished, half of them continued dancing, even without the music. The rest looked confused and stared at each other. One of them sat down and threw her headband offstage.

None of this bothered the audience. They were delighted. There were a lot of sighs of "Oh, how cute!" as they clapped and cheered. Mimi came forward and said something to the kids. They all lined up and took a bow. There were more cries of "Aww." People were snapping pictures with their phones.

"Mimi Cloverley and her dancing reindeer! Aren't they the cutest things you've ever seen?" Annie said into the mic. "And now, it's time for the Christmas Trolley Tour!" She gazed over the crowd to the trolley. Ben was already in the driver's seat. She waved to him, even though she knew he couldn't see her.

Ben took a last look around the trolley. All the riders were in their seats, and Jackson and Emma were in their places just behind him. Jackson was holding the box of cookies on his lap. Everyone was ready!

Ben clanged the bell, and the trolley was off. Down Main Street, left on Second Street at the city hall. A police car in the parking lot of the police station flashed its lights at them. Left again on State Street, where all the shops were lit up and decorated. Dave Meyers was standing in the doorway of the hardware store, waving. So were Darlene and Cammie and Paula at the café, along with the Women's Club volunteers at the thrift shop. They'd decided to stay open late in case the crowd brought in more business. The trolley was getting a great send-off.

Ben turned right on First Street and passed the high school. Its electronic signboard read, "Welcome Christmas Trolley! Varsity football at Woodsville Friday Nite! Go Macklin!" All the riders, being alumni, students, or parents of future students at Macklin High, cheered. Down to Pine Avenue, then left.

This was where the holiday lights began. Several neighbors on the street had joined together to create a stunning display of snow-capped mountain peaks, spread across all their roofs. Their yards were covered in clumps of white foam to look like snow. A Swiss cottage with a cuckoo clock sat in the middle of each driveway. The riders pointed and snapped photos excitedly.

Ben checked his watch, hoping he'd timed it correctly. He'd talked to everyone on the street earlier in the week. He slowed the trolley to a crawl as he counted down the seconds. Three, two, one ... and the cuckoo clocks burst open. Cuckoos on springs popped out to the recorded strains of "Cuckoo! Cuckoo!" The trolley riders cheered and applauded.

The trolley crisscrossed street after street, each more dazzling than the last. The photo op on Columbus Street was a big hit. Ben was glad for the chance to catch his breath. He'd practiced his script over and over, but it was different reciting it to the crowd of passengers. He knew none of them would care if he stumbled, but he'd always taken pride in his work, and he wanted to be the best tour guide possible. Even if he actually was the *only* tour guide.

As the tour continued, he started to relax. The riders were laughing at his jokes, and seemed to appreciate his comments about the history of Macklin. As he turned down one street after another, he could hear appreciative gasps and cries, along with comments such as "The Smiths really need to fix that roof."

Oakmont Avenue was next, and Ben looked for Grace Iwamoto's house. He'd found an angel for her roof, and the stack of presents between her house and the Belmonts' actually looked very impressive. To his surprise, Ben saw Grace standing in front of her house, hanging on to her walker with one hand for balance. She was holding a thermos with the other. She waved frantically at Ben with the thermos. He could see that she was crying.

"Another photo op!" he shouted into the microphone as he slowed and parked. "We know you've still got a lot of pixels to use! Ten minutes, people!" All the passengers happily got off the trolley again, and began posing in front of the waterfall of lights across the street from Grace's house.

"Grace, what's up?" Ben asked.

She handed him the thermos, still crying. "Hot chocolate for you. Ben, you have to help me. I don't know what to do. I've lost Ellie."

"Who's Ellie?" he said. "Just calm down and tell me about it."

"Ellie lives next door to me," Grace sobbed. "She's three. Her parents are having a Christmas lights party and they asked me to babysit. I brought her out here to see the lights and wait for the trolley. I was fixing her a cup of hot chocolate when it happened."

"What happened?"

"Ellie was looking down the street and she saw the house with the sleigh." Grace pointed down the block, where Ben saw a large, brightly lit wooden sleigh in someone's front yard. "She said, 'It's Santa's sleigh!' and she pulled away from me. Then she ran down the street. I tried to run after her but I couldn't keep up. I kept yelling, 'Ellie, stop!' but she didn't. When I finally got to the house with the sleigh, she was gone."

"You need to call the police. Did you do that?" Ben asked.

Grace nodded. "Yes, I got hold of Chief Newton, and they sent a patrol car out, but they can't look everywhere. I thought, you're on the trolley, you're driving slower and looking carefully at all the houses, maybe you'll see her."

Grace wiped her eyes with the sleeve of her jacket. Ben put his arm around her. "She's so little. She could be any place. What if she's hurt? I was so stupid to think I could handle a three-year-old. Her parents are so worried. *I'm* worried. Anything could happen to her." Grace was trembling.

"I'll look for her," Ben promised. "What was she wearing?"

"A red quilted jacket and a little fuzzy white hat," Grace replied.

"I'll ask everybody on the trolley to keep an eye out. She's probably just in someone's yard looking at the lights. Besides, this is Macklin. If someone sees a lost little girl, they'll stay with her and call the police." He hugged Grace and ran back to the trolley.

Ben picked up the microphone. "Attention, riders!" he called out. "We have a lost child on this street. The police are searching for her, but we've been asked to look out for her, too. She's three years old, and her name is Ellie. She's wearing a red jacket and a fuzzy white hat." The passengers looked at each other and murmured in concern.

"Each side of the aisle should look in a different direction," Jackson suggested.

"That's a great idea," said Ben. "Attention, riders! Those of you on this side of the aisle," he announced, pointed to his left, "look this way." Pointing to his right, he said, "If you're on the other side of the aisle, look that way."

"I'm going to send out an alert," said one of the passengers, tapping on his phone as Ben started the trolley up again. Other passengers did the same. Everyone in town would soon know about the lost child.

Ben continued with the tour, but he was anxiously scanning every house and yard as he drove. How far could a three-year-old go? They should be able to see the white hat, if she hadn't taken it off.

He came to the street his parents' house—well, really his house now—was on, and suddenly realized that in all the planning for the trolley tour, he had forgotten to put up any lights of his own. Vowing to change that tomorrow, Ben motored slowly down the street. The house to the right of his had a scene of heavenly angels in its front yard. The angels were holding different instruments—violin, flute, horn, and harp—while Christmas songs played through a loudspeaker. White lights dazzled all around them. The lawn looked like it was covered in luminous white clouds.

Suddenly Ben saw something. A small movement in the sea of clouds. He slowed the trolley. "Did you see that?" he asked Emma.

She squinted, and they both saw it. Something white definitely moved, in a spot where anything white should have been still. Ben pulled the trolley to the curb and jumped off. He worked his way through the clouds. Up close, he saw that the clouds were made from a metal tubing frame covered in sheer white cloth. They were lit from within by battery-powered lights. Some resembled large boulders, and some were almost as tall as Ben. He kept losing sight of the spot of movement as he pushed his way through.

Now he could hear a small voice, singing along with the music. He pushed his way between two clouds and saw Ellie, in her red coat and white hat, sitting with her back against another cloud, while she watched the angels. Her face was covered with tears.

"Hi, Ellie!" Ben said. "I'm Ben. I drive the Christmas trolley. You remember, you went outside with Mrs. Iwamoto to see the trolley and the Christmas lights? Well, we've come to give you a ride home on the trolley." He worked his way up to her through the clouds and started to pick her up.

"NO," she shouted.

"But, Ellie, you can't stay here. Mrs. Iwamoto is worried about you. She misses you. You have to come home with us," he pleaded.

"My mommy said never to talk to a stranger," little Ellie said emphatically.

Ben thought for a moment. "Do you know your phone number?"

"Yes!" Ellie said proudly. "Six one four three five one one."

Ben took out his phone and dialed. "Hello?" he said loudly. "Is this Ellie's mom? This is Ben Grover from the Christmas trolley. I have Ellie here and I want to give her a ride home on the trolley. But she's being a very smart girl and she won't come with me without your permission. Can you talk to her?" He could hear Ellie's mom screaming with joy as he handed Ellie his phone. Ellie listened for a minute.

"Okay, mommy," she said, and handed the phone back to Ben. "Mommy says I should go with you. Except the angels are so pretty."

"The angels will be here for three more weeks," he told her. "Maybe your mommy can bring you back to visit them."

"That would be fun," Ellie said. She sniffled. Ben looked at her tear-stained face. He didn't have any tissues. Making a mental note to bring tissues from now on, he took off his tie and wiped Ellie's face with it. He hated to do it with his new tie, but he couldn't let Ellie go home looking like that.

Everyone cheered when Ben returned with Ellie. Emma put a Santa hat on her and held her tightly on her lap. Ben gave Jackson his phone and told him to call the police station and Grace Iwamoto, to report that Ellie was safe.

Now that they'd found Ellie, the passengers were more enthusiastic than ever. Ben continued down street after street, each one blazing with gorgeous lights. He felt a lump in his throat. Macklin might be tiny, but it had plenty of holiday spirit! He felt amazingly proud of his hometown.

Finally, Ben turned onto the last stretch of the tour, Spruce Street. Everyone on the trolley gasped in delight. A huge sign proclaiming "Santa's Workshop" floated above the street. Both sides were a winter wonderland of glistening white lights. Colorful animated displays of elves, toys, mine trains, and workbenches dotted all the yards. Holiday music poured from hidden speakers. Emma tightened her grip on Ellie. She wasn't taking any chances.

"Oh, wow!" cried Emma, as they passed an animated display of Santa's elves using a conveyor belt to load a vintage airplane, in lieu of a sleigh. Santa, in the pilot's seat, was wearing flight goggles and a jaunty red scarf. A red-nosed reindeer sat in the co-pilot's seat, turning its head from side to side.

"This is *way* beyond wow," answered Jackson. "It's like we're really in Santa's workshop!"

The trolley tootled back down Main Street, with the passengers cheering and waving. Ben drove triumphantly up to the Macklin House and parked.

Ellie's parents, Grace Iwamoto, and Chief Newton were on hand to welcome Ellie. Both of Ellie's parents hugged Ben. Ben hugged Grace again. "I knew you would find her," Grace whispered.

Annie was waiting to greet the riders and direct them across the lawn, to a table with hot chocolate and more cookies. All her anxiety evaporated as the first people stepped off. "This was an adventure! This was so much fun! It really puts Macklin on the map!" were the first sentences she heard. And the accolades continued. Everyone loved the trolley tour!

Annie had a cup of hot chocolate waiting for Ben before he started the second tour. "We all heard about Ellie," she said. "I can't believe you found her!"

"I can hardly believe it myself," he answered. "And the tour was amazing! A hundred times better than I thought it would be!" He reached in his pocket and pulled out a few crumpled bills. "Some of the riders gave me tips. Add this to your fund!"

Annie started laughing. "They were awed by your immense knowledge of Macklin history!"

Ben laughed, too. "They were awed by your fantastic Christmas trolley!" He realized he was holding his tie. It was soggy and crumpled from Ellie's tears. Annie noticed it, too. "Your tie?" she said regretfully.

"I'm sorry," said Ben. "She was crying and I didn't have anything else to use."

"That's okay," Annie said, handing him another small bag. "I made an extra."

CHAPTER 20

December 2

DANIELLE CAME INTO ANNIE'S OFFICE AT TEN O'CLOCK the next morning. Annie was still thinking about last night's trolley tour. She hadn't heard a single unhappy comment. Everyone had loved it! The trolley tour was a success! It was going to work!

"I have a bunch of kids from the high school out front," Danielle explained. "They want to meet with you."

"Me?" Annie said. She couldn't think of any reason someone from Macklin High would want to see her. If they wanted a donation, they'd come to the wrong place. She pulled her dark blue blazer off the back of her chair and went out to greet them. There were four of them, two girls and two boys. They all looked very serious.

One of the girls, who had frizzy hair and wore black-framed glasses, spoke. "We're from the Macklin High School senior class," she said. "We wanted to tell you in person."

"That's very considerate of you," Annie said, still unsure of what this was about.

One of the boys, who wore a letterman's jacket with a football letter, said, "We've chosen 'Christmas Trolley' as the theme for our Winter Formal on December ninth."

The second girl had long blond hair and wore a silver megaphone charm, with small gold music notes on it, on a chain around her neck. *A song leader*, Annie thought. Amber had one of those charms. "We added a dollar to the price of the tickets," the girl explained. "We're going to donate the extra dollar to your fund for the Macklin House."

The second boy, who had long black hair and was wearing eyeliner, added, "We all went on the field trip in eighth grade, and saw the Macklin House. We want to help save it."

"Your class would do that for us?" Annie said. They nodded solemnly. "You're incredible. I can't thank you enough! Your generation is going to save the world. Do you know that?"

"All we want to do right now is save the Macklin House," said the girl with frizzy hair.

"What do you need from me?" Annie asked.

The girl with the long blond hair answered, "Photos."

Annie remembered her high school dances. Photos were an important part of the ritual. "Here's what we'll do. I'll drive the trolley over to the school one afternoon, and you can take photos for the yearbook. I know everybody will want pictures with the trolley on the night of the dance, so we'll block off the area around the trolley stop at five p.m. You can have an hour for photos with your dates and your friends. You can stand by the trolley, or sit in the trolley, or hang out the sides, but you can't climb on the roof. Anybody climbs on the roof, you're all banned. And—thank you! You're the best!" She shook all their hands as they left. Then, she sat down on one of the chairs in the lobby. *I did the right thing when I bought the trolley,* she thought. *I knew it would bring the town together! Even the teenagers want to help!*

She couldn't wait to tell Ben about this at lunch. Just then, her phone rang. It was her mother.

"Annie! Guess what?"

"Hi, mom," Annie said.

"We're going to drive up on Saturday. To see your trolley tour," her mom said excitedly.

"You and Dad?"

"All of us," her mother said cheerfully. "Amber and Tom are coming with the kids in their motorhome. We'll stay with the Cooleys and drive home on Sunday." The Cooleys lived down the street from her family's old house. They were her parents' best friends.

"That's wonderful, Mom," Annie said. "I'll make sure I get all of you tickets for the six-thirty tour." She felt both happy and dismayed as she hung up. Happy that her family was coming for the trolley tour. Dismayed, because they'd have to meet Ben. Well, re-meet him. What would they think? What would *Ben* think?

Across the town square, Ben had just arrived at Meyers', planning to run some reports for Dave and help out with the noon rush. Dave was uncharacteristically silent. Usually, he was chatty with his customers, but today, he was speaking in monosyllables. He looked like his mind was a million miles away. After Dave had given a customer the wrong change twice, Ben finally said, "Dave? Is everything okay?"

"Thanks for asking, but it's not your problem," Dave replied.

Ben was troubled. "Tell me what's going on. I won't share it with anyone else, I promise."

Dave looked skeptical. "Not even Annie. Unless she could help," Ben offered.

Dave went into his office and came back with two folding chairs, which he set up next to the front counter. This unnerved Ben more than anything else. *It must be serious if we have to sit*, he thought. He wondered if it was a medical issue. Dave wasn't young.

"It's about Adam," Dave began. Ben waited.

"He and Stacey went to New York a few years ago to try to make it in the music business. They live in this tiny fourth-story walk-up in Brooklyn. They sublease," Dave explained.

Ben imagined something similar to his apartment in San Francisco, with worse weather.

"He called me last night and they're losing their apartment, and they want to come back to Macklin," Dave continued.

"That sounds great!" Ben said enthusiastically. "I mean, do you get along? Are you close?"

"They're going to move in with me. That's fine. But they want to start a music store."

"A music store?" Ben tried to picture it.

"They'd give lessons. Rent out instruments, sell sheet music. Have their pupils give little concerts," Dave explained.

Ben thought back. Annie had taken piano lessons at some point. He'd spent a number of excruciating hours listening to her practice. "I don't remember a music store in Macklin," he said cautiously. "But it sounds like an interesting idea. Would they have any competition?"

"No, there's nothing like that here now. But they don't have any money. Adam asked me if I could help them out, just for a while. He wanted to know if I'd seen any cheap space they could rent."

"I've noticed some empty warehouses down by the river," Ben said, "but they'd probably want something right in town."

"The thing is," Dave continued slowly, "I'm just barely making a profit, you know that. I've even been using my savings to keep the store going. I've been thinking about it all morning, and the only way I can see to help them out is to put a mortgage on the building. And that kills my profit. His mother can't help. She hasn't got a dime."

Ben relaxed. No one was dying. This was a solvable crisis.

"How big an area do you think they'd need?" he asked.

Dave pulled at his hair in frustration. "Maybe a thousand square feet?" he suggested. "They'll need a soundproofed room for the lessons. Space to display instruments. Shelving for sheet music. Bathrooms. A performance area."

"They don't need that," Ben said. "They can hold their recitals at the Macklin House. The families will love it." *Oh God, I'm starting to sound like Annie,* he thought.

"So where can we find a cheap place like that?" Dave said. "They want to move next week."

"Hi, Dave!" someone called out. Elaine Gilpin came in, wearing her construction outfit. She had on a khaki tank top over ripped jeans, with knee-high leather boots. She had a matching khaki contractor's belt around her waist, and large abstract-shaped earrings made out of copper wire. "I'm putting up drywall. Can you help me find the drywall tape?" She surveyed the store cautiously. "That snowman isn't around here, is it?"

"It's outside," Dave assured her. "Your feet are safe."

"Go help Elaine," Ben said to Dave. "I'm going to run some numbers."

He was secretly excited. *This is just what I used to do in business*, he thought. *I can fix this. I don't know how yet—but I can fix this!*

CHAPTER 21

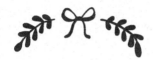

December 3

SATURDAY MORNING DAWNED BRIGHT AND CLEAR. IT WAS going to be a perfect night for Annie's family to see the Christmas lights. Annie spent the morning frantically cleaning her little cottage. Even though her parents weren't staying with her, she wanted the place to look spotless. They'd come up for a weekend a few months earlier, just after she'd moved back to Macklin. That was before she'd redecorated. Now, she wanted to show off her cute, cozy home.

Her parents arrived around one o'clock. "Macklin hasn't changed a bit!" her father announced happily.

"Yes, it has!" her mother countered. "It has its very own Christmas trolley tour now! Just like Disneyland!"

Annie wasn't sure Disneyland had a Christmas trolley tour, but wasn't about to argue. She proudly showed her parents around her cottage. They were suitably impressed. "Have you put this on Instagram?

You could be an interior designer!" her mother proclaimed. "If you moved to Palm Springs, we've got tons of friends who would hire you!" Amber and Tom were driving more slowly in their motorhome, and planned to arrive around three. Annie took her parents to the café for lunch. Paula was their waitress.

"Hi, Mr. and Mrs. Mulvaney," she greeted them. "Remember me? Paula?"

Her father looked confused. Her mother thought for a moment, then brightened. "Paula Stanley! You look just the same!"

Paula laughed. "Not really, but thanks. Annie told us you're here for the trolley tour."

"We wouldn't miss it," Annie's father said proudly.

"Be sure to try some of my cookies when you're on the trolley," Paula told them. "And buy one of the t-shirts. Our friend Cammie designed them."

"And I'm supplying the coffee and hot chocolate," said Darlene, coming up to their table to fill their cups.

"Darlene Ridgeway!" Annie's mom squealed. She hugged Darlene. "How are things? You should move to Palm Springs. We love our retirement community."

"I can't afford to retire," Darlene said. "Besides, I like it here. Annie's really getting everyone involved in this trolley tour. The whole town is excited!"

Annie blushed. "It's true!" Paula exclaimed. "The lights are gorgeous, there's entertainment every night, and Ben does a great job with the tour. My daughter plays an elf on the trolley, and he's taught her a lot about meeting the public."

"Who's Ben?" Annie's father asked.

"Ben Grover? You remember him. He was in Annie's class in school. He's back in Macklin," Paula explained.

That was a relief, Annie thought. She hadn't had to bring him up herself. She could just introduce him casually when the time came.

Her father brightened. "Oh, *him,*" he said. "The kid who always left his bike in the driveway. Right behind my car." And just then, Darlene appeared with complimentary pie for everyone. The conversation turned to dessert. Annie was saved from any further discussion of Ben. After lunch, Annie's parents went off to meet the Cooleys. They were planning an early dinner at the Cooleys' house and would come back for the first tour at six-thirty. "I wish they would move to Palm Springs," her mother said wistfully. "They don't know what they're missing!" Annie wondered briefly why her mother didn't get a job at the Palm Springs Chamber of Commerce.

Amber showed up at the Macklin House by herself around three o'clock. "Tom's taking the kids out for tacos and then over to the playground to wear them out before the tour," she explained. "I told him you and I needed some time together. Actually, after five hours in the motorhome with all of them, I need a glass of wine. Do they serve wine at that café?"

"No wine, but they have good coffee," Annie assured her. She tidied up her desk and told Danielle to look after things. They walked over to the café. Paula was at the hostess station.

"Amber!" Paula shrieked. "I got your text this morning. It's like old times!" They hugged each other and compared photos of their kids. Paula seated them in what she declared to be "the best booth," and they traded gossip about their fellow former song leaders. Annie half-listened while she ate a burger. What would her parents think of Ben? What would *he* think of *them*?

Amber and Paula moved on to other people they'd known in high school, and made plans to meet up later at the trolley tour. Paula finally brought their check, almost apologetically. "I'll get this," Amber said. Annie suspected she wanted to leave Paula a big tip.

"Tom just texted me," Amber added. "They're going to meet up with Mom and Dad and the Cooleys, and all come to the tour together." She looked at her watch. "It's only four o'clock. Could we visit that thrift store you're always telling me about?"

Annie would like nothing better. It *was* like old times, going shopping with her sister. "Are you looking for anything special?" she asked.

"Clothes for the kids, or some weird stocking stuffer for Tom. And we need some cups for the motorhome. How about you?" Amber replied.

"I could use some stocking stuffers, too," Annie admitted. "I've been working so hard on the tour I keep forgetting Christmas is coming." Amber promptly found some puzzles for Savannah and Scott, and a yo-yo for Tom. She examined a pair of matching children's sweaters in beautiful Scandinavian designs, but regretfully put them down.

"I'd love to get these!" she confided to Annie. "But I know Mom is knitting them Christmas sweaters."

Annie nodded. "She already gave *me* a Christmas sweater."

"She's knitting matching ones for Tom and me, too. Every week she shows up with a hat, or a scarf, or a shawl. You don't live nearby, so she doesn't give you all this stuff."

"Just hold on for a year, and then she'll be done with knitting and on to something else."

"Flower arrangements," Amber predicted gloomily.

They dawdled through the thrift shop, trying on tops and shoes. Annie found a pair of antique-looking silver earrings. "These would be great for Danielle's Christmas present!" she told Amber. "Danielle wears a lot of black, and she *loves* silver jewelry." She was paying for them at the cash register when Amber suddenly grabbed her arm. "Time to go!" Amber announced.

Annie pulled out her phone and realized it was almost five-thirty. "Oh, my gosh!" she told Amber. "I need to be on-site in ten minutes."

Annie slipped the earrings into her purse, and they started across the town square. They came to the gazebo, and Amber stopped. "The gazebo!" she exclaimed. "Where I had my first kiss!" Annie rolled her eyes. "We can take a minute, can't we?" Amber urged. "Let's go up."

They climbed the steps up to the gazebo's floor, which was several feet above the ground. From here, they had a good view across the town square to the trolley stop in front of the lit-up Macklin House. A number of early arrivals were standing near the trolley, admiring it.

"Is that him?" Amber pointed toward Ben, who was wearing his red shirt and standing guard at the front of the trolley.

"Yes, that's Ben," Annie answered.

Amber studied him critically. "He turned out better than I expected," she said approvingly. Seeing Annie's look, she continued, "I remember him as this scrawny kid with big ears."

"The last time you saw him was in eighth grade," Annie said.

"None of us looked like anything in eighth grade. Except you," she added generously.

"Well, yes," Amber said modestly. It was true. Amber had shot up to her full height of five foot ten in eighth grade, and to their mother's horror, had dyed her hair blond. She'd looked like a teenage model. Annie, in eighth grade, had looked like an awkward eighth grader.

Then, they saw their parents and the Cooleys approaching the trolley from Main Street, along with Tom and the kids. They were all wearing souvenir trolley tour t-shirts. And they were headed straight for Ben. Annie clutched Amber's arm.

"They must have parked behind the Macklin House!" she gasped. "Dad's talking to Ben! What's he doing?"

Their father and Ben were walking around to the back of the trolley.

"They're looking at the engine," Amber reported.

"Why do guys always want to look at the engine?" Annie said through gritted teeth.

"They just do," said Amber. "Annie! Dad's not going to say something like, 'Do you want to marry my daughter?'"

"How do you know that?"

"He's oblivious to those things. I had to show him the wedding invitation to make him realize Tom and I were serious." Amber frowned and tugged at the pockets of her jacket. "Oops, I forgot something at the café. You go on ahead and meet everybody. I'll catch up in a few minutes." She turned around and headed back toward the café, leaving Annie to deal with the family alone.

By the time Annie approached the trolley stop, Ben was talking to her mother. They were facing away from her. Wanting to hear what he was saying, she hung back out of view and pressed herself against the side of the trolley.

"Ben, that is a darling tie," her mother was saying now. "You know, people don't wear ties the way they used to."

"Annie made it," Ben said. "She made the elf costumes for Jackson and Emma, too. They'll be here in a minute. I'm their elf mentor."

"Really?" Annie's mother said. "What does an elf mentor do?"

"I teach them customer service. How to greet people, how to shake hands, how to treat our passengers. They're great kids!"

"I'm sure you're very good with them. I can't wait to see their costumes."

"Annie told me you were in the knitting club," Ben added. "I'll bet you make a lot of cute things, too, Mrs. Mulvaney."

"This trolley was a mess when Annie bought it," he went on. "She painted it and did all the repairs. Hey buddy, no climbing on the seats." Ben scooped up Scott, who was trying to balance himself on the top of a seat back, and put him on the ground. "You have an incredible daughter, Mrs. Mulvaney." Annie, overhearing this, was too stunned to move. What was he going to say next?

"Ben, just call me Lynette. And you know my husband, Dan."

Now Ben was showing her father and Tom the storage compartment on the other side of the trolley. She heard Tom say, "Look at all that space! I wish we had something like that in *our* motorhome!" Then, she heard Ben say, "Hey, buddy, no climbing up the back of the trolley." Annie decided she had better come out of hiding.

"Annie!" her mother said in her usual astonished voice. "You're here! Did you and Amber have a nice visit? Ben says this tour is fantastic and he saved us seats right up front, so we can hear everything he says."

"That was so nice of him," Annie managed to say. Just then, she heard, "Testing," from the stage, and then Brent Preston's booming voice. "Good evening, Macklin!"

"Good evening, Brent," the crowd yelled back.

"We've got a special treat tonight for all you Macklin High graduates. How many alumni do we have here tonight?" Two-thirds of the crowd raised their hands.

Annie stared at the stage. "This isn't on the schedule," she said. What was Brent doing?

"Tonight, we have with us two of your favorite Macklin High song leaders performing their routine just as they did in the old days! Let's welcome Amber Mulvaney Hollings and Paula Stanley Andrews!"

The music of the Macklin High fight song began to play. Amber and Paula, wearing their white song leader sweaters emblazoned with a red capital M, bounced onto the stage. They'd abandoned the rest of their original song leader costumes, short red skirts and white boots, for jeans and tennis shoes. They waved red and white pompoms, and started to sing and dance to the school fight song:

Let's sing a song for Macklin High School
We want our team to fight, fight, fight!
And when our team has won the battle
Let's take the trolley tour tonight!

The crowd began to clap and sing along.

They changed the words for the trolley tour! They planned this, Annie thought. *That's why Amber went back to the café.*

Emma was standing beside her, looking appalled. "This is the most embarrassing thing my mother has ever done!" she wailed.

Jackson, next to Emma, was watching every move. "Why are you embarrassed? Your mom can really dance! Look at her go!"

Emma hit him over the head with the night's box of cookies. Annie strategically grabbed the box away from them. Paula, still dancing, suddenly seemed to lose her footing. She went down, but managed to twist her body into doing the splits. She bounced back up as the crowd cheered.

"I can't go on the trolley tour tonight," Emma moaned. "I can't ever show my face in public again."

"Emma," Jackson said. "Your mom is awesome. Everybody's clapping! They love it!"

Fortunately, just then, the song ended. Amber and Paula took a bow. Brent came back on stage.

"All right!" he said. "And you know we've got our very own Macklin High football coach, Rick Jordan, over there playing Santa Claus. He got some practice delivering presents to Macklin last night when our Macklin Bulldogs beat the Woodsville Wildcats twenty-one to nothing! Let's hear it for Coach Rick!"

More cheers. "And now, it's almost time for our first trolley tour of the evening, and for those of you not going on this superb ride, we've got the Rotary Club's banjo group to entertain us." Brent waved the banjo players on stage as Ben clanged the trolley bell. Time for the tour to start.

Amber ran up, still in her song leader sweater. "I can't believe I can still get into this!" she said happily.

"But not the skirt?" Annie asked.

"After two kids? No way," Amber laughed.

"Annie? You're coming on the tour with us, aren't you?" their mother asked.

"Um," Annie managed. "I usually ..."

"Of course, you're coming," Amber announced. She gave Annie her I'm-the-big-sister-and-I-know-best look. "Your friend over there can handle the money." She pointed at Grace Iwamoto.

"Of course, I'm coming," Annie said. "I just have to run over there and tell Grace. Don't let anyone else take my seat!"

CHAPTER 22

December 4

ANNIE AND HER FAMILY MET FOR AN EARLY BREAKFAST AT the café before her parents and Amber and Tom started home. She couldn't believe how well their visit had worked out. The lights had been spectacular. Ben had been flawless on the tour. Not to mention all his compliments, when he didn't know she was listening. She'd hugged Amber ten times in appreciation for her song leader routine.

"I'm so proud of both of my daughters!" their mother said. "Annie, the trolley tour is just as wonderful as you said it would be. That Ben is really an excellent tour guide. We have a lot of tours in Palm Springs if he ever wants to move."

"He's not really a tour guide," Annie said. "He's ... sort of doing me a favor because he's out of work right now."

"He's a smart guy," her father commented. "What does he do in real life?"

"He was a project manager at Jupiter Computer," Annie said proudly. "On track to become a vice president." So there, she thought. He's not just an elf mentor. Her father looked suitably impressed. "You did a great job putting this all together," he commented. "Seriously, think about relocating. I love Macklin, but this town isn't big enough for your talents."

Amber gave Annie a thumbs-up sign when their parents weren't looking and said, "Keep me posted!"

"I will," Annie promised. She had a lump in her throat as she watched them all drive away. She *did* miss them. But she had her own plans for the future. Once she came up with one hundred thousand dollars.

It was a good thing the trolley didn't run on Sundays because she needed a day to catch up on her chores. Annie had just put a load of laundry in the washer and was trying to think of an excuse to call Ben and thank him for being so nice to her family, when her phone rang. It was Ben, and he sounded desperate.

"I need help!"

"Do you want me to call 911?"

"No, it's not that kind of help. I'm at home. Can you come over? I don't know what to do," he said anxiously.

"Okay," Annie said. If he didn't need 911, she reasoned, he could wait until she changed her clothes and put on fresh makeup. It was always a good idea to take food in an emergency, so she threw some cookies and popcorn into the trunk of her Honda Civic. She tried to figure out what the problem might be as she drove over to Ben's house. Everything had seemed okay when they'd parted the night before, after the last trolley tour.

She found Ben in his wood-paneled family room, surrounded by cardboard boxes. He was wearing one of his many Jupiter Computer logo polo shirts and a pair of board shorts. His hair was sticking up, and he looked like he was at his wits' end. He grabbed both of her hands. "You're here!"

Annie looked around. Other than the boxes, she couldn't see anything unusual. No smoke, no fire, no flood. "Ben, what's the matter?" she asked cautiously.

"You know how I've been trying to clean out the house." She nodded. "So, there's a bedroom down the hall that we never used after I went off to college." She nodded again. "And this morning—I opened the door!"

"Was it full of ants?" *I should have brought ant spray*, she thought. There were always ants in Macklin.

"No! It was full of these!" He gestured around the room.

"Boxes of stuff?"

"Not just stuff! Christmas stuff! Ornaments, and tree lights, and little miniature houses, and throw pillows, and books, and wreaths, and a red and green afghan if you still need one for Santa's chair. And that's just what I've opened so far! I'm not a Christmas guy! I need help!"

"Oh, this is no problem," said Annie, handing him a cookie. "We'll go through the boxes and see what you want to keep, and what you want to throw away or donate."

"There's just so much of it. Do you think my mom was a hoarder?" asked Ben. He watched Annie open the box nearest to her. It was full of wrapping paper. She was wearing jeans and yet another Christmas sweater. This one showed the Empire State Building with a wreath at the top. Santa Claus was climbing up one side. King Kong was climbing up the other.

"She might have been a Christmas hoarder, but that's normal," Annie assured him. "Everybody has a lot of holiday decorations. People buy things, and then the next year they can't remember where they put them, so they buy more. Then they end up with a storage unit."

Ben was still looking at her sweater. "How many of those Christmas sweaters do you *have*?" he said. Every time he saw her, she was wearing a different one. He was starting to wonder if Annie was a Christmas hoarder.

"Probably as many as you have logo polo shirts," she answered.

"These are great shirts," he said indignantly. "They gave them away for free at one of the sales meetings. I took ten of them. I never had to worry about what to wear to work."

Annie stood up and carried the wrapping paper over to the kitchen counter. "Where did all this Tupperware come from?" She opened one of the lower cabinets. Tupperware containers of all sizes fell out. "Your mom sure had a lot of Tupperware. Maybe she *was* a hoarder."

Ben sighed. "The ones on the counter aren't hers. Grace Iwamoto told her friends at the senior center that I'd put up Christmas lights for them. They're all calling me now to put up their lights and fix their computers. They were friends of my parents. I just can't charge them anything. It wouldn't be right. So they give me food instead."

"They cook for you?"

"They love it. Mrs. Stanislaus told me this is the first time in years she's been able to fix any of her old recipes. She says nowadays everybody in her family's always on some diet. The asparagus diet. The grasslands diet. The Renaissance diet."

"The Renaissance diet? You're making that up."

Ben shrugged. "No, she explained it to me. The theory is that the explosion of art during the Renaissance was because of what they ate."

Annie looked skeptical. "I thought most people in the time of the Renaissance didn't have *enough* to eat," she said.

"So did I," Ben agreed, "but her husband swears by this diet. She says she wishes he'd go on the plumbers' diet. Look at all this!" He opened his refrigerator. "Lasagna, meatloaf, chicken soup, carrot cake …"

"That's a lot of food," Annie observed.

"There's more in here," he said, opening the freezer section. "Beef stroganoff, lamb chops, chicken curry. And then there's this!" He proudly opened one of the kitchen cupboards.

"A bottle of Glenlivet?" Annie said incredulously.

"That was from Jerry LaFontaine. I attached a sound bar to his TV, and he said I'd saved him three thousand dollars and deserved some good scotch."

"That's impossible. It doesn't cost that much to install a sound bar," Annie said.

"No, but he was going to buy a three thousand dollar hearing aid that Medicare won't cover, and now he says he doesn't need it."

"If you can figure out something the seniors need in January, you'll never have to shop again," Annie said. She looked around the family room. "Now, the first thing we need to do is move some of these boxes out, so you can set up your tree."

"My tree?" Ben was taken aback. "I don't *have* a tree."

"Did your mom put up a real tree?" Annie asked.

Ben shook his head, saying, "She had one of those artificial ones. It wasn't very big." Looking at all the boxes, he suddenly felt guilty. He could easily have come home to help her put up the tree.

"You didn't find the tree in the bedroom?" Annie insisted.

Ben looked puzzled. "No, this is all there was. There's no artificial tree in the garage, either. There were boxes of outdoor lights, but that was it."

"Then, we need to get you a tree!" Annie exclaimed.

The Boy Scouts had a Christmas tree lot at the Presbyterian Church. They drove up in Ben's minivan and found the Scouts selling mistletoe, hot dogs, and fudge, along with trees. Annie was excited. She loved real Christmas trees, and the Scouts had a huge selection. Small trees, big trees, giant trees meant for a mansion like the Macklin House. Plain trees of all varieties. Trees flocked in white and pink.

The sun was shining, the air was crisp, and it was a perfect day to find a Christmas tree. Annie and Ben bought hot dogs and started looking at trees. A small Cub Scout approached them, holding a box of mistletoe. He was clearly terrified.

"Go on, Andy," said the boy's father, who was standing next to a table about ten feet away that was covered with mistletoe.

Andy stared at his shoes and said in a monotone, "Would—you—like—to—buy—some—mistletoe."

"Good job, Andy," said the father.

"We'd *love* to buy some mistletoe," Annie said. Andy looked astonished and held out the box. Ben reached in his pocket. "How much?" he asked.

"One—dollar—each—piece."

Ben handed him a dollar. Andy turned around and ran back to his dad, waving it. "I got a dollar! I got a dollar!" he exclaimed.

"Good job! Now go give him his mistletoe."

"Oh!" Andy said. "I forgot." He ran back to Annie and Ben. "Here you are. Thanks!" He handed a clump of mistletoe to Ben. Ben handed it in turn to Annie.

"For the Macklin House," he said. "You need some mistletoe over there."

Annie felt like saying, "How about some mistletoe at your house?" but she kept quiet.

Allan Tolbert was wandering around the tree lot, acting as an unofficial host. He was thrilled to see Annie and Ben. "Guess what happened yesterday!" he said eagerly. "We got five donations to our GoFundMe page."

"That's great, Allan," Annie said, hugging him. "So what's our total now?"

"Three hundred and fifty dollars, but I know it'll go up. I've been mentioning it at the end of my sermon every Sunday."

"Ben's going to buy a tree," Annie said.

"Pick out a big one," Allan said. "The Scouts are donating ten percent of their tree sales to the Macklin House fund. And everybody's talking about the trolley tour! It was a great idea, Annie!"

Annie and Ben finished their hot dogs, and walked up and down the aisles of the tree lot. The air was fragrant with pine and spruce. No snow on the ground, of course, but there were plenty of flocked trees. It was almost like being in a mountain forest.

"These trees are so fresh!" Annie exclaimed. "How about that one?"

"It's not quite what I'm looking for," said Ben. For someone who wasn't a Christmas guy, Ben was turning out to be surprisingly finicky about his tree. He rejected tree after tree as too tall, too short, too fat, too skinny, too wobbly, too pointy, or, finally, too green.

"Too *green*?" Annie was losing patience. This was like taking a toddler to the ice cream store. "They're all green! Except the flocked ones!"

"I just had a different green in mind."

"Remind me never to go with you to look at paint samples. Enough of this!" They'd been walking through the tree lot for almost an hour, and had seen every tree at least twice. She pointed to three trees immediately in front of them. "Those are all nice trees that would fit in your family room. Choose one of them!"

"This is hard," he said. "I've never bought a Christmas tree before."

"I'm going to count to ten. Pick a tree by the time I'm done. One, two, three ..."

Ben closed his eyes. "That one," he said, pointing into space.

They tied the tree to the top of the minivan, bought a box of fudge from the Scouts, and drove back to Ben's house. Other drivers, also carrying trees, honked and waved at them. Some gave them enthusiastic thumbs-up signs. One of them rolled down his car window as he waited at a stop sign.

"Hi, Ben!" he yelled. "Really liked your jokes on the trolley tour!"

"You're a celebrity!" Annie told him. She waved at another tree-carrying car.

Ben turned red. But Annie could tell he was pleased.

The tree looked perfect in Ben's family room. Ben put the lights on the tree, and they started decorating. They unpacked box after box, finding red and green glass balls, dangling icicles, and strings of smiling gingerbread men. They found a Christmas village, which they set up on the coffee table in the living room. The more they unpacked, the slower it went. Once they got past the glass balls and the gingerbread men, every ornament seemed to have a story. Ben looked at a tiny pair of skis labeled "Mammoth Mountain."

"This is from the first time I went skiing!" he said. "I'd forgotten all about it. My mom told me I could have *one* souvenir from the gift shop. I think I spent an hour picking this out."

Annie held up a small Golden Gate Bridge. "Wow," he said. "That's from a trip to San Francisco. We saw everything! The Golden Gate Bridge! Alcatraz! Chinatown!"

"Oh, look at this!" Annie said. She'd unwrapped a small cardboard picture frame covered with glued-on pieces of macaroni that had been spray-painted gold. The frame held one of Ben's school photos. She turned it over and read aloud, "Benjy Grover, age six."

"That was in first grade," said Ben. "We were in Mrs. Evans' class."

"Remember how she wouldn't let us sit together because we were always talking?"

"We were always in trouble," Ben admitted. He was studying the photo. His four front teeth were missing. "I look ridiculous."

"I have one of those, too," Annie said reassuringly. "I had these braids that came down to here." She inadvertently pointed at her chest.

"Here's a chain I made out of construction paper," said Ben. "And a snowman made out of Styrofoam balls." He shook his head. "Are you *sure* my mother wasn't a hoarder?"

"She was a devoted mother with an only child," Annie reassured him. "Oh, I found your Christmas stockings!" She held up four hand-made stockings. Each had a different design. They were labeled Steve, Carol, Benjy, and Buddy. Buddy had been the Grovers' cocker spaniel. "What happened here?" Annie held out Buddy's stocking. The toe had been chewed to pieces.

"I put a bag of dog treats in his stocking one year on Christmas Eve," Ben remembered. "I didn't think he could jump high enough to get to them. We came in the next morning and he'd eaten the whole bag. Plus half the stocking." He took the stocking from Annie. "I guess this can go in the trash pile."

"No! You can't get rid of Buddy's stocking!" Annie grabbed the stocking from Ben and clutched it against her heart. "He was part of your family! You have to keep it!" She marched over to the fireplace and hung it up.

"I should have known," said Ben. "A woman who spends her life taking care of an old Victorian house would never let me throw away Buddy's stocking."

"By the way," Annie said as they opened the next box, "I want to thank you for yesterday. Showing my family all around the trolley, and saving them seats up front. You were great!"

"Hey, your family's really special. They drove all the way up here to take the tour. I wanted to make it a special night for them," Ben replied.

"You did! Everything was perfect!" Annie couldn't think of anything else to say. You just couldn't come out with, were you nice to them because you're interested in me, or just because you're polite?

Ben looked thoughtful. "You know something? Going through all this stuff? I miss my mom and dad."

"They'd be proud of you, Ben," Annie said seriously. "You're a good person."

"A good, jobless person," he sighed.

"You'll find something," Annie said sympathetically. "Besides, if you hadn't come back to Macklin, you wouldn't be driving the trolley."

"Well, there is that," he conceded. "It's just that—I was really *good* at my job." He looked down at the logo on his shirt. "This is who I was. The guy at Jupiter who had all the answers. The guy who could solve any problem. Now I'm just—plain Ben Grover. An elf mentor."

"Ben!" Annie said. "You're way more than that. You're still the guy who can solve any problem. You put up lights for Grace Iwamoto—"

She waved at the Tupperware on the counter. "You're helping all those senior citizens. You've increased sales at Meyers' Hardware. You're figuring out something for Dave and Adam and Stacey, so they can move back here and start their music store. Jackson and Emma idolize you." She paused to collect herself. "And—and—I couldn't do the trolley tour without you. If you weren't here, there wouldn't *be* any Christmas trolley."

"You're the one who thought of it!" Ben said, laughing. "I'm just a little cog in Annie Mulvaney's plan for the Macklin House to become the greatest museum in the universe!"

Annie threw a spool of ribbon at him. He threw one back at her. They went on like this for several minutes, until they ran out of ribbon and started on the boxes again.

When Ben opened the last box, and found the big star that went on the top of the tree, they decided they'd done enough for the day. They ate the lasagna from the refrigerator. They spread the afghan on the couch, and watched a holiday movie on TV. They made popcorn. They watched another movie.

After the second movie ended, Annie said, "I've got to go." Ben walked her to the front door. "This was fun," she told him.

"I'll tell you a secret," Ben confessed. "I didn't really care that much about which tree we picked out. I was just enjoying walking around the Christmas tree lot with you." They looked into each other's eyes. "I think your Christmas spirit is rubbing off on me," he said.

"I think it was there all along," Annie replied. "It just got buried for a while." Both of them looked like they wanted to say something more, but the moment passed.

"Well, drive safely," Ben said. "Text me when you get home."

"Ben, it's only ten minutes away."

"I know, but I don't want to worry."

Annie drove home smiling. It had been a great day. Something was happening between them. She was sure of it!

CHAPTER 23

December 6

ON MONDAY MORNING, BEN DISCOVERED THAT HE'D added another skill set. By ten a.m., four senior citizens had called him to ask if he could bring them a tree from the Boy Scout tree lot. He was starting to wonder if some of his pub buddies in San Francisco would like to relocate to Macklin. There seemed to be no shortage of odd jobs for able-bodied young men with minivans.

Meanwhile, he was thinking about Adam and Stacey's music store. There had to be a way to make this work. He sat at his computer until midnight, scanning through reports he'd pulled from Dave's accounting software. He knew there was an answer, if he could just find it.

Ben arrived early at Meyers' on Tuesday morning. He disappeared into the office, and emerged about an hour later holding a pile of spreadsheets.

"Let's go over to the café for some coffee," he said to Dave. "I want to show you something."

There weren't any customers yet, so Dave locked up. He put a sign on the door with an arrow pointing down the street, and wrote, "If you need us, we're at the Macklin Café" on it. The senior citizens, as usual, were lounging on the patio furniture. Several of them waved coffee cups and dollar bills in the air.

"Are you going to the café? Can you bring us some refills?"

It was the breakfast shift at the café, and Darlene brought them coffee as they slid into a booth. "Do you need menus?" she asked. They shook their heads, no. "Dave, you let me know if you need anything," she said.

Dave took a gulp of his coffee. "Okay," he said. "Are we totally broke?"

"Not at all," said Ben. "I've found a solution for you and Adam." He suddenly felt like he was in his element again, giving business advice. He put one of the spreadsheets in front of Dave.

"You're going to lease a thousand square feet of your building to Adam and Stacey for their music store," he said triumphantly. He held out a diagram of the building. "Probably at this end by the thrift shop. That would be the easiest section to reconfigure."

Dave's looked stunned. "I can't do that," he said. "Can I?"

"We're going to reduce your inventory by twenty-five per cent," Ben explained. "Dave, look at these numbers. You're carrying twice as much inventory as the typical hardware store of your size. See this chart?" He laid the spreadsheet patiently in front of Dave. "These items aren't selling. They might have sold in the past, but they don't sell now. They sit on the shelves and take up space. That's one reason your profit is so depressed."

"But we've *always* sold those," Dave protested.

Ben produced another chart. "These are your biggest sellers. Other than the holiday lights, which bring in fifty percent of your revenue."

Dave studied the spreadsheet. He looked perplexed. "Half of these aren't even hardware," he said. "They're just … junk gadgets."

"I think that's 'lifestyle accessories,'" Ben said dryly. "That's what people are buying now."

"I only sell these things because Darlene keeps telling me I should carry them."

As if magically summoned, Darlene appeared with the coffee pot. "Look at this," Dave said to her. "These are my sales for last month. Why would anyone buy twenty-five hard-boiled egg peelers?"

"Wedding shower party favors," Darlene said instantly. She filled their coffee cups and walked away.

Ben and Dave looked at each other.

"I should have known that," Dave said ruefully.

"No, you shouldn't," said Ben. "So we're going to drop all these other things that aren't adding to your bottom line. That frees up space for the music store. You're still making the same amount of money. Once Adam and Stacey get their music business going, you can charge them a little rent." He paused to catch a breath. "It'll add to your customer base, too. You'll have all these parents bringing their kids in for lessons, with nothing to do for half an hour except browse around looking at hardware."

Dave stared at Ben. "This is brilliant," he said. "You really think this will work?"

"It'll work," Ben promised. For a moment, he felt a jolt of panic. What if it *didn't* work? It was different at Jupiter, where a customer was just one of a hundred other customers. Dave was his friend. Dave's store was a Macklin institution. This plan couldn't fail.

But he knew it was the answer. He could feel it.

"It'll work," he said again. "You can tell Adam and Stacey to start packing."

CHAPTER 24

December 8

BY THE SECOND WEEK OF TOURS, THE CHRISTMAS TROLLEY had taken on a life of its own. Everyone in Macklin seemed to be hanging out in the town square now, whether they were going on the trolley tour or not. They ate at the café. They brought picnics. People organized holiday sing-alongs. The thrift shop was staying open until eight o'clock every night. So was the hardware store, where Dave and Ben were promoting the Christmas lights as being "Just Like the Ones You See on the Trolley Tour!"

A Christmas craft fair sprang up in the town square. The stalls opened around noon and closed up when the second trolley tour ended. Brent Preston had made a few half-hearted announcements about vendor permits, but wasn't following up on them. He and Police Chief Mike Newton had conferred, and decided not to disturb holiday commerce.

Annie was amazed at the variety of things people were selling. She'd never realized how many creative people there were in Macklin, just waiting for a chance to showcase their work. Wanting to promote the Macklin House, she tried to visit three or four stalls every day. She admired some crafts more than she did others, but you never knew where networking would lead.

James Adams, an elderly retired man with a neatly-trimmed white beard, who was one of Annie's docents, had a popular stall selling hand-carved wooden toys. He also made small boxes inlaid with different kinds of wood.

"I love these," Annie told him. She was wandering through the craft fair on her way to meet Ben at the café for lunch.

"They're puzzle boxes," James explained. He picked up one of them and showed Annie a secret compartment.

"Not only are they beautiful, they're useful, too!" Annie exclaimed.

"You're supposed to hide your special jewelry in there," said James. "Like, maybe your wedding ring."

"When I get a wedding ring, I'll call you," she said. Further down the row, she found Ruth Sandberg, another one of her docents, selling painted ceramic flower pots filled with poinsettias. Holiday quilts were popular, along with dried holly arrangements. Angie Morgan, with Peanut as her mascot, was selling homemade organic dog treats. She seemed to feed Peanut as many treats as she sold, but he wasn't complaining.

At the far end of the craft fair, Annie came to a booth where a young couple about her age was standing next to a display of hand-blown glass ornaments. She instantly fell in love with their rich colors. "Where do you make these?" she asked them. "Do you have a studio?"

The girl had real flowers in her hair, the guy had long hair and a beard, and they both were wearing shabby paint-stained clothes. They looked like they belonged in an artists' colony in Mendocino. Annie had no idea what they were doing in Macklin.

The guy said, "I built a glass-blowing kiln out in back of our house. It's, uh, kind of illegal, but no one's stopped us yet."

The girl said, "When we get a little more money we're going to rent a space."

"They're fabulous," Annie said. "I may be back." She realized she was late for lunch. Her lunchtime was totally flexible, but Ben had to get back to the store to relieve Dave.

"It's a good thing I don't have room for a bigger tree," she told Ben as she settled into their booth, "Otherwise I'd buy out their whole stock. And it's too bad they don't have a real studio where they could sell things year-round. Macklin needs an artists' co-op!"

"Could you sell something like that at the Macklin House?" asked Ben. By now, they'd developed a routine for lunch at the café. Annie ordered a salad, Ben ordered a sandwich, and they shared.

Annie thought it over. "Maybe in one of the second-floor rooms? Or could we enlarge the gift shop?" They brainstormed ideas as they finished eating.

Cammie was on the lunch shift, and she kept hovering anxiously near their table. Annie wondered if something was going on with Jackson. After Cammie had come over four times wanting to know if they needed anything else, she finally asked, "Cammie, how are things?"

This was evidently the opening she'd wanted. Cammie looked from one of them to the other and said, "Ben? Could I borrow your minivan?"

Ben looked baffled but agreeable. "My van? Sure. What do you need it for?"

Cammie shifted from one foot to the other. Annie was reminded of Jackson. "I need to bring something to the craft fair."

"Is it something big? Do you need help?" asked Ben.

"It's not big, but there's a lot of it. Would you mind?"

"Of course we'll help," said Annie. "What is it?"

Cammie hesitated. "It's—my art."

"Your art?" Annie was intrigued.

"I used to do oil painting in art school," Cammie explained. "When I had Jackson, it was all I could do was take care of the two of us. I couldn't keep up with my art classes. Once in a while, I'd paint something, but I never thought it was very good. Then you asked me to design the logo for the trolley. And everybody loved it! People kept saying I was talented." Cammie swallowed. "They kept asking me, 'Why aren't you drawing? Why aren't you painting?' I had some paintings I'd done over the years that I just kept wrapped up and shoved under Jackson's bed. I looked at them again, and I thought, these aren't bad! Maybe I *am* talented. So I got out my paints a few weeks ago, and, well, I did some more. I'm going to put them in the craft fair and see what happens."

"Cammie!" Annie exclaimed happily. "I can't wait to see them!"

"When can we do this?" asked Ben. "This afternoon?"

"I'm off at two. Can you meet me at my house? They're having a movie after school today, so I don't have to pick up Jackson until later. We could get the paintings and bring them back here before I have to get him and go on the dinner shift."

"Perfect," said Annie. "Give us your address."

Cammie's apartment was easy to find. It was one unit in an older stucco fourplex on the south side of town. Annie thought the building, and the area, looked run-down. Ben, used to San Francisco real estate, thought it was a good deal.

"This is a great apartment building! Look! She has her own parking space!" he exclaimed.

Cammie shyly showed them into her apartment. It was a small one-bedroom. Cammie's paintings were stacked up in the living room. Annie looked at them quickly, planning to spend more time once they got them to the craft fair. She glanced briefly into the bedroom. It had a Golden State Warriors poster on one wall. Toys and video games covered the single bed. Obviously, this was Jackson's room. Annie figured Cammie must sleep on the couch.

She noticed a lot of papers tacked up on the bedroom walls, and went to take a closer look. They were cartoons, signed by Jackson. Cartoons of superheroes, sports stars, and sci-fi aliens. Jackson had inherited Cammie's artistic talent. But he was using it in his own fashion. From what she'd seen of Cammie's paintings, her style was soft and romanticized. Jackson's cartoons were sharp and comic.

Ben was looking through the paintings. Some were as large as three feet square. Cammie had tacked them onto wooden stretcher frames. "These are beautiful, Cammie," he said. "I don't know much about art, but I like them."

Annie joined him. "They're all scenes of Macklin!" she exclaimed. Several of the scenes were landscapes, recognizable as the roads and farms around Macklin. Cammie had also at one time or another painted Meyers' Hardware, the café, and the gazebo in the town square. One painting was of city hall on the Fourth of July, with American flags everywhere. One showed the old iron bridge down at the river. There were several of the Macklin House at different times of the day.

"I did a lot of these when I was in art school," Cammie explained. She pointed at the ones of the Macklin House. "These are new ones I did from photographs. I talked to that kid, Zach, who's doing the video. He took a bunch of photos for me. We didn't really have a way to take photos of anything else, so they're all of the Macklin House."

"Everyone will love them," Ben predicted. "Let's get them in the van. Do you have anything to set up on?"

"Oh," Cammie said worriedly. "I didn't think about that."

"I have an idea," said Ben. "We sell folding tables. I can get Dave to loan you some tables and we'll put a sign on them that says, 'Tables courtesy of Meyers' Hardware.'"

"Who's going to watch the stall for you while you're on the dinner shift?" Annie asked.

"Oh," Cammie said again. "I didn't think about that, either."

"Grace Iwamoto can do it," Annie suggested. "And she loves art!"

Annie called Grace while they loaded the paintings into the van. Grace was thrilled and said she'd meet them at the craft fair.

Dave was less thrilled when Annie called him. "I don't remember where the tables are. I put them somewhere when I brought in the Christmas lights. If Ben were here, he could go look for them. He told me next year, I need to make a diagram of where everything went." Dave did not sound happy at the prospect of making a diagram.

"He's not an employee, Dave. You're not paying him," Annie said. "Sometimes, he has other things to do. Like helping Cammie."

"Well, if you can find them, you can borrow them," Dave said, and hung up.

Cammie was nervous on the drive back to the craft fair. "Maybe I shouldn't do this."

"Of course you should," Annie told her. "You're a lot better than you think you are. You just need some self-confidence. And I saw Jackson's cartoons when we were in your apartment! He draws really well! Has he ever taken an art class?"

"Well, no," Cammie admitted. "He wants to take an after-school class in drawing, but ... it won't work out." Annie immediately realized her mistake. Cammie probably couldn't afford the after-school class. An idea came to her. "He draws great cartoons. I wonder if he would design a coloring book for me."

"A coloring book?" Cammie and Ben said simultaneously.

"About the Macklin House," Annie said. Ben rolled his eyes. "For kids. A souvenir they could take home and color. We have a pamphlet for grade school kids, but nothing for younger ones."

"Toddlers shouldn't be at a museum like the Macklin House," Ben pointed out.

"True," Annie agreed, "but their parents bring them anyway. If you have three kids, you can't just leave the little one in the car. Maybe we could have a playroom!"

"Maybe you should ask Jackson, not his mom?" Ben suggested, rolling his eyes again. Every day Annie had a new idea. The Macklin House was going to rival the Smithsonian by the time she was finished with it.

"Oh! Annie!" Cammie said excitedly. "Does Ben know anything about you-know-what?" Annie drew a blank. Ben waited.

"You know! Darlene and Dave!"

"Darlene and Dave?" asked Ben.

"Cammie thinks Darlene and Dave are ... an item." Annie couldn't think of another way to describe Cammie's theory.

"Hmm," Ben said. "She does bring muffins over to the store every day. Last Friday, she brought pancakes. Dave told me Darlene advises him on his merchandise. And when we went for coffee on Tuesday, she asked him if he needed anything, but not me." None of this sounded particularly romantic to Ben, but Cammie was thrilled.

"See? I was right!" she said excitedly.

"Dave said he was going to fix the front windows in the café, too," Ben mused. "Could that mean something?"

"Good work, Ben!" Cammie punched him on the shoulder. Fortunately, they arrived at the town square before Cammie could ask anything else. They were lucky enough to find a parking spot in front of the hardware store. Cammie and Annie carried some of the artwork across the street to the town square. They picked a spot at the end of a row of booths where there was still space. Grace found them trying to sort the paintings by size and subject.

"I love these!" Grace beamed happily. She turned over a painting of some rose bushes on the town square and looked at the price tag. "Cammie! Is this what you're asking for this painting?"

"I wasn't sure about the price," Cammie said. "Is it too much?"

"No! It's too little," Grace said firmly. "Go look around the stalls. There are at least two other painters. They're charging more and their work isn't as good."

Cammie hesitated, but Annie said, "Hurry! We need to price these before you go to work."

Ben came up, carrying a metal folding table under each arm. He set them down and breathed for a moment. "I forgot how heavy these are," he said.

By the time Cammie returned about fifteen minutes later, they had the tables set up and covered with the paintings. "You were right," she said. "My prices are way below the others." She looked excited.

"Don't ever undervalue your work," Grace admonished her.

Cammie shifted from leg to leg again. "Do you really think they'll sell? I'm kind of hoping ..." She took a deep breath, and then went on.

"I'm hoping I can make enough so Jackson can take that after-school class. Like, my art would pay for *his* art."

"Just wait," Grace said. "But you need a sign—'Custom Art by Cammie'—or something like that. With your email."

Cammie's eyes widened. "Really?" she said.

"You have to market yourself," Grace told her. "I learned that from Annie and Ben." Annie and Ben exchanged dumbfounded looks. "Like they're doing with the trolley. You need something catchy to make people remember you."

"You seem to know a lot about this," said Cammie. "Were you an artist?"

"I used to make pottery," Grace explained. "I had some of my things in a gallery in Carmel. Back in the old days." She looked at her hands. "I'm too arthritic to do it now. That's why I love to go to craft fairs like this. It's fun to see what people are making."

Cammie was impressed. "Was that, like, your career?" she asked.

"Oh, heavens no," said Grace. "You have to eat. I worked at city hall. Forty years. I issued marriage licenses. I speak Japanese and Spanish, so they loved me."

"Forty years!" Cammie said. "You must have a lot of stories."

"Everybody has a story," Grace replied. "You just have to ask."

"That's what we should do!" Annie said happily. "An oral history project! We could interview older people in Macklin. Get them to talk about their lives. Zach could photograph them. We could have an interactive exhibit. We could ..."

"One thing at a time," Ben interrupted. "First, the trolley tour. Then, the rest of your ideas."

Cammie's phone buzzed. "Oh, gosh, I have to pick up Jackson," she said, looking at the time.

Grace patted her arm. "I'll price these for you. Just leave everything to me. I'm going to make you the hit of the craft fair!"

CHAPTER 25

December 9

THE NIGHT OF THE WINTER FORMAL, ANNIE MADE SURE to arrive at the trolley stop at four o'clock. She pulled the "No Parking" chain and poles out of the storage compartment, and blocked off the street around the trolley. Annie figured she'd have all the kids photographed and off to the high school gym, before the patrolman assigned to security for the trolley tour showed up at six. And what was the worst that could happen? He'd give her a ticket for blocking the street?

Groups of students were already arriving, and wandering around the craft fair while they waited. Annie thought they all looked wonderful in their formals and tuxedos. As they milled around, waiting to get in line at five o' clock for their photos, a group of boys approached her. One of them came forward. He was a few inches taller than Annie, and had red hair and freckles. His tuxedo had a blue cummerbund, probably to match his date's dress. He looked nervous.

"Are you Mrs. Mulvaney?" he asked anxiously.

"Ms. Mulvaney," said Annie. "And your name is?"

"Josh," he replied. "I have a favor to ask."

"Go ahead, Josh. I'll help you if I can."

Josh gulped, but plowed ahead. "I want to propose to my girlfriend on the trolley."

"You want to what?"

"Propose to my girlfriend. It's really romantic, the trolley. So I was hoping ... could you give us a little more time when it's our turn?"

Annie looked at Josh in consternation.

"We've been dating since sophomore year," he added.

The other boys were hanging around the edge of the conversation. Annie thought fast. She didn't want to squelch young love, and the trolley was indeed romantic. She could speak from personal experience. But she couldn't let the trolley turn into Macklin High's version of a hot proposal spot, either.

"Josh, what class are you in?" she asked.

"I'm a senior," he replied.

"I'm sorry. I can't let you propose on the trolley. I'm the executive director, and this is the rule. No one is allowed to propose to someone on the trolley unless they're a high school graduate. I have to see their diploma."

Josh looked crushed. "But—but Mrs. Mulvaney—" he began.

"Ms. Mulvaney," corrected Annie again. *How old do these kids think I am, anyway?* she wondered.

"I'll *be* a high school graduate. In June."

"Yeah, bro, if you pass calculus," one of the other boys called.

"You're not a high school graduate now," Annie said, shaking her head. She gazed around the trolley. "Which one is your girlfriend?"

Josh pointed to a large group of girls who were squealing over someone's selfie. One gown was blue. That had to be her.

"Ask her to come over here. I want to meet her," Annie said. Josh left and Annie turned back to the students waiting in line. She processed three couples before Josh returned. His girlfriend looked sweet and pretty. She had blue eyes that matched her dress, and was wearing a silver heart-shaped locket. *Undoubtedly a gift from Josh*, Annie thought. "This is Caroline," Josh said proudly. "Caroline, this is Mrs. Mulvaney."

"Ms. Mulvaney," Annie said automatically. "Caroline, I've been talking with Josh, and I just want you to know that he's one of the most considerate, romantic boys his age I've ever met. You're very lucky that he's your date. Now get in line for your pictures."

Caroline beamed at Josh. Josh beamed at Caroline. Annie wondered where Ben was. With all these happy couples around, she missed him. *Wouldn't it be fun if we were one of those couples*, she thought. Then, she put the thought out of her mind. She couldn't get distracted by these fantasies. The first trolley tour of the night was about to start.

CHAPTER 26

December 10

THE SATURDAY NIGHT TOURS WERE OVER, AND THE crowd in the town square was heading home. Ben gave Annie a ride in the trolley back to the parking lot next to her cottage. After a week of tours, he was exhausted and only wanted to fall into bed. They made a date to meet at the café for breakfast.

Annie felt tired but not sleepy. She fixed herself a glass of Pinot Noir and started writing down her latest ideas for the trolley, none of which, she admitted to herself, were likely to happen. A Valentine's trolley. Ghost trolley tours on Halloween (she could put Zach to work on those). A Fourth of July trolley.

Annie sipped her wine and read over her list. She was trying hard not to think about Ben or the one hundred thousand dollars she needed. Then she heard the trolley bell clang. Annie stopped writing, and listened. She heard it clang again.

Is Ben here? she thought. That didn't seem logical. He'd ring the doorbell. *I'd better go see what's going on.* She was still dressed, so she quickly threw on her coat. She fumbled in a drawer for a flashlight, and opened her front door.

There were a few security lights in the parking lot but not enough for Annie to see the trolley clearly. Then, the bell clanged again, and she made out a figure in a dark jacket bending over the engine compartment. The person was too large to be Ben. "Hey!" she yelled. "Get away from my trolley!" Annie's heart pounded. Any thoughts of personal safety had disappeared. She felt like a mother protecting her child. No one was going to harm her trolley!

The person slowly stood up—Annie could see now that it was a man, wearing a heavy jacket and a wool hat—but immediately went back to doing something in the engine compartment. Annie started running toward the trolley, hoping to scare the man away. Just as she reached the parking lot, the trolley's engine roared into life. He'd hot-wired it. The man jumped onto the trolley, grabbed the steering wheel, inexplicably waved at her, and drove out of the parking lot.

Annie was really angry now. She felt in her coat pocket as she ran. She had her car keys and her phone. Her Honda Civic was sitting there in the parking lot. She jumped in, gunned the engine, and zoomed out after the trolley.

"You're not going to steal our Christmas trolley!" she muttered between clenched teeth. It wasn't hard to follow the trolley, with its Christmas lights all around the roof. The thief reached the corner, clanged the bell, and kept going through a red light. Fortunately, it was so late that there wasn't any traffic, because Annie followed right behind him. The trolley picked up speed as he continued down the block. Annie wondered how fast the trolley could actually go. They'd never driven it very fast, but the thief was steadily pulling away from Annie's Honda.

Annie pulled her phone out and called Ben. *Thank God for Bluetooth,* she thought. His phone rang and rang. Just when she thought it would go to voicemail, he picked up. "Are you okay?" he said groggily.

"Ben, wake up!" Annie said urgently. "Someone's trying to steal the Christmas trolley. I'm following him."

"*What?* I'll call the cops," Ben said, now wide-awake. "Tell me where you are. And stop following him! It's probably some kid who took it on a dare, but you never know."

"It's not a kid. It's an older guy. I'm at Tenth Street and Miller Avenue."

"I'll call you back in five minutes." Ben hung up. Annie continued following the trolley. She was getting worried. She wanted to pull up alongside it, to see if she could get a better look at the driver, but the streets were narrower in this part of town. The trolley was having some near misses with trashcans at the curb. Suddenly, the driver hit a large plastic trash bin. The trolley kept going, but the bin bounced into the middle of the street, dumping bags of trash in its wake. Annie swerved just in time to avoid a collision. She steered back into the middle of the street as the trolley made a tight left turn into a cross street. Annie had to brake hard and turn quickly to follow him.

She remembered the trolley's GPS system. It showed a map of the immediate area with a moving icon for the trolley. The thief was taking advantage of the GPS display to find a way to shake her off his tail. Annie's car didn't have a built-in GPS, and she was too busy driving to use the one on her phone. Grimly, she pursued the trolley. She knew she was being foolish, but she couldn't help herself. There were plenty of places in Macklin where you could hide a trolley. If she lost track of it, the police might never find it.

Her phone rang. It was Ben.

"I got hold of Chief Mike Newton. He was parked at the police station, so it'll take him a few minutes to catch up to you. He's got radar in his cruiser, and he'll track you with that when he gets a little closer. I'm on my way, too. I'm trying to cut across the south end of town to get to Tenth and Miller. Where are you now?"

Annie squinted at the street signs, and said, "DuPont Street. Ben, I think I know where he's going. DuPont runs into Gold Hills Highway, where the fairgrounds are."

"That's the county road that goes out past those farms on the way to the lake," said Ben. "Where my dad used to keep his boat."

"Right!" said Annie. "If he's trying to hide the trolley somewhere, it'd be the perfect place. Half those farms have abandoned barns and corrals."

"Or he might be headed for the lake. I heard some people live out there in their RVs."

"He just turned on to Gold Hills Highway!" Annie exclaimed. "Yuck, no lights out here. I hope a cow doesn't wander across the road. Can you call Mike and update him?" Her anger was giving way to fear. Gold Hills Highway was a twisty, two-lane country road in the middle of nowhere. Maybe it *hadn't* been such a good idea to follow the trolley thief. Maybe it had been a really *bad* idea. "I wish you were here," she said.

"Me too," he answered. She heard him mumble "This town needs a helicopter," before he hung up. A jackrabbit suddenly ran across the road. She hit the brakes hard to avoid hitting it.

Up ahead, the trolley was slowing down a little. The road was getting bumpier. Annie had to struggle to keep her car on the pavement. "Brent Preston needs to run for county supervisor and fix these roads," she said aloud. Then, her lights flashed on a road sign. "Macklin Lake, two miles."

Her phone rang. "Mike's on the highway about ten minutes behind you," Ben said breathlessly. "He says not to get out of your car, no matter what happens."

"I won't," Annie promised. "We're definitely headed for the lake!"

"I'm about a mile behind Mike, but he's driving faster," Ben continued.

Up ahead, the trolley was turning left. "I have to hang up," Annie said. The fields on either side of her were fenced. The trolley driver must have turned in at a gate. She slowed down, looking for a side road. Now she saw clumps of trees to her left. She could just catch quick glimpses of the trolley's rear lights among the trees. Slowing even more, she suddenly came to an entrance to a side road. In daylight, it would have been easy to spot. Tall wooden fence posts on either side held up a sign above the road that read, "Macklin Lake." She turned onto a dirt road with scrubby trees on either side.

The lake had been a favorite gathering spot for teenagers when she had been in high school. Annie remembered the road ended at a parking lot next to a boat ramp and a bait shack, where a walking trail led along the lakefront to the shuttered Blue Heron Restaurant. She could recall picnic tables, and a dilapidated restroom. She tried to call Ben again, but had no cell service. Hopefully, Mike really *was* able to find her with his police radar.

Annie had been slowly catching up to the trolley without realizing it. Now, she almost rear-ended it as she went around another curve. They'd come to the parking lot. She expected the trolley would stop, but it kept on going.

She glanced frantically into her rear-view mirror, hoping for a sign of Mike or Ben. Where were they? The thief motored slowly on. Now she could see a group of RVs sitting near the edge of the parking lot, close to the water. The thief drove the trolley toward the RVs and began to ring the bell.

A few people came out of their RVs, waved briefly at the trolley, and went back inside. The trolley made a circle around the parking lot. Annie was losing her fear. "This guy's just showing off!" she said. Then, he changed course. He was headed straight for the boat ramp.

Annie's anger came roaring back. She rolled her driver's side window down. "You're not going to run the Christmas trolley into Macklin Lake!" she yelled furiously out the window. She thought quickly. There was one road leading into the parking lot, and the police would be coming up that road. The only other way out, except on foot, was the boat ramp. The guy could drive around the parking lot all night, but he either had to go out the way he came, or down the boat ramp. And he was *not* going down that boat ramp.

Annie flipped on her high beams, pushed her accelerator to the floor, and veered to the left of the trolley. For a moment, she was even with it as she got her bearings. Then, she accelerated again and pulled out in front. She raced ahead to the entrance to the boat ramp. Her tires screeched as she turned her car sideways across the opening, and slid to a stop. She turned off the motor and waited.

The trolley kept coming, and for a horrifying moment, Annie thought the thief might ram her car. She braced for the impact. But the trolley skidded to a stop about ten feet away, just as Chief Newton tore into the parking lot with his lights and sirens at full blast. His police cruiser pulled up next to the trolley. The chief stepped out of his car and advanced toward the trolley, holding something in front of him. Annie gasped. She was about to scream, "Don't shoot him!" when a bright light hit the trolley. Mike was pointing his Maglite at the driver.

The thief climbed stiffly out of the trolley and put his hands in the air. The chief approached him, still shining his Maglite in the man's face. Now that Mike was on the scene, Annie felt it was safe to get out of her car. She ran toward the trolley, wanting to make sure it hadn't suffered any damage. Then, she stopped in shock beside Mike, staring at the thief in the merciless glare of the Maglite as Mike read him his rights.

"*Ted?*" she said incredulously. "Ted Worley? You stole our trolley?"

It was Ted, looking sheepish. "Yes, it's me," he admitted. "Can I sit down?" he asked Mike. "I have bad knees."

"No," Mike answered. "You should have thought of that before you stole this trolley. You're under arrest."

"Why did you do this?" asked Annie. "You seemed like a nice guy, except for your forgery problem."

"I wanted to drive the trolley," Ted said plaintively. "It sounded like so much fun when you interviewed me. I've never driven a trolley. I was just going to, you know, take it around the block a couple of times."

"I need you to put your hands behind your back, sir," said Mike, who was trying to handcuff Ted.

"I can't do that," said Ted. "I have problems with both my shoulders." Just then, Annie saw car lights turning in from the road. Ben had arrived.

"Then, put your hands in front," the chief said in exasperation. He led Ted to the police cruiser as Ben drove up. "Annie, do you want to press charges?"

"I'm not sure," she said. Nothing had really happened to the trolley, and Ted seemed non-violent, if a little nutty. "Can I let you know in the morning?"

"Sure," said Mike, bundling Ted into the back seat of his cruiser. He took a last look around the parking lot and sighed. "Just another night of mayhem in Macklin."

Ben ran up to Annie and threw his arms around her. "You caught the guy! But what were you thinking?"

"I was dumb," Annie admitted, hugging Ben. Now that it was over, she couldn't believe what she'd done. "I shouldn't have tried to follow the trolley. It could have been a real criminal."

"I know!" Ben exclaimed. "I was really worried about you. What if something had happened to you? I'd never—I'd never forgive myself!"

"But what—what else could you have done? You called the police and you followed me," she said.

"I could have talked you out of chasing him."

"It's okay, Ben," Annie said. "We caught him! We got the trolley back!"

"Ted would probably have brought it back on his own."

"It's too bad he didn't," said Annie. "Now, we've got to figure out how to get it back ourselves."

CHAPTER 27

December 11

ANNIE AND BEN MET FOR BREAKFAST AT THE MACKLIN Café the next morning. Annie had ordered a cheese omelet for protein and energy. They'd been up most of the night making multiple trips to the lake, to bring the trolley and both of their cars safely home again. They were getting a lot of attention while they waited for their meal. Plenty of people in Macklin owned police scanners, and it seemed that most of them had followed the whole chase on their radios. They were interrupted every few seconds by neighbors stopping at their booth to gush, "You were so brave!"

Annie was wide-awake in spite of only having slept about two hours. She had thrown on a Christmas sweater she'd just bought at the craft fair. A Christmas tree stood on a multicolored rug. Two opened boxes sat under the tree. A mouse perched on one of the upper branches, holding a large piece of cheese in one paw and a remote control in the other. An orange tabby cat was furiously chasing a Roomba beneath the tree while the mouse smirked.

She was still full of excitement from the night before. "I can't believe we did that! We helped foil a robbery! We helped catch a carjacker! We saved the trolley from going into the lake!" She frowned at Ben. "Why are you eating banana cream pie for breakfast?"

"Potassium," Ben answered. He looked terrible. His eyes were bloodshot, and he'd downed three cups of coffee in rapid succession, trying to wake up. He looked sternly at Annie. She seemed to have forgotten that her life could have been in danger. This morning she was thinking of the escapade as a thrilling adventure.

"You could have been hurt! You could have been kidnapped! You never, never, never follow someone who's stealing something!" Ben told her.

"He's right, and it won't happen again!"

They looked up to see Chief Newton, who was still on duty. His usual crisp uniform looked like he'd slept in it. "I brought you a present." He held out a police wheel clamp. "Put this on your trolley when you aren't driving it. I don't want to chase after it again."

Ben slid over in the booth and Mike sat down next to him. He looked hopefully at Ben's coffee. Ben signaled to Cammie to bring another cup.

"What's going to happen to Ted?" Annie asked.

"That's up to you. Right now, he's in the city jail. He doesn't seem to have any money to pay for the bail bond."

"Ohhh," Annie said. "That's terrible. Nobody will bail him out?"

"Don't even think about it," Ben warned her.

"Do you want to press charges?" Mike asked her.

Annie sighed. "I guess not. Nothing really happened, except a joyride. Could you give him community service?"

Mike nodded. "Great idea! I'll put him on trash duty for the trolley tours and release him." Mike swallowed his coffee in one gulp and got up. "Use that thing!" he said, pointing to the wheel clamp as he left.

Cammie stopped at their table with their bill. "I heard Dave Meyers' son is coming back to town," she said. "Is that true?"

Ben nodded. "Adam and Stacey. His son and daughter-in-law from New York. Dave's going to lease them some space in his building."

Cammie looked around conspiratorially, and then said, "Darlene asked me this morning where Dave was."

"We don't know," Annie said. "We were up all night."

"Chasing a thief who tried to steal the trolley," said Ben.

"Oh, my God!" Cammie said. "That's the most exciting thing that's ever happened in Macklin!" Sensing that this might not have been the most appropriate reaction, she added, "Was anybody hurt?"

"No!" replied Annie. "And we caught him! We saved the Christmas trolley!"

"Are you selling any of your paintings?" Ben asked, trying to change the subject.

"I almost forgot!" Cammie said happily. "Mayor Preston bought the one of the old bridge. He wants to put it in city hall. Can you believe it? I'll have a painting in city hall! Me!"

"Cammie, that's wonderful!" Annie exclaimed. "Promise me you'll never give up your art again."

"I won't," Cammie said. "Just think, a few months ago I was just a waitress. Now I'm a logo designer and a painter. All because of the Christmas trolley!"

Annie stood up. "We should take a better look at the trolley now that it's daylight," she said. "I don't think there's any major damage, but we might need to touch up the paint."

"Let's go see," said Ben, dragging himself out of the booth, along with the boot. They walked down the street past Meyers' toward the corner. The senior citizens were sprawled on the patio furniture again, with their coffee and the newspaper. They waved. Some of them started clapping. "Our heroes!" they yelled.

A woman in a pink shawl was peering at the crossword puzzle. "Annie!" she called out. "What's a seven-letter word for a Christmas tree?"

"Conifer," Annie said.

"What's another name for Santa Claus? Two words. Lots of letters," came from another woman, wearing a red ski parka. She was balancing a piece of pie on her lap along with the paper. She waved her fork at Ben. "Apple cranberry," she announced. "Try it. Antioxidants."

"Kris Kringle," Annie said. She heard a dog growl, and noticed Jerry LaFontaine. Jerry was cradling a small basket in his lap. Suddenly a small, tawny head shot up. The dog growled again, this time at Ben.

"Peanut!" Ben exclaimed. "What are you doing out here? Angie didn't give him to you, Jerry, did she?"

"No, I'm just watching him while Angie's shopping," Jerry replied. "Dave banned him from the store. He said even if Peanut was a comfort dog, he bit someone."

"That was me," said Ben, holding up his thumb. Peanut growled again.

"It's okay, Peanut," Jerry said soothingly. "Those mean people aren't going to hurt you."

Annie and Ben exchanged astonished looks. "We aren't mean!" Ben protested. "I was rescuing the polar bear! And he bit me!"

Just then, Angie came out of the hardware store. She reached into her green cloth shopping bag and pulled out a small packet. "Peanut! Look what mommy found for you in the Camping section! Freeze-dried fish!"

Annie's phone beeped. "I forgot!" she gasped. "I've got a board meeting this morning."

"On Sunday?" Ben asked.

Annie sighed. "We're conferencing in Brad and Sophie. Brad says it's the only day this week he can meet. Tomorrow he's having high tea with a duchess."

The crossword puzzle workers, interested, looked up. "Not Kate. Not Meghan. I asked him," Annie told them. They went back to their puzzle. "Then he's leaving for a castle in Scotland, where apparently he won't have an internet connection."

Ben scoffed. "Scotland has perfectly good internet service. He's hoping you'll let him out of the meeting. We ran into this all the time at Jupiter."

"What did you do?"

"You could make him give a presentation at the meeting," Ben suggested.

"That would drive everybody else away," said Annie. "For now, we'll just put up with meeting on Sunday." She looked at Ben. "Go home and get some sleep."

"I'll put the boot on the trolley first," he said. "AND DON'T TAKE IT OFF."

"I promise," Annie said as she waved good-bye to Ben, and walked up the steps to the porch of the Macklin House. She was starting to feel like she could use a nap herself, but this meeting came first.

The board members were already in place when she entered the conference room. Only Allan, still at church, was missing. She could see Sophie on one laptop screen, wearing a chic green silk scarf. Brad, in a heavy wool fisherman's sweater on the other screen, was impatiently marking sentences in a book with a yellow highlighter. Annie wondered if he owned the book. Knowing Brad, it was fifty-fifty.

Annie pulled out a chair at the conference table, and faced Natalie and Ron and the laptops expectantly. Natalie slid her gavel out of her purse. "I'm exhausted," she complained. She brushed dust off her pink tracksuit. "Our friends, the Logans, are downsizing. They told me I could have everything in their garage for the thrift store, and I've been moving boxes all morning. It's a good thing I have my brand-new SUV. The seats fold down and they're *completely automatic.* You press a button, and they go up. You press a button, and they go down. You press a button, and they move to one side. I don't know how anyone manages without these new features."

Annie heard Ron mutter, "For the price of that car, the seats should jump up and sing." She ignored him.

Natalie banged her gavel. "The meeting is called to order. This is our December board meeting, and Annie's going to bring us up to date on our fundraising goals."

"Thank you, Natalie," Annie said. "To date, we've had sixteen trolley tours, with an average attendance of fifty riders per tour. We've had five hundred adult riders, and three hundred and thirty children. So far we've raised thirteen thousand, three hundred seventy-five dollars. A few kind people gave us extra donations. Then we've made an additional ten thousand five hundred dollars from sales of souvenir t-shirts at fifteen dollars each. They're very popular. We really appreciate the t-shirt donation from Preston Automotive."

Natalie looked pleased. Ron looked irritated.

"We've also made seven hundred thirty dollars from coffee, hot chocolate, and cookies. Our total is twenty-four thousand, six hundred five dollars. With twenty more tours to go," Annie continued.

"And our expenses?" asked Ron. He was tieless this morning but was wearing a green-and-white striped button-down shirt under a gray flannel blazer. Annie guessed he was going to show a house to a client after the meeting.

"The only costs we have are insurance on the trolley, and gas. Everything else has been donated." Annie sighed inwardly. She personally thought the expenses were extremely low, but she knew Ron was going to complain. "The insurance is five thousand dollars for the life of the event," she continued. "So far, we've spent around eight hundred dollars on gas. Our net is eighteen thousand, eight hundred and five dollars."

"Aren't you forgetting something?" Ron asked disapprovingly. "What about advertising?"

"It's all digital," Annie explained. "We're just using our regular Facebook and Instagram and Twitter accounts." She looked around at the board members before summing up. She'd gone through the numbers several times, and she could hardly believe what she was about to say.

"We'll probably make around fifty thousand dollars from the tours if all goes as planned."

"Wow!" Natalie exclaimed. After a few seconds, Brad glanced up briefly from his book, while Sophie said, "That's amazing!"

Everyone clapped except for Ron. "That's more than I expected," he grumbled. "But even with the additional pledges from individual donors, we'll be short of where we need to be. This idea is never going to work."

"Ron," Annie said firmly. "Think of the glass as half-full. A month ago, we needed one hundred thousand dollars and had nothing. Today, we still need one hundred thousand dollars. But we're on track to have fifty thousand of it in two weeks."

"I'd say that's a major achievement for this town," offered Natalie. "Thanks to all of Annie's hard work. And if we've got fifty thousand, all we need is another fund-raiser or two and we'll have our money."

"Philip would be proud of us," Sophie added. "Wouldn't he, Brad?"

After the Skype pause, Brad put down his book. "I never thought I'd say this, but I have to agree with Sophie."

Natalie wrote a note in large letters, which she passed to Annie. "They agree," it read. "Pigs fly."

"I still think it's a long shot," Ron said unhappily. "I'm going to look for other options."

"Ron, you know if there are other ideas out there, the board would love to see them," Natalie said. "Annie, do you have anything else for us right now?"

"I guess you've all heard that someone borrowed the trolley last night for a joyride out to Macklin Lake. Police Chief Newton captured the man, and he's in custody now. The trolley had some minor damage, but nothing that can't be repaired quickly. Chief Newton loaned us a police boot to put on the wheels to prevent further thefts." Annie hoped that she'd sounded official enough.

"That's my point!" exclaimed Ron. "If something happens to that trolley, no more tours. No more money."

"Ron," Natalie said patiently. "The trolley is fine. I saw it myself. The glass is half-full, remember?" She banged her gavel. "This meeting is adjourned!"

CHAPTER 28

December 13

ANNIE HAD BEEN RIGHT WHEN SHE PREDICTED THE TROL-
ley tours would keep Emma and Jackson occupied. They diligently
finished their homework every afternoon in Dave's office, and the snowman had been out on the sidewalk, undisturbed, since the tours started.
Ben had to admit that he missed their practical jokes at times. Rudolph
was still in the store, much to Dave's disgust, but the kids had removed
the motion sensor and the coin jar. They were definitely taking their
elf jobs seriously.

He was trying to figure out the instructions for a new line of doorbells with cameras on the Tuesday afternoon following the trolley chase,
when Emma wandered over to his worktable.

"I'm done with my homework," she said, forestalling his question.
She picked up one of the doorbell pieces and turned it back and forth,
examining it. "What's this?"

"One of our new doorbells," Ben explained. He was trying to follow the directions, but the translation made no sense. "You will instant see huge green finger," he read aloud.

Emma inspected the other pieces. "It looks like that wire goes in there," she said, pointing.

"You're right," Ben agreed. "Do you like electronics?"

"Oh, yes!" she answered eagerly. "It's fun to put things together. It's kind of like a 3-D puzzle. That's why I like coming here after school. Dave has all these tools! And all these electrical things." She gestured at the doorbells. "You can take them apart and see how they're made."

Suddenly Emma looked horrified and clapped her hand over her mouth. "Don't tell Dave I said that!" she pleaded.

Ben looked up. Maybe he could do some more mentoring. "Your secret's safe with me, as long as you put whatever it is back together again. So, you like to figure out how things work. Did you ever think about engineering?" he asked.

Emma's face brightened. "Maybe," she said. Then she hesitated. "You know we have to do a science fair project in April."

Ben remembered. A science fair project was required in seventh grade. He'd built a telescope.

"I want to do something special. Not like just growing two plants and comparing them." Emma made a disgusted face. "That's for little kids."

"Okay," said Ben.

"What I'd really like to do," she continued, "is to build a robot. A real robot. Not some toy thing."

"Is Jackson interested in building this robot?" Ben asked.

"He'll do it if I want him to," Emma replied.

"I know the feeling," said Ben. "That would be an awesome project, Emma."

Emma still looked hesitant. "My mom says it's too complicated and too expensive."

"Your mom's a great person but she doesn't know anything about robots," said Ben. "I was on a robotics team in college. It wouldn't be that hard to design a simple robot. I could help."

"Really?" Emma said excitedly. Then, she looked crestfallen. Her next question got to the heart of the matter. "You don't think it's—not a good project for a girl?"

"Of course not!" Ben said immediately. "There were two girls on my robotics team. They were the smartest ones on the team. If you want to do this, go for it."

She sighed. "Sometimes I wish I was more like my mother. She bakes all these fantastic cakes and cookies. Everybody loves them. I try and try, but they never come out the same for me."

Ben thought this over. "You *are* like your mother," he said. "She likes to bake things, right?" Emma nodded. "Well, when you bake, uh, cookies, what do you do? You take a lot of different, uh, ingredients and mix them together. You put this ingredient and that ingredient together, and you come out with something different."

"I guess," Emma said.

"It's the same with building a robot. You take your electronic components and you figure out how to put them together to make the robot do what you want it to do. It's like when your mom bakes something. You're just using different materials."

"I never thought of it that way," Emma admitted. "Could we really build a robot? How much do you think it would cost? For materials?"

Ben started mentally calculating. Then he had an inspiration. "Emma! If I know *my* mother, I've probably got two big tubs of robot parts in our garage. She never threw anything out. Let me look tonight. Some of the electronics will be obsolete, but I bet I'll have enough for most of your materials."

Emma looked like she was about to cry. "Oh, thank you, Ben!" She threw her arms around him and hugged him. "You're the best thing that ever happened to us! Except for Annie. I'll never forget this!"

"It's okay," Ben said in embarrassment, patting her on the back. "Look, it's five o'clock. You and Jackson need to get your dinner and get changed. This is going to be an exciting night. Adam and Stacey are going to perform on the stage before the first tour."

Just then, Jackson walked in. "This is a dumb book," he announced. "I don't know why we have to read it." He held up a middle school version of "Romeo and Juliet," translated into modern English.

"You'll appreciate it when you're older," Ben told him. "Hey, Jackson. I heard you're a good artist. I heard you like to draw cartoons."

"Yeah …" Jackson said. Ben couldn't tell if he was embarrassed to admit that he was an artist, or afraid Ben would put him to work painting something.

"So Emma and I were talking about building a robot for the science fair."

"Yeah …"

Ben put down the doorbell. "The thing is," he said, "if you're building a robot, you need a good design. Judges don't want to see something that just looks like a bunch of nuts and bolts. They like designs that look really cool. So we were thinking, maybe you could put your drawing skills to work and come up with a few prototypes."

Jackson became interested. "It would depend on what the robot has to do," he said. "Like if it's a flying robot, it'll need wings. But I don't think we could build a flying robot."

"That would be pretty advanced for seventh grade. Why don't you and Emma talk it over for a few days, and then you could sketch out some options."

Jackson was already thinking. "Maybe it could have multiple arms."

"Put down all your ideas. But, right now, go get your dinner. The trolley tour starts soon," Ben reminded him.

The kids passed Adam coming in the store as they went out. "How's it going?" Adam asked. "Dad just went over to the café to pick up some food. He said Darlene made apple pie today."

Ben looked around carefully to make sure Emma and Jackson couldn't overhear, and then said to Adam, "Cammie thinks Darlene likes your dad."

"Really?" said Adam. "Wouldn't that be great? He needs something in his life. Besides this store."

"Darlene probably needs something in her life besides the café, too," Ben agreed. Well, he'd put the idea out there, and Adam hadn't dismissed it. Where was Cammie, the matchmaker, when he needed her?

Adam looked thoughtful. "I don't think Dad's really gone out with anybody since he and my mom split up. And that's been what, ten years? It was because of the store."

Ben tried to look noncommittal.

"He just worked all the time, you know how he is. Even when the store wasn't open, he'd be over here unloading shipments and stocking the shelves. I remember Mom telling him, 'Why don't you become a contractor? They don't work on weekends.'" Adam thought. "Maybe Stacey and I can sort of nudge things along."

"I heard you're performing tonight," said Ben.

Adam smiled broadly. "Looking forward to it. Our first show in Macklin!" He checked his watch. "Got to go set up!"

"Time for me to get ready, too," said Ben. "Here comes your dad."

Dave was carrying a takeout bag from the café. It looked heavier than usual. He handed Ben a turkey sandwich. "Thought you'd need dinner. Look what Darlene gave me!" He pulled out a whole apple pie. Ben and Adam exchanged glances as they inhaled the fresh-cooked scent. Adam looked amused as he left the store.

"That really smells good," Ben commented. "Darlene makes great pies. Does she know Adam's playing tonight?"

Dave was running the day's sales report. "I'm not sure," he said.

Ben intercepted the sales report from the printer. "She *has* to see Adam and Stacey. It's their first concert in Macklin. We want a big crowd for them. She can take half an hour off. Go back over there and tell her about it. I'll close up."

"Okay," said Dave, looking slightly confused. He stared hopefully at the pie.

"I'll put it in the refrigerator," Ben promised.

THE CHRISTMAS TROLLEY

Once he'd run the final report and closed up the store, Ben headed for the Macklin House to change into his shirt and tie. Tonight, he was wearing the green one. Annie was just finishing up, too.

"You look really nice tonight," she told him, straightening his Christmas tie.

"So do you," he answered. Annie was wearing the red sweater her mother had knitted for her over a white tank top, with a pair of jeans. She had on her Christmas light bulb necklace and earrings.

"I can make the necklace light up," she told him. "See?" She pushed the button on its little battery. Ben started laughing. "We can add you to the tour!" he exclaimed. "And for our last stop, ladies and gentlemen, here's Annie Mulvaney, a human holiday light!"

Annie rolled her eyes.

"No, don't turn it off!" Ben added. "It looks great with your eye—uh, sweater." The necklace sparkled in the twilight as they walked over to the trolley stop together. Ben saw Darlene and Paula conferring at the cookie station. He decided to consult Annie.

"Since Cammie thinks Darlene likes Dave, Adam and I told Dave he has to go to the show. Maybe they'll run into each other. What do you think? Is this all in Cammie's mind?"

"It could be," Annie replied. "Cammie's really into love and happy endings. But Darlene seems really attentive to Dave when they run into each other." Annie was secretly wondering what Cammie thought about Ben and herself. Had Cammie detected any signs of romance? "So, here's your job. If Dave's at the show, you make sure he ends up somewhere near Darlene."

"How am I going to do that?" Ben asked.

"You'll think of something. It'll be easy. He won't even know what's happening." They parted ways at the trolley stop. Annie walked over to the stage to make sure Brent was there for emcee duties, even though she wasn't really worried. Brent may have been a small-town politician, but he was a politician. He loved being the emcee. She found him sitting on the edge of the stage, wearing one of the trolley tour shirts with "Donated by Preston Automotive" discreetly incorporated into the design on the back. Brent was handing out business cards and chatting up his voters. "Hi, Annie!" he said happily. "Are we ready?"

People were already milling around, browsing through the craft fair and running into their neighbors. Annie turned on the microphone and handed it to Brent, who stood up and moved to the center of the stage. "Good evening, Macklin!" he shouted. "May I have your attention, please?" The crowd stopped talking and drifted away from their shopping, moving closer to the stage. "Tonight, we've got two special acts for your entertainment. Let's welcome our first group. Mimi Cloverley and her dancing Snowflake Fairies!"

Everyone pressed in closer, right up to the edge of the stage. Annie headed in the opposite direction, over to her ticket table. The Women's Club members had volunteered to help her each night with the tickets, and some were better at this than others. Elaine Gilpin was on duty tonight, though, so Annie had no worries. Elaine's cash total would be correct down to the last penny.

Since the dancing reindeer had proved so popular, Mimi had choreographed a second routine for her nine toddlers, to the tune of "The Dance of the Sugar Plum Fairy." They were now "Snowflake Fairies," wearing all-white jumpsuits. Each had a slightly different cardboard snowflake attached in back. Mimi had imported the older sister of one of the fairies to play the Snowflake Queen. Enamored with her role, the Snowflake Queen leaped among and over the fairies, waving her arms in sweeping gestures. The toddlers happily tumbled back and forth, while the Snowflake Queen leaped closer and closer to the edge of the stage. Suddenly, she leaped and twirled at the same time, and fell backward off the stage. One of the toddlers stood up and cried, "Come back!" All the others took up the cry. "Come back! Come back!"

Someone in the audience caught the Snowflake Queen, and helped her back onto the stage. All the toddlers clapped in delight. One of them turned to the audience, held up her arms, and said clearly, "See? She came back!"

The snowflake dancers lined up and bowed clumsily, to great applause. They managed to walk off the stage in a more or less straight line.

Over at the ticket table, Annie was helping Elaine check off ticket reservations. She glanced at the stage and saw Adam and Stacey setting up. They had brought an electronic keyboard with two bass speakers. She picked out Ben, in his green shirt. He was standing next to Dave and Darlene, toward the middle of the crowd.

Annie suddenly wanted to be down there with them, instead of working the ticket table. She glanced at Elaine. Tonight Elaine was wearing a white quilted satin jacket over a red silk camisole and white silk capris. She'd accessorized with pearl earrings and a pearl pendant. Next to Elaine, Annie felt extremely underdressed in her Christmas sweater and light-up jewelry, even if it *was* the sweater her mother had knitted for her. However, Annie was still the one in charge, underdressed or not. "Elaine," she asked, "could you take over here? I need to go talk to Ben." She pointed toward the crowd.

"No problem," Elaine answered cheerfully. Annie quickly got up and pushed her way through the spectators toward Ben. Brent was back on stage. "Now for our second act!" he announced. "Adam and Stacey Meyers! They've just moved here from Brooklyn, New York to open a music store. Adam is Dave Meyers' son and a graduate of our own Macklin High. Stacey is his beautiful and equally talented wife. They met in college, and he finally convinced her to move back here to our wonderful town. Let's hear it for Adam and Stacey!"

The crowd was buzzing with anticipation. A new musical duo, straight from New York!

"Annie!" Ben said, smiling as she reached his side. "Who's collecting the money?"

"Elaine's doing it. I wanted to see Adam and Stacey perform," Annie answered.

"That's great! Looks like they're just about ready."

Stacey picked up the microphone and came up to the front center of the stage. She was wearing a flowing chiffon top, jeans, and cowboy boots. Adam, at the keyboard to the side, looked serious in a black t-shirt and black jeans. "Hi everybody!" Stacey shouted. She tossed her long hair. "We're Adam and Stacey. Or Stacey and Adam. We're so happy to be here in Macklin and sharing our music with you tonight!"

The crowd cheered. Stacey looked at Adam. He hit a few introductory notes on his keyboard and they launched into "Jingle Bell Rock."

The audience erupted. "Oh, my God!" Annie said. "They're really good." Dave was grinning from ear to ear and looked incredibly proud.

People started clapping in time to the music, and suddenly everyone was dancing on the grass. Ben turned to Annie and held out his hands. "Annie!" he said. "Dance with me!"

Annie laughed happily and they started dancing. Had they ever danced before? Both of them were just average dancers, but they were caught up in the music. Annie couldn't remember when she'd felt so happy. It wasn't just that she was dancing with Ben—it was the whole spirit of the celebration.

They kept dancing through another five songs, crowd-pleasing numbers that kept everyone on their feet. Then, Adam and Stacey stopped to take a break. Adam gestured to Dave.

"Dad!" he called. "Dad! We want you to sit in on this next song."

"What's he doing?" said Ben. Dave shook his head, but Adam kept motioning him to come up on the stage.

"He wants you to go up there," Darlene said. "Go on." She gave Dave a slight push. Dave looked sheepish but climbed up on the stage. Adam pulled out a clarinet that he'd hidden on the other side of the stage.

"What on earth?" said Annie.

Dave looked from Adam to Stacey. He finally took the clarinet and blew a few tentative notes. Adam stepped up to the microphone.

"This is our last song tonight. Most of you know my dad, Dave Meyers. We asked him to join us for this song." The audience cheered. Several people yelled, "Go, Dave!" Dave looked embarrassed. "I'm out of practice," he said. "I can't play."

"Sure you can," said Adam. "How else are we going to start our band?"

Dave looked horrified. "We're starting a band?"

"Dad," Adam said patiently. "This is California! We can do anything we want! Come on, Stacey will cue you when to come in."

Adam played an introduction and Stacey began to sing, "Have Yourself a Merry Little Christmas." As if it were the most natural thing in the world, Ben took Annie in his arms and they began to slow dance. At the end of the song, Stacey turned to Dave and motioned him forward. Adam started again at the beginning of the song, with Dave playing a solo.

Annie and Ben couldn't believe it. Dave was good. Not at the level of Adam or Stacey but astonishingly good.

"Did you know Dave could play the clarinet?" Ben asked.

"No!" said Annie. "I had absolutely no idea!"

"All this undiscovered talent in Macklin!" Ben said in amazement. "And we never knew!"

"Like Grace Iwamoto says," Annie answered. "Everybody's got a story. You just have to ask." She put her head on Ben's shoulder as Dave's clarinet soared and they kept dancing.

The song ended. Annie and Ben stood looking at each other, no longer in each other's arms but holding hands.

"Annie …," Ben said.

He's going to kiss me, she thought. *I know it.*

She felt someone tugging at her sleeve. It was Jackson. Now she saw Emma pulling at Ben.

"The trolley tour!" Jackson hissed. "We're behind schedule! We've got to get over there NOW!"

For the first time since she'd bought the trolley, Annie had a heretical thought.

That damned trolley.

CHAPTER 29

December 17

ALL WEEK LONG, EVERYONE IN MACKLIN HAD BEEN KEEP-ing an eye on the weather. It usually didn't rain in Macklin until January. It never snowed. But every so often, high, gusty winds would come roaring down from the foothills. And Macklin was in for one of these cold, powerful windstorms.

Each day, the temperature grew colder and the wind picked up. Annie could see the tops of the pine trees across the square blowing back and forth on Saturday night, as the first trolley tour left. She had moved her ticket table to the Macklin House porch to keep it out of the wind. Fortunately, the evening's entertainment, the Rotary Club's banjo and fiddle group, was still drawing an enthusiastic crowd. But most of the craft fair vendors had closed up for the night, and there were only a few small children waiting to visit Santa.

Annie zipped up her puffy silver down jacket, and walked over to the coffee booth to talk to Paula and Darlene. She wrapped her green wool scarf more tightly around her neck. Her mother had made it for her in the knitting club. It was beautiful wool, but too warm for most nights in Macklin. Annie had written her mom a grateful thank-you note for the scarf, but had privately wondered how often she'd wear it. Now, she was extremely happy to have it.

Paula and Darlene were pouring cups of coffee and hot chocolate as fast as they could. Annie noticed in astonishment that Dave was helping. Maybe there was something to Cammie's theory after all!

Paula beckoned to Annie. "Brent wants to see you." She waved toward the stage, where the banjo group was just wrapping up their act. "Who needs Nashville?" Brent shouted over the microphone. "Give it up for our very own Macklin Rotarians!" Brent jumped down from the stage and caught up with Annie.

"Do we have any more entertainment tonight?" he asked.

"No," Annie replied. "We were going to leave the sound system on for an open mic night, but it doesn't look like anyone wants to perform as yet."

"Okay," Brent said. "You won't need an emcee for that. I'll take a last walk around, and then I'm going home."

"You're a wonderful emcee," Annie told him. "You're doing a great job! Let me get you a cup of coffee before you go." She walked him back to the coffee booth and got him some coffee and a cookie.

"You know," he said as he bit into his cookie, "if this takes off, the Macklin House is probably going to need a truck."

"Brent!" Annie laughed.

"I'm serious! If I see a good used truck with low miles, I'll keep you in mind," he said as he walked off with his coffee. Annie sighed ruefully. Yes, the Macklin House could use a truck. She couldn't keep asking Ben to pick up things in his minivan. And just then, she saw Ben himself coming up the walk from the trolley stand, clutching his jacket and struggling against the force of the gale. "This wind is getting pretty bad," he said. "Do you think we should cancel the second tour?"

Annie winced. In spite of the weather, customers were already lined up, and she really didn't want to lose the ticket money. Every dollar helped. "Go sit in the trolley and see what it's like inside," she suggested. "The driver's seat is right in front, out in the wind. It might be warmer in the passenger seats."

Ben returned in a few minutes. "It's not too bad," he said. "The sides kind of block the wind. Do we have any blankets?"

"Actually, we do!" Annie said, brightening up. "Macklin's emergency response team stores a lot of supplies at the Macklin House. Including blankets!"

Ben corralled Emma and Jackson. Twenty minutes later, they had a pile of blankets available for any riders who needed extra warmth. The passengers shivered as they boarded the trolley, but seemed to think of the upcoming ride as a great adventure.

"It'll be like a sleigh ride in wind instead of snow," Ben told them as he maneuvered the trolley into the street. The trolley shuddered in the wind. Ben was glad he was driving the big, sturdy trolley instead of a small car.

As he drove further along their route, though, the wind seemed to grow even stronger. Small tree branches blew into their path. Ben could see some of the light displays waving wildly. He started to feel nervous. This was worse than he'd expected. The passengers were still enthusiastic, pointing out flying palm tree fronds and roofs with lost shingles.

More debris flew into the road, as Ben turned down Brewster Street. This was a crowd-pleasing street in an older part of town. Tall spruce trees lined both sides of the street, and all were strung with garlands of white lights. Tonight, the trees were swaying dangerously back and forth in the wind. Usually, Ben could count on carolers standing along the street to serenade the trolley. But tonight, the homes were shut up tight, and the sidewalks were deserted.

Ben saw the taillights of a single car up ahead of him. Suddenly, a huge gust of wind shook the trolley. He fought to keep it under control. There was a loud cracking sound as one of the spruce trees broke in two. Ben saw the car up ahead swerve, but not in time. With a giant boom, the tree fell across the road and onto the car. The impact knocked the car up on its right side. Ben yelled, "Hold on!" and slammed on the brakes.

The trolley skidded slightly, but came to a stop about twenty feet away from the shattered car.

Dense branches covered the squashed top of the car and blocked the door on the driver's side, which looked folded in half. The taillights glowed incongruously from beneath the branches. For a moment, there was no sound except the wind, as everyone on the trolley stared at the scene in stunned disbelief.

Then a man in the front row of seats yelled, "That's Brent Preston's car!" As soon as he said it, Ben recognized Brent's vintage Mustang. Adrenaline took over. Ben stood up and turned around to face his passengers. "Everyone stay on the trolley! Except you, you, and you. You come with me." He pointed to three men sitting close to him who looked fairly young and strong. Then he grabbed Emma and Jackson, who both looked like they were going to cry. "Do *not* leave this trolley. Pass out cookies. Keep everybody in their seats." He pulled out the first-aid kit from under his seat, and jumped down to the ground, followed by the three men. One was already pulling out his phone to dial 911.

As soon as they reached the downed tree and wrecked car, they knew they had an impossible situation. The man with the phone groaned in disgust. "I can't get any signal," he said. "The wind must be affecting the cell towers." They could see Brent in the driver's seat, unconscious, his seat belt holding him in place. Blood was trickling from a wound where he'd hit his head as the tree pushed the car up in the air. His cup of coffee had toppled out of the cup holder and landed next to the passenger door.

"Pull the tree away!" said Ben, grabbing hold of the trunk. They tried, but even with the four of them, it was too heavy to move. With the car crumpled up and sitting at an angle, there was no way to get Brent to safety.

They pulled on the branches again, and looked at each other helplessly.

"If we can't get through to the fire department or the police, we're on our own," said Ben.

"If we could move the tree, we could push the car upright and get Brent out through a window. We'd need a winch to pull that tree off, though," said one of the men.

"I've got a chain," said Ben.

"A chain?"

"In the storage compartment. If we wrapped it around the tree and hooked the other end to the trolley, we might have enough power to move the tree." Ben's heart was pounding as he ran back to the trolley. His hands were shaking as he fumbled with the cover on the storage section, but he steadied himself as it popped open. He pulled out the chain and one of the end poles, and grabbed a screwdriver out of the emergency kit. Jackson, Emma, and the rest of the passengers peered anxiously over the side. "STAY ON THE TROLLEY! WE'RE GOING TO TRY SOMETHING!" Ben yelled.

The men dragged the length of chain from the trolley to the tree, bracing themselves against the wind. The parking tickets snapped off the chain, and blew off into the distance. The padlock still hung open on the chain. Ben wrapped one end of the chain around the tree and locked it to itself. *No key to unlock it later*, he thought, *but this will either work, or it won't*. Hooking the chain up to the trolley was going to be harder.

Ben looked at the raised handrail that ran along all four sides of the trolley. It wasn't much, but he couldn't see any other place to attach the chain. He wrapped the chain around the front railing several times, and stuck the screwdriver through it. He hoped that would hold the chain in place. He extended the rest of the chain down the aisle. Then, he placed the pole in the middle of the aisle where the chain ended, and hung the last link in the chain over the hook on the pole. He motioned the three men back into their seats.

"EVERYBODY LISTEN!" Ben shouted. "I'M GOING TO BACK UP THE TROLLEY. PICK UP THE CHAIN FROM THE AISLE AND HOLD ON TO IT. YOU PEOPLE AT THE BACK, HOLD ON TO THE POLE. I HOPE THAT'LL GIVE US SOME EXTRA FORCE TO MOVE THAT TREE! DON'T LET GO OF THE CHAIN!"

The passengers immediately did as he had asked. Ben slid into the driver's seat. Clenching his teeth, he started up the trolley and put it in reverse. Ben backed up as slowly as he could, until the chain was taut. "Here we go," he muttered. Slowly, he put on the gas. The trolley stood still. "PULL!" Ben yelled. He pressed down on the gas pedal, and they heard a metallic noise. For a moment, Ben thought the chain was pulling the railing off. Then, a shout went up from the passengers, and he realized it was the sound of the tree branches scraping on the car as they were pulled away. Back, back, back the trolley went, until the tree was free of the car and lying in the road. "It worked!" yelled one of the passengers, as they all dropped the chain. Everyone cheered and clapped.

"WE NEED TO PUSH THE CAR UPRIGHT," Ben shouted. No time to be politically correct at this point. "EVERYBODY WHO'S UNDER FIFTY, COME WITH ME."

His passengers were all swarming off the trolley anyway, regardless of age. Jackson and Emma asserted themselves and drew an imaginary circle well away from the car. "Everyone over fifty or under twelve goes here," they said, herding anyone looking remotely elderly or childlike into their space.

Ben was left with ten people, both men and women. They all lined up alongside the car. Ben said a silent prayer that the car wouldn't fall back on anyone when they tried to move it. "COUNT OF THREE," he said. "ONE, TWO, THREE!" They pushed. The car teetered for an instant and then fell dramatically onto its four wheels. Brent's body shifted and his arm hit the horn. The noise seemed to bring him back to consciousness. He opened his eyes groggily. "What—what happened?"

"A tree fell on your car," said Ben. "We need to get you out of there." He could see that Brent's head was still bleeding. "Can you move your arms and legs?"

"I think so," said Brent, wiggling his fingers. "My right leg really hurts, but it moves."

Ben reached through the broken window and unlocked the door. Using the crowbar from the trolley, they were able to pry the car door open far enough to pull Brent out. Ben and three of the other men carried Brent over to the trolley, while some of the passengers made a bed of blankets across one row of seats. Brent was obviously in a lot of pain, but only moaned once, when they lifted him onto the trolley.

"I'm a nurse," volunteered one of the women. She bandaged the wound on Brent's head, and tried to stabilize his leg as much as she could. Ben coiled up the chain and left it next to the tree. The wind was starting to rise again and he wanted to get out of there as soon as possible.

"Hurry, Ben," said Emma. "His head's still bleeding and his leg's really swollen."

The other passengers were all back in their seats, ready to go.

Jackson stood next to Brent, who was stoically trying not to moan in front of his voters. "You'll be okay, Mr. Preston," Jackson assured the mayor. "Ben won't let anything happen to us."

Ben guided the trolley back through the wind-swept streets toward the Macklin House. It was closer than the hospital, and the police officers on crowd control duty would be able to call an ambulance. He steered around fallen branches in the streets, and a life-sized plastic reindeer that had blown off a roof and come to rest in the middle of an intersection.

"I still can't get phone service," one of the passengers yelled.

Ben risked a quick glance back at Brent. His eyes were closed and he wasn't moving. Blood was still oozing through the bandage on his head.

As they approached the town square, Ben started madly ringing the trolley's bell. He hoped someone would hear their urgent cry for help.

From the Macklin House porch, Annie heard the bell. "Something's wrong," she said aloud. "They're not due back yet. And Ben wouldn't ring the bell like that unless there was a problem. Oh, God, I hope they weren't in an accident."

She had a terrible vision of Ben lying on the ground, dead. Then, rationality returned. Ben was driving the trolley. He *couldn't* be dead.

Annie saw the trolley coming down the street toward the Macklin House. She saw Ben in the driver's seat, and felt an incredible sense of relief. Ben was okay! But he kept ringing the bell. Something was definitely wrong. She raced down the walkway to the street as the trolley slid into its parking space. Ben jumped off. He had scratches on his face and his arms, and he looked dirty and exhausted. The passengers were all yelling at once. "We need an ambulance!"

"It's Brent Preston," said Ben. "A tree fell on his car."

"Oh, my God," said Annie. She waved frantically at the nearest police officer, who was idling next to his patrol car on the corner. "Help! We need an ambulance!" she shouted. Startled into action, the officer ran up with his police radio.

"Neal!" Annie exclaimed, reading his name badge. "We need the paramedics!" By now, Annie had seen Brent, who looked barely conscious. The bloody bandage didn't bother her, but the sight of Brent lying immobile was completely unnerving. Brent was always talking, moving, shaking hands with people. *Brent's dead, not Ben,* she thought irrationally.

Then, the patrolman leaned over the side of the trolley. "I called an ambulance," he said. Brent moaned. Annie sighed in relief.

Ben was trying to get all the riders off the trolley in an orderly fashion, and failing completely. Emma and Jackson ran out of the crowd and clung to Annie. She hugged them tightly. Then, she said to Emma, "Go find your Mom and Darlene. Tell them to give free coffee to everybody who was on the trolley."

No one was leaving until the ambulance arrived, and they might as well have a hot drink in the meantime. Annie heard the story in bits and pieces as she helped Paula and Darlene with the coffee. The details were jumbled, but everyone was clear on one point: Ben had made them band together to save Brent.

With everyone off the trolley, Ben sat down in the driver's seat to wait for the ambulance. The woman who'd bandaged Brent's head crouched down beside him, periodically taking his pulse. "He's going to be okay," she said reassuringly. "We just need to get him to the ER."

Just then, Ben heard the ambulance siren, and a moment later, he saw its headlights as it came down the block. It parked behind the trolley, and two EMTs jumped out with a stretcher.

"You guys did a good job," one of them told Ben approvingly, as they carried Brent off the trolley. "If you hadn't found him when you did, it would have been another story."

They hustled Brent into the ambulance, and drove off with their siren blaring. The sound faded into the night, and the crowd slowly broke up.

Annie saw Jackson and Emma standing with Paula, who was handing out the last of the coffee to Neal, the patrolman. Suddenly worried, Annie asked Paula, "Did anyone call Natalie?" Neal nodded, gulping his coffee. "Chief Mike called her and went over to their house. He's driving her to the hospital."

"What a night!" Paula said. She looked at Emma and Jackson. "You two need to get home and go to bed. Thank goodness that was the last tour for a few days!"

Finally, everyone was gone, except Annie and Ben. The night air was really freezing now, and the wind still howled. "It's too cold out here," Annie said, as she steered Ben up the porch steps of the Macklin House, into the lobby.

Suddenly, the night's events seemed to catch up with Ben. He turned pale and his hands started to shake. Annie got him to one of the benches in the lobby, and he sat down. He looked like he was about to faint. "Just stay there," Annie told him.

It was all crashing in on him—the car wreck, the tree, rigging up the chain, that awful, tense moment when he started backing up the trolley. How had he done all that? Suddenly, he felt Annie's hand on his shoulder. "Drink this," she said, as she sat down beside him. She was holding a cup of sugary hot tea. "You're a hero, Ben. You saved Brent Preston's life."

"With the Christmas trolley," he said in wonder.

"With the Christmas trolley," Annie agreed. She placed her hand over his and held it there until he stopped shaking.

CHAPTER 30

December 17

"BEN," ANNIE SAID FINALLY. "YOU'RE NOT IN ANY SHAPE TO drive home."

He'd drunk the tea as they sat silently on the bench for several minutes, still holding hands.

"I have a perfectly good couch in my sitting room and plenty of extra blankets," Annie continued. "Stay at my place tonight."

"Are you sure?" Ben said. "That would be great. I—I really don't think I could drive right now."

He still looked shaky. Annie held his arm as they walked over to her cottage. The holly wreath on her door had blown off and was tangled in a bush six feet away.

"The streets will still be full of branches from the storm, anyway," Annie said as she opened the door. "If I'd realized how bad the wind was going to be, I never would have let you take the trolley out."

"But then we wouldn't have found Brent," said Ben. He sat down on the couch, still dazed. "You know, I almost took a different street. I kept thinking, I should cut the tour short and just get back. But I didn't. It was fate."

"Whatever it was, you found Brent and got everyone on the trolley to help. Now you need to rest."

Annie pulled all her spare blankets and pillows out of the closet, and handed them to Ben. She went into the kitchen and poured out a large glass of scotch. Ben needed to sleep, and she figured this was the best way to knock him out for the night.

"I found an old bottle of scotch," she said, handing him the glass. He'd already wrapped himself up in the blankets, and his color was coming back. "Drink this. It'll relax you," she added.

He was starting to drift off, but sat up. "Is it twenty years old?" he asked.

"No. It's just old," said Annie. Ben drank the whiskey in three gulps, and his eyes started to close. Annie shoved a pillow under his head as he collapsed on the couch. She tucked the blankets tightly around him.

"You know why I didn't take the other street?" he said sleepily. "I knew you'd feel bad if they didn't get the full tour. I didn't want to disappoint you."

"Oh, Ben," Annie said. "I was so afraid that something had happened to you."

"Annie," Ben said. He halted. Then he mumbled, "If it's windy next year, we have to cancel the tour."

She wanted to say, "I love you." But he was already asleep.

Ben was still sleeping when Annie got up the next morning, so she was able to quickly shower and get dressed. She'd made a pot of coffee and was cooking pancakes when Ben stirred. He sat up dazedly, and then was suddenly wide-awake.

"Brent Preston! The trolley!" he exclaimed. "Is Brent okay? Is the trolley okay? We didn't wreck anything on it when we pulled that branch off, did we?"

"Everything's fine," Annie assured him. Phone service was back, and she had already called the hospital to check on Brent. "Brent's doing well and seems more upset about his car than he is about his broken leg. He's being *very* mayor-like. He's holding a press conference at ten o'clock in his hospital room."

"A press conference? We only have two reporters in town."

"Which works out really well," said Annie, "because the hospital only allows two visitors at a time." She flipped the pancakes onto a plate. "Do you want some eggs, too? That's about all I have."

"That sounds fantastic," Ben answered. The drama of Brent's rescue was fading, replaced by the much happier experience of sitting on Annie's couch while she cooked breakfast. *I could just sit here and watch her all day*, Ben thought.

Someone knocked on the door. Puzzled, Annie went to answer it. It was Jackson, with Emma behind him. Neither of them looked any the worse for the previous night's events. If anything, they were more energetic than usual.

"Hi, Annie," Jackson said, and then added to Emma, "Oh, good! Ben's here too." Emma widened her eyes, but didn't say anything.

"On the couch," said Ben. "I'm here. On the couch."

"You need to come out in front," said Jackson. "There's a TV van. From Sacramento."

"They're taking pictures of the Christmas trolley," said Emma. "We need to get our elf costumes out of the office. They want film of us with the trolley."

"WHAT?" Annie and Ben yelled together.

"They want both of you to be on TV, too!" Jackson exclaimed.

Annie and Ben looked at each other.

"Brent probably woke up this morning and put out a press release," Ben muttered.

"I told you. You're a hero. And it's free publicity! I'll sneak over to the Macklin House and get your other shirt. Emma, Jackson—tell the TV guys we'll be there in twenty minutes," Annie said. She followed them out the door, leaving Ben to gobble up the pancakes.

Annie was right, he thought. This could be great publicity, even though he sure didn't feel like a hero. He'd just done what had to be done. He swallowed the last of his breakfast, wishing that he and Annie might have had a little more time alone together that morning.

The TV reporter was a young Asian woman wearing black pants, a coral-colored jacket, and four-inch stiletto heels.

"I'm Cindy Nguyen from 'Fast Break at Five,' on Channel Five," she said. "That's my cameraman, Bill. We cover local news from all over the valley."

They were setting up in the parking lot near Annie's cottage, where the trolley was parked. Emma and Jackson, in their elf costumes, were helping Bill carry his equipment over from the TV station's van. Ben, wearing his red dress shirt and tie, and Annie, wearing one of the trolley tour t-shirts, were waiting patiently next to the trolley. "I saw this *incredible* story on Twitter this morning from somebody named Brent Preston," Cindy continued breathlessly. "He says he's the mayor of Macklin and was saved from death last night by a—Christmas trolley?"

"I told you," Ben said to Annie.

"And this is the trolley? And you're the hero who was driving?" Cindy motioned for Bill to start filming, and held her microphone out to Ben.

"Well, yes," he answered.

"We were on the trolley, too," said Emma. Cindy ignored her. "Tell me what happened."

"The wind was really bad," Ben explained. "We were following Brent's car, and a tree blew over on top of it."

"How did you feel when you saw Mayor Preston's car had been hit?"

"I felt scared," Ben said awkwardly.

Cindy wanted more. "You must have felt like this was a life-and-death situation," she said encouragingly. Ben looked helplessly at Annie. "How were you able to get the tree off the car?"

"With a chain," Jackson put in.

"And you pulled the tree off by improvising with a chain?" Cindy looked impressed. "What made you think of that?"

"We had the chain in the trolley's storage compartment," Ben explained. "It came with the trolley, and we just never took it out. I remembered it was there. We had to try *something*. We hooked one end of the chain to the tree, and the other one to the trolley, and I backed the trolley up, and the tree moved."

"Then we helped push the car upright, and Ben pulled Mayor Preston out," Emma contributed.

"You must have felt like the spirit of Christmas was flowing through you as you pulled that tree off," Cindy said to Ben.

Ben couldn't remember feeling anything except panic, but he knew this wasn't what Cindy wanted to hear. "Something like that," he said. "You need to tell your viewers about the Christmas trolley tour. Annie Mulvaney started it." He pointed at Annie. "Tell her about the Macklin House."

Annie took the microphone and gestured toward the house. "The Macklin House is a registered historic landmark. We need one hundred thousand dollars to restore it, and bring the building up to code."

"She's the director of the museum," Ben added.

"We needed a fund-raiser, and I came up with the idea of using the Christmas trolley for a tour of Macklin's holiday lights. Your viewers may not have seen them, but they're absolutely spectacular. The tour costs twenty dollars for adults and five dollars for kids, and it runs every night through December twenty-fourth. All the money goes to the Macklin House Trust."

"What a worthy cause," said Cindy, and swerved back to Ben without missing a beat. "Tell us how you felt when you started backing up the trolley. You knew it was a race against time to save the mayor."

Jackson broke in. "Ben told all of us on the trolley to pull on the chain together. Like we were rowing, in a lifeboat from a sinking ship!" Ben was taken aback by this, but Cindy looked interested. She turned the microphone to Jackson and Emma. "And what was going through *your* minds as you pulled on the chain?" she asked encouragingly.

"That we really needed to pull hard to save Mayor Preston," said Emma. "Because you don't get many chances to save somebody's life. And that's the most important thing you can ever do."

Cindy beamed into the camera, having finally struck interview gold. "This is Cindy Nguyen from 'Fast Break at Five,' with all your local valley news, reporting live from Macklin, California, where a town's Christmas spirit and this Christmas trolley miraculously saved their mayor's life!"

She motioned for Bill to stop filming. "Thanks so much!" she gushed. "Here's my card. If you ever have any more life-and-death events, call me first!"

CHAPTER 31

December 18–19

ANNIE AND BEN WATCHED CINDY'S SEGMENT ON "FAST Break at Five" that afternoon. Cindy had edited out Annie's comments about the Macklin House. She'd substituted an interview with Brent Preston himself from his hospital bed, along with several cell phone close-ups of Brent's bloody face. Brent had been only too happy to provide dramatic details of the car crash and his rescue. He managed to throw in a plug for "our remarkable town of Macklin and our historic Macklin House," but that was as much free publicity as Annie got. She was seriously discouraged.

"I should have listened to Zach," she said morosely. "If that trolley had been full of blood-covered zombies, they'd have made it the lead story on the evening news."

"This is what happens on TV," Ben said, trying to console her. "We still have another week of tours. We're completely sold out. You're going to hit your fifty thousand dollars."

"That's still only half of what we need," Annie said.

"It'll work out somehow," Ben replied. "It *has* to work out. I have faith in you. It's your dream, Annie. It's been your dream ever since we were kids."

"You were right. The Macklin House is a pile of junk."

"No! *You* were right," Ben said emphatically. "It's a living piece of history. The trolley tour made everybody realize how special it is. Don't give up now!"

Neither of them mentioned Ben's night on Annie's couch, or what words had been left unsaid between them.

When the trolley tours are over, Ben thought, *I'll plan a special evening for the two of us. Where we can be alone together and really talk.*

When the trolley tours are over, Annie thought, *I'll tell him how I feel.*

Annie felt better by the next morning. So Cindy Nguyen hadn't mentioned the Macklin House on her broadcast. They were doing fine without TV coverage. She could hardly believe that in six days, the trolley tours would be over.

Ben spent that Monday cleaning up the trolley after its Saturday night heroics. It was covered in dust and debris from the wind, so he hosed it down and scrubbed every inch. There were gashes in the wood where the chain had scraped, and scratches in the paint. The front railing was bent in spots. *We'll have to wait until next year to fix that,* he thought. He refused to think that there might not be a next year for the Christmas trolley.

Needing some wood putty, Ben walked over to Meyers'. The senior citizens greeted him once again from the front of the store. They were wrapped up in wool stadium blankets from their various alma maters, and were happily toasting marshmallows on a portable fire pit. Ben wondered how Dave ever managed to sell anything from his patio display.

"Good work, Ben!" one of the men called out. The others clapped.

"We saw you on TV!" added one of the women. "You looked so cute! I called my sister in Los Angeles and told her, 'That's the young man who put up my Christmas lights! Doesn't he remind you of the guy who was in that movie on Netflix last week?'"

The man next to her commented, "That doesn't narrow it down much."

"The one with the dog," the woman insisted.

"That doesn't narrow it down much, either."

"Well, the guy was very cute, just like Ben," she said.

"Uh—thanks," Ben managed to say, escaping into the store. With only six days to go before Christmas, he'd expected things to be slowing down. Instead, there seemed to be a rush of last-minute shoppers. Stacey had taken over the cash register. Ben felt a quick pang of dismay, even though Dave had told him to take the day off. He'd been replaced! And by someone who was singing holiday songs in a lovely soprano while she rang up sales.

Stacey caught sight of him and waved her arms frantically. "Ben! Can you go over to the light displays on the back wall and help some people? I have no idea what they want!"

Ben made his way to the back of the store, passing Rudolph, who was still unsold but now majestically mounted on the wall in Outdoor Living, where he was too high up for Jackson and Emma to reach him. Ben found Sonia and Ray Martinez among the Christmas lights, looking at a giant penguin. The six-foot tall penguin was wearing a top hat and a cheery red scarf and was lit up from the inside. He also had a family: Mrs. Penguin, in a red bonnet and round black-framed glasses, and three penguin children wearing red-and-white striped ski hats. Mrs. Martinez was clearly in love with the penguins. Ray clearly was not.

"Ben!" Mrs. Martinez cried happily. "Aren't these the most adorable things you've ever seen?"

"They're three hundred dollars," Ray interjected.

"But they'd look so darling on the front lawn. Wouldn't they, Ben?" She looked at him imploringly. "And you might even put our house on the trolley tour next year if we had them!"

"We might," Ben agreed, thinking. Maybe he could talk some of the other well-known people in town into letting him showcase their homes on the tour. The Prestons, Coach Jordan, Chief Newton—"You know, they wave," he said to Mrs. Martinez.

"They *wave?*" Ray covered his eyes and shook his head.

"Let me show you," said Ben. The penguins were already plugged into a power strip. He turned the power switch on. The penguins lit up, and their stubby wings moved back and forth in a movement somewhat resembling the royal wave of Queen Elizabeth II. Mrs. Martinez was entranced.

"Maybe we could just buy one," Ray suggested hopefully.

"They only come as a set," Ben said, trying to sound apologetic.

"We'll take them!" Mrs. Martinez exclaimed.

"I'll see what I can do about putting your house on the tour next year," Ben promised.

"We're going home," Ray announced, picking up the male penguin. "Before these penguins have any more babies."

Ben escorted them up to the cash register, and then noticed it was starting to get dark. Annie had told him she was going to the Macklin Women's Club's annual holiday dinner that night. *I should stop in before she leaves and tell her how the repairs on the trolley are coming,* he thought. He knew it was a flimsy excuse to see her, but he hurried over to the Macklin House anyway.

Annie was sitting at her desk, getting ready to leave. The Women's Club holiday dinner was always a festive event, so she was wearing a dark green silk jacket over a lacy cream knit sweater, with a cream wool skirt. For jewelry, she had picked a silver necklace strung with snowflake shapes, with matching earrings.

The Women's Club had raised two thousand dollars for the Macklin House from their thrift shop, and Annie was presenting them with a framed certificate of thanks. She had made the certificate herself with a program on her computer, using an old photo of the Macklin House as a background. Pleased with the results, she slipped the frame into her handbag as Ben came in. Her face lit up. "Ben!" she cried happily. "I just went over the ticket sales again. I think we're going to do it! We'll make fifty thousand dollars! We'll be halfway to our goal. If Ivan starts work just after New Year's, I think we can convince the county to hold off closing us down. That buys us some time to figure out how to get the rest of the money!"

"Oh, Annie," Ben said. "You've done it!" Then, before he could stop himself, he added, "And you look amazing tonight."

Annie blushed and smiled. "I was just about to leave for the dinner." She hesitated. "I wish I didn't have to go to this tonight. It's been so overwhelming the past few days. I wish I could just have a glass of wine and listen to Christmas music." *With you*, she thought.

Ben was suddenly conscious of his rumpled work clothes and dusty shoes. Annie was in her element, executive director of the Macklin House, looking professional yet elegant. It suddenly came to him that the trolley tour was ending in a few days. Annie was going to go on being the executive director, and he'd still be a guy helping out at the hardware store while he looked for a job. He wouldn't have any excuse to meet Annie for breakfast, or drop in at the Macklin House to talk about the trolley route, or listen to her compliments about how well he was doing as an elf mentor. He could see it plainly—Annie was a rising star, and he wasn't. Okay, he'd saved the mayor's life. But no one would remember that in a month.

Annie was looking at him, as if she hoped he'd say something. "You'll have fun once you get there," Ben encouraged. "You *love* the Women's Club." Both his and Annie's mothers had been members. "Remember the dinner when we got our scholarships?"

"Oh, yes," Annie said. "We had to give a speech about our goals in life. I was so nervous I couldn't eat a thing."

Ben was surprised. "You didn't eat? I had four desserts. My mom didn't even notice." He said this with a certain amount of pride. "Besides, you're one of their thrift shop's best customers. How many holiday sweaters have you found there?"

"Only three!" Annie said, laughing. As much as she wanted to spend the evening with Ben, she knew where her duty lay. "I'll bring you a piece of cake. But just one!" she promised him, as she headed for her car.

With that, Ben was on his own for dinner. He considered going home, since he had a tuna casserole and a bowl of spaghetti and meatballs in his refrigerator, courtesy of another grateful friend of Grace Iwamoto. On the other hand, he was tired from all that work on the trolley. And the café was right across the street.

He started down the walkway from the Macklin House to the town square. The streetlights and the holiday lights had come on, and the whole square was lit up. He could even catch the faint scent of the pine trees in the square. He had parked the trolley in its usual spot, in front of the Macklin House by the staging area.

Someone was sitting in the front seat.

A middle-aged Black man, wearing a tan sport jacket over a white shirt. No tie. The man was rubbing his eyes and squinting at something on his phone.

A man Ben recognized.

Ed Waters.

"Hello, Ed," Ben said cautiously.

"I've been looking for you, Ben," Ed replied. "We need to talk."

CHAPTER 32

December 19

BEN SAT ACROSS FROM ED IN THE CORNER BOOTH AT THE café. Close enough to the fireplace to feel the warmth of the fire, but far enough from the door that no one was likely to notice them. "How'd you find me?" he asked.

Ed sighed. "Miranda in accounting is Facebook friends with somebody whose sister saw this news clip on a local TV show about how you saved some guy's life with a Christmas trolley," he answered. "I drove over from San Francisco today." He was flipping through the menu. "They only charge seventy-five cents for coffee? How do these people stay in business?"

"Barely," said Ben. "Ed. Why are you here?"

Ed put down his menu. "I want you to come back."

"Come back? To Jupiter?"

Ed took off his reading glasses and set them down next to his plate. "Denton signed their contract, and now they want to start ramping up as of January first. You've got the skill set, you've got the relationship, and I don't have anyone else who can handle the job."

Ben was shocked. "This is pretty sudden," he said carefully.

"Ben. I've been trying to contact you for a week. Denton is *your* client. You brought it in. You're the one to handle it. We need you."

My old life, Ben thought. *A bigger apartment. I can add to my whiskey collection. I can go to Bali.*

"This is full-time? Not a contract job?" he asked.

"Full-time, salaried. Just like before," Ed replied.

I'll be the Jupiter guy again. I'll be the guy who solves the problems. Not just Ben Grover making do on unemployment.

"I want to be a vice president," Ben said.

"Done," said Ed.

"I want a ten percent raise over my previous salary. And I want four weeks' vacation," Ben added.

"You'll automatically get three weeks if you're a VP," countered Ed.

"Four weeks," said Ben. "You know I'll have to work around the clock for the next few months. I'll need some time off once we get through the implementation phase." *San Francisco. The big city. Annie will be impressed.*

"You always were a good negotiator," Ed said resignedly. "Four weeks."

"I want a ping pong table in my office."

"No," Ed said flatly. "If you want a ping pong table, buy a house with a basement. I'll have Sallie overnight a signing package to you."

He put on his glasses and looked at his menu again. "They only charge six dollars for a hamburger? Including fries? How do these people stay in business?"

CHAPTER 33

December 20

BEN SPENT A SLEEPLESS NIGHT. HE TOSSED AND TURNED, alternately thinking of all the exciting things he could do once he was back in San Francisco, and what he'd need to do to get the Denton project up to speed. He finally rolled over and fell asleep around four o'clock. It was a shock when his alarm went off at seven.

He headed over to the hardware store, still going over his ideas. The senior citizens waved at him, but he was lost in thought. He needed coffee. The café was busy with its usual morning crowd. Ben smelled cinnamon rolls and bacon as he entered. Cammie was working the breakfast shift, and she was bursting with news.

"Ben! Two more of my paintings sold!" she said excitedly. "I'm like—a real artist!"

"That's great, Cammie! Congratulations!" Ben exclaimed. "I'm so proud of you!" Cammie was beaming as she showed him to a booth.

Ben didn't want to say anything about his *own* news until he had the written offer in his hands. He desperately wished he could tell someone. He wished he could tell ... Annie.

He felt a lump in his stomach. Last night, he'd been so sure she'd be thrilled. This morning, he wasn't so sure. What *was* he going to say to Annie?

"And look!" Cammie whispered. "I was right!"

"Right about what?"

"Darlene and Dave! Don't they look like they're in love?" she said, pointing to another booth. Darlene and Dave were sitting side by side, going over some sheets of graph paper on the table. They were smiling and laughing. They didn't necessarily look like they were in love, but they did look happy.

For some reason, that made Ben feel even worse. He went over to the booth. They both looked up.

"Take a look at our plans," Dave said, holding out one of the sheets of paper. *What am I going to say to Dave?* Ben thought. "We're going to take out the booth in the corner and build a stage."

"A stage?" asked Ben.

"The entertainment over at the trolley tour is so successful, I told Dave we need a place where people can perform year-round," Darlene explained. "Like Adam and Stacey. And you," she added, patting Dave's arm. Ben's eyes narrowed. Maybe Cammie was right.

"Like me," Dave said hesitantly. He seemed to be trying to adjust to his new persona as Dave the musician, instead of Dave the hardware store owner.

"The café's going to be completely different," Ben said, looking around.

"It's time for a makeover," Darlene said enthusiastically. "We'll have paintings by local artists, like Cammie, on the walls. Then I want to replace the hostess stand with a glass-fronted counter. We'll sell some of the pottery and glass pieces from the craft fair, and James' wooden boxes, and we can change out the merchandise monthly."

"And bags of Paula's cookies!" Dave added.

"That sounds great," Ben said weakly.

"Oh, I've got the latest sales report," Dave said. He pulled a spreadsheet out of his shirt pocket. "Look at this! We're twenty percent ahead of sales for this time last year. That's because of you, Ben. You're doing a fantastic job with the holiday lights. We even had a three hundred dollar sale!" Dave pointed happily at one of the columns of figures.

Ben looked at the spreadsheet. "Those were the waving penguins I sold to Mrs. Martinez. I didn't have anything to do with it. She'll buy anything. Once back in seventh grade Annie and I filled up a wagon with Girl Scout cookies and took it in to school, and she bought all of them!"

"Sonia Martinez isn't dumb," said Dave. "She was preventing a cookie riot at recess. And she wouldn't have bought those penguins if it hadn't been for you. She told Stacey you promised her you'd put her house on next year's trolley tour if she bought them. Ben, listen. The store's doing well enough now that I could actually hire you. I know it's not as good as your job at Jupiter …"

Ben turned pale. Had someone overheard his conversation with Ed?

"… but there's a lot of opportunity. When we reorganize after the holidays to make room for the music store, we could add a line of small tech products. Just think about it for a few days."

Oh, God, Ben thought. *How am I going to tell everyone?*

"That's really generous of you," he said. Then, he heard someone call his name.

"Ben!"

He turned around to see Grace Iwamoto, maneuvering her walker down the aisle. "If you stop on my block tomorrow, I'll have coffee and some fudge for you."

The lump in his stomach was growing bigger. *This isn't going to be easy*, he thought. *But I'll never get a chance like this again.*

CHAPTER 34

December 21

BEN MET ANNIE AT THE CAFÉ FOR LUNCH THE NEXT DAY. He ate mechanically, still thinking about the Denton contract. The offer hadn't arrived yet, but he trusted Ed. Ed never promised anything he couldn't deliver.

He was going to need assistants. Four or five people. Who could he bring over from other work groups? He mentally ran through a list of Jupiter's employees. Maybe he could rehire a few of the other people who'd been laid off.

He was also dreading the inevitable moment when he'd have to tell Annie his plans.

"Ben! Have you heard a word I said?" Annie waved her hand in front of his face.

"What? Oh—um—sort of."

"It's like you're a million miles away."

"I just have some things on my mind today," he said lamely, hoping to distract her. She looked concerned.

"Is everything okay? Is it something with your mom's house?" she asked.

"No, it's—just some personal stuff," he said. Now Annie looked even more concerned.

"Ben, if there's anything I can do ..." she began.

At that moment, the door to the restaurant opened and Tim Hood, the mail carrier, came in. He was holding a thick overnight letter in his hand, and he made a beeline for Annie and Ben's booth.

"Hi, guys," he said cheerfully. "Ben, I know this is supposed to go to your house, but you're always here at lunch, so I thought I'd just drop it off."

"Thanks, Tim," Ben said, taking the envelope. Annie stared at it. The Jupiter Computer logo was clearly visible in the return address space.

"You got mail from Jupiter?" she asked. "Is there a problem with your unemployment?"

Ben was pulling the envelope open as she spoke. There it was, on paper. His offer. He looked at Annie, who still looked concerned. He sighed. Might as well get this over with.

"It's a job offer," he said.

Annie was confused. "A job offer?"

"I met with Ed Waters on Monday night," Ben said.

"You met him?" Annie was even more confused. "Where?"

"He's been trying to get in touch with me and somebody saw that news clip on 'Fast Break at Five.' Ed drove over here and made me an offer. It was right after you left for the Women's Club dinner. You remember that Denton contract I told you about? They want me back, to run the project. At a ten percent raise in salary. And I'll be a vice president."

Annie was staring at him, stunned. She was trying to keep from bursting into tears. What had she been thinking? That all their time together over the past few weeks, the Christmas trolley, would be enough to keep him in Macklin? Ben Grover, who had announced to her in eighth grade that he intended to make his fortune in the big city? He looked so happy. Well, he looked *sort* of happy. This was his dream. And she wasn't part of it.

Annie swallowed hard and asked, "What did you say?" although she already knew the answer.

"I said yes. It's a really good offer, Annie. It's all I've ever wanted in a job."

"When do you start?"

"The first of January. I can stay through the end of the trolley tours on the twenty-fourth. Then I need to pack up and head back to San Francisco." *There*, he thought. *I did it. I told Annie.* He waited hesitantly for her reaction.

She managed to smile. "I'm so happy for you, Ben."

He smiled back. "It's going to be great."

Annie took out her wallet and put some money on the table. "I have to get back," she said. "I guess I'll see you at the trolley tonight." She was managing not to lose her composure.

"See you tonight, Annie," he said. He watched her walk out the door. He pulled his papers from Jupiter out again, and spread them across the table.

It was all there. A ten percent pay raise, a VP title, four weeks' vacation. Everything he'd ever wanted.

Then why did he suddenly feel so miserable?

CHAPTER 35

December 22

NEWS TRAVELED FAST IN MACKLIN. BY THE NEXT MORN-
ing, it was common knowledge that Ben was leaving. Dave Meyers
looked completely dismayed when Ben arrived at the store. "I was
hoping you'd stay," he said. "I know Macklin isn't San Francisco, but
there are a lot of great things about this town. You've really made a
difference the past few weeks. You and Annie."

Customers kept him busy, but every time he waited on someone,
Ben felt a pang of regret. He knew most of them by name now. They
were more like friends than customers. They liked to hang around and
talk. They asked for his opinion. They even *valued* his opinion. It would
be completely different once he went back to Jupiter. There, he'd deal
with CFOs and project managers who only wanted to see the bottom
line. Five minutes later, they'd be off to their next meeting.

Adam and Stacey stopped by to look at flooring samples for their
music store. They wanted something to set their area apart from the

decades-old brown laminate in the rest of the shop. "Are you really leaving?" Stacey asked anxiously. "We don't want you to go! You're the one who figured out a way for us to get our music store. If it wasn't for you, we'd still be broke in Brooklyn."

"You'll come back for our opening, won't you?" Adam asked. "And you'll come back when the café's finished? We're already thinking about music for opening night."

Angie Morgan arrived, looking around furtively as she slipped up to the cash register. She opened her coat slightly, and Peanut's head popped out. His eyes widened and he looked ready to growl, but Angie quickly shoved a dog treat in his mouth.

"I just wanted to say thank you," she said. "You saved Peanut's life."

Ben doubted that, but nodded appreciatively. "Take care of him, Angie. Don't go near the Outdoor Living department. We still have that deer head."

Mrs. Martinez came in, and she wasn't happy.

"Are you sure about this, Ben?" she asked.

He gave his standard answer. "It's everything I've ever wanted."

"Are you sure about that?" she said. "Are you *really* sure?"

"I'm sure," he replied.

"You'll never get another chance like this, Benjy," she told him.

"I know," he answered. She stared at him reproachfully for a moment, and then set off down the aisle. Ben felt puzzled. Had he missed something in that conversation?

The elves were in a surly mood when they showed up for the trolley tour. "We don't care if we go on the tour or not," Jackson announced. "If you won't stay with us, we're not going to stay with you."

"Who's going to help us with our science fair project?" Emma asked bitterly. "You said you'd help us build a robot."

"You said you'd show us how to hack into a keyless auto entry system," muttered Jackson.

"I DID NOT SAY THAT!" exploded Ben, who was feeling irritable himself. "I said I'd show you how to take one apart and put it back together."

"Everybody leaves Macklin," Emma grumped.

"And they never come back," added Jackson.

"I'll only be in San Francisco," Ben told them. "We can email. We can Skype."

"You know our moms can't afford high-speed internet," said Emma.

"You'll be like the emigrants," Jackson said gloomily.

"What emigrants?" asked Ben. The conversation was getting beyond him.

"Annie's ancestors," explained Emma. "She told us about them. She found it on Ancestry.com. They all left Ireland in 1850 to come to America. And no one in their village *ever heard from them again.*"

"I wish that would happen to *my* relatives," said a woman waiting in line to board the trolley.

Emma and Jackson glared at Ben for the rest of the night and refused to laugh at his jokes. Annie barely spoke to him as she set up for the first tour. She looked tired and sad. The passengers were subdued. Even the entertainment, the middle school chorus, didn't have the usual holiday sparkle.

Ben drove his two trolley tours, but something had changed. Somehow, his Christmas spirit was gone.

While Ben was driving the trolley, Annie had other things to worry about. There was her personal life, and there was the Macklin House. Both of them seemed to be on a course for disaster.

Natalie Preston had phoned her at lunchtime. "Ron called me. He has a proposal he wants to bring before the board. TONIGHT."

"Tonight?" Annie was upset. "Doesn't he have to give us ten days' notice?"

Natalie sounded grim. "He's calling a special meeting under the emergency provisions of the trust. We'll meet at seven p.m. at the Macklin House."

"Did he tell you any details?" Annie asked Natalie.

"Only that it's a serious proposal that will take care of our financial problems, and that the board needs to review it without delay."

"We've been talking about the deferred maintenance for two months now," Annie said slowly. "If Ron has a proposal, why is he just bringing it up now?"

She thought back over the last few board meetings. Ron had never been enthusiastic about the trolley tour, but he'd done his part in looking for other sources of money. He seemed to truly care about the Macklin House. She knew he made a trip to Sacramento once or twice a month. Maybe he'd found a state grant after all.

"Who knows," said Natalie. She'd never liked Ron much to begin with, but if you were the wife of the mayor, you tried to get along with everybody. "I emailed Brad and Sophie, and they'll be available."

"That'll be the middle of the night for them," said Annie. "That makes no sense. Couldn't we do it tomorrow morning instead?"

"He insisted it had to be tonight," Natalie said.

Annie had the uncharitable thought that Ron wanted to keep discussion of his proposal to a minimum, and was hoping that Sophie and Brad wouldn't join in. No, it was more likely that there was a deadline involved. She couldn't remember when the state budget expired, but she knew it wasn't December thirty-first. But if it was a private donation, the donor would want to complete it by the end of the tax year. That made sense.

"I'll get the laptops set up for Skype," she said. "I'll see you tonight at seven."

The only good thing about the emergency board meeting was that it gave Annie an excuse to avoid Ben. She put James Adams in charge of the ticket money that evening, and didn't go near the trolley at all. Instead, she sat at her desk and reviewed everything that had happened with the Christmas trolley. Money raised, money spent, the number of tickets sold, the other benefits to the town. Annie wanted everything at her fingertips in case the board, especially Ron, asked her any questions.

She was trying hard not to let anyone see how devastated she was by Ben's decision. She forced herself to concentrate on the trolley. *What kind of proposal could Ron have?* she wondered.

The doorbell chimed, and Annie realized it was almost time for the meeting. Allan and Natalie had arrived together. As she let them in, she could hear singing from the stage and applause from the crowd. The first trolley tour had already departed, so there was no chance that she would catch sight of Ben. She felt a little relieved. She didn't need anything distracting her from the meeting ahead.

Allan looked worried. He liked things to be orderly and peaceful, and an emergency meeting was neither. Natalie looked exasperated. "I hope this is worth it," she said to Annie. "I'm missing my book group's holiday meeting. I have a darling little carryall that holds everything I need for book group. It fits perfectly in this special storage compartment of my SUV. You know, that car is so well-designed. It has a space for everything."

"That's nice, Natalie," Annie said. She supposed, if she stayed in Macklin, she would someday have to buy a car from Brent. In about twenty years, when her Honda gave out.

They all saw Ron coming up the walkway to the front door of the Macklin House, carrying a briefcase. His mouth was set in a straight line, and he paid no attention to what was going on behind him on the lawn. He nodded at them as he came up to the door but didn't smile. Ron was all business tonight.

"Come on in, Ron," Annie said, trying to set a friendly mood. No one spoke. Allan was fiddling with the laptops, and suddenly, Brad appeared on one screen. He was wearing a bathrobe, and his hair was sticking out in all directions. He was holding a large mug with the string of a teabag hanging out. A few seconds later, Sophie appeared on the other laptop. In contrast to Brad, she was wide-awake. She was wearing a black cashmere sweater, and her hair looked perfect. She was holding a champagne glass. Annie suspected Sophie hadn't gone to bed yet.

"We're all here now. Sophie and Brad, thanks so much for joining us," Natalie began, banging her gavel on the table. "The meeting is called to order. Allan, would you take notes?" Allan nodded, pulled out a small notebook, and began to write.

"Ron would like to present a proposal to us. Go ahead, Ron," Natalie continued.

Ron reached into his briefcase and took out some black three-ring binders. He passed them out to the group.

"Brad and Sophie, I emailed this to you earlier. Did you have a chance to read it?" he asked.

"Not yet," said Sophie, after the customary Skype delay. "You can explain it."

"I didn't get to it, either," said Brad. "I was in the British Museum all day."

"I thought you were in Scotland," Sophie said accusingly. "What are you doing on that sabbatical? Are you working, or are you sightseeing? I still pay taxes in California. Those are *my* tax dollars you're using for this boondoggle."

"It is *not* a boondoggle. I'm doing serious research on Victorian concepts of animal behavior—"

"That's a boondoggle if I ever heard of one. I'm going to call your department head," Sophie said indignantly.

"LET RON GO ON," Natalie said, banging her gavel again.

Ron opened his binder. Everyone else did the same thing. The first page had a picture of the Macklin House under the heading, "Macklin House Development Project."

"This is a proposal that was brought to me by a developer," Ron began. "It will solve our cash flow problems, while keeping the Macklin House intact."

Everyone waited.

"It's a very common approach to the use of older properties. We sell the property to the developer with the provision, under the city's historic building guidelines, that the outside of the building remains as is. The interior will be converted to condominiums. The HOA fees will pay for the maintenance of the building and the grounds. Since the inside is completely renovated, that takes care of the deferred maintenance. We still have our historic Macklin House, but without any future expenses," Ron said. He looked at the others in satisfaction.

"But it won't be a museum," said Annie.

"Not as it is now," Ron acknowledged. "If you'll look at the proposal, you'll see they plan to keep one room on the main floor that will be dedicated to the Macklin family. Photos of Philip, photos of the current interior, maybe a few pieces of furniture. Some storyboards explaining the history of the house."

"That wouldn't allow for any educational exhibits," Annie said.

"Or tours," Allan put in.

"Ron," Annie said. She was trying to stay calm. Calm and persuasive. "I can see what the developer has in mind. But Philip Macklin's will is very specific. He left the house to the city to be used as a museum and to educate the future citizens of Macklin about the history of their town. I am quoting."

"Annie," Ron said angrily. "This is happening all over. Small museums just don't have the funds to stay in business. Especially in a town like this. This way, at least we preserve the structure. Don't you think that's what Philip Macklin would have wanted?"

"You have no idea what my great-great-great-great-grandfather would have wanted!" This came from Sophie. They all turned to the laptop screens. Sophie looked angry. Brad appeared to have fallen asleep.

"Well, Sophie, there's another piece to this," said Ron. "The heirs, meaning you, control one-third of the Macklin House Trust. That's in addition to your own trust fund, of course. I need to make it clear. This proposal will bring you, personally, a lot of money." He paused. "And to be honest, with interest rates as low as they've been lately, and the cost of living in Paris ... you see my point."

"Everything starts with the will," Annie said. "We have to act according to the will. And the will states *specifically* that the house is to be used for a museum. To educate the citizens of Macklin."

Allan said, "We'd have to consult our legal counsel. But I've read the will. I agree with Annie."

Ron looked really angry now. "Annie," he said. "Financially, this is our best chance. I'd like to keep the Macklin House as it is. We all would. But it can't be done. Your trolley is a great little idea, but it's not going to raise all the money we need. And even if we somehow come up with all of it, what happens next year? Or the year after that? This is an *old house*. It's going to need constant upkeep. You're young. You don't understand how this works. You don't want to admit that I'm right. You just want to protect your job."

"It's not about my job," Annie said, staring him down. "It's about what's right."

"As for the educational part—we all went on that field trip, but if we weren't on the board, how much attention would we pay to the Macklin House now?" Ron went on. "How much do *you* remember about that field trip, Annie?"

Oh, way more than you can imagine, she thought. "That's exactly why we need the Macklin House as it is now. A museum. With tours, and lectures, and all kinds of programs for people. The way Philip envisioned it."

Natalie banged her gavel. She looked around at the group. After a few seconds, Brad suddenly jolted awake. "We need to take a vote," she said. "I'm going to do this one by one. We are voting on the proposal Ron has presented to us tonight. Ron?"

"Yes," Ron answered.

"Allan?"

"No."

"As chairman, I'm voting no. Brad?"

Brad had fallen asleep again. Natalie banged the gavel. After a few seconds, he woke up. "Brad. How do you vote on this proposal?"

"I vote yes."

"Sophie?"

They waited for her answer. Annie counted: three, four, five seconds. "I vote ... no."

"The motion is defeated," Natalie announced. She added, "Brad, you can go back to bed now," and disconnected him.

"Is that it?" asked Sophie.

"Yes. The meeting is adjourned," Natalie said. Sophie's screen went blank. The four of them in the conference room looked at each other, but no one moved.

Ron was fuming.

"I truly believe the board has made a mistake tonight," he said. "You are never going to raise the money you need." Ron paused. "I think," he continued, "that I have a major difference of opinion with the majority of this board. I don't feel I can continue to serve as a board member." He glared at each of them in turn.

"Ron," said Natalie. "You did what a board member should do. You brought the proposal to us. It was voted down. Now we go on."

"No," he said bitterly. "I can't support the board's position. I'm resigning." He stood up and closed his briefcase.

"Are you sure, Ron?" asked Natalie. He nodded. "I'll need it in writing."

"Here," Allan said, offering his notebook. Ron quickly wrote, "I resign from the board of the Macklin House." He handed the paper to Natalie with a dramatic flourish.

"You're making a *big* mistake," he said as he picked up his briefcase. "You'll come back to me in six months desperate to do this deal." He stormed out.

Annie and Natalie and Allan looked at each other in silence for a moment. Finally, Annie said, "Do—do the two of you really think we're doing the right thing? Maybe Ron was right. Maybe I just can't face giving up this job."

"Oh, that's a load of ... ," Natalie cut herself short.

"Ron just doesn't like to lose," Allan said. "He thinks he knows more than everyone else about everything."

"He's always disagreed with me, even on simple things," Annie said with a perplexed frown. "He never seemed to like me, and I don't know why."

Natalie and Allan stared at each other. "I thought you knew," said Allan.

"Knew what?"

"He didn't want you to get the job," Natalie explained. "He wanted us to hire his girlfriend."

"His girlfriend?" This was a whole new story. Annie thought back. She'd gone to a barbecue sponsored by Ron's real estate office, a few weeks after she'd been hired. She vaguely remembered a tall blonde woman wearing a dress that was far too exotic for a summer barbecue in Macklin. "Chelsea somebody?"

"That's her," Natalie said. "She lives in Sacramento, and Ron thought if we offered her the job, she'd relocate. She had absolutely no qualifications. We were so thrilled when you applied, Annie. You had the perfect resume, and he couldn't say no. But he's never forgotten it."

That explains Ron's trips to Sacramento, Annie thought. "Is she in real estate, too?" Annie asked.

"No, she designs kitchens for high-end clients. You can see why Macklin didn't appeal to her."

"And isn't this interesting?" said Allan, as he opened his three-ring binder to a page with renderings of the future condominiums. "Doesn't Chelsea work for In the Know Interiors?"

"She sure does," replied Natalie. Even upside down, Annie could clearly read the fine print below the drawings. *"Custom Designs from In the Know Interiors."*

"What now?" Allan asked.

"We find another board member," explained Natalie. "Now, who in Macklin would like to join the board of a destitute historic mansion that needs one hundred thousand dollars?"

"I have an idea," said Annie. "How about Mrs. Martinez? I mean, Sonia Martinez?"

"I like it," said Allan. "I worked with her on Macklin's homeless outreach program. She had good ideas, and she got along with everybody. And she'd definitely believe in our educational mission."

"She'd be great!" said Natalie. "We need new donors, and she knows everybody in town who's under forty."

THE CHRISTMAS TROLLEY

The three of them looked at each other. They were all thinking the same thing. Mrs. Martinez' ex-students would do anything she asked them to do. If she told them to donate, they'd donate.

Natalie was already tapping her phone keys.

"You have her number in your phone?" Annie asked in astonishment.

"Oh, yes," Natalie said ruefully. "Brent Junior had detention every other day when he was in middle school. We're on a first-name basis. Sonia! It's Natalie Preston. Brent Junior? He's doing great! He's married! He's a bank manager in Bakersfield!" She listened. "I know," she said. "I can hardly believe it myself. Keep your fingers crossed. Sonia, I'm here at the Macklin House with Allan Tolbert and Annie Mulvaney. I'd really like to talk to you about something. Are you free for coffee some time tomorrow? Two o'clock at the Macklin Café? Perfect!"

She put her phone on the table and smiled. "I think we've found our new board member!" she said.

CHAPTER 36

December 22

LATER THAT NIGHT, BEN RETURNED HOME AFTER THE LAST trolley tour. The house felt cold and somehow lonely. He poured himself a glass of Glenlivet and collapsed on the couch in the family room.

He had tours coming up on the twenty-third and twenty-fourth, and then he planned to hit the road early on Christmas morning. He knew there was going to be some kind of a celebration in the town square the night of the final trolley rides. A week ago, he and Annie had discussed the party eagerly, but now his heart wasn't in it. *Maybe if I say I have to pack I can leave early,* he thought.

Ben took another sip of his whiskey, and decided to light a fire. He took a lingering look around the family room, realizing he would be gone in a few days. The Christmas decorations he and Annie had put up stared accusingly at him, bringing back memories of the day they'd hung them up. He could see Annie opening each carton excitedly, admiring all his childhood ornaments. His eyes strayed to the mantel.

The mistletoe they'd bought at the tree lot was hanging out of Buddy's stocking. That had been such a fun day ...

Ben pushed these thoughts aside and surveyed the room again. He decided the decorations and the tree could stay where they were until his next trip back. But he plugged in the lights on the tree, hoping to make the room more cheerful. He noticed that there were still a few unopened boxes in the corner.

"I guess I could go through some of these while I finish my drink," he said aloud. He picked up the nearest box and carried it over to the couch.

It was a collection of his mother's old jackets. He sorted through the box, thinking she'd probably packed them up to make more room in her closet. The box could go to the thrift shop now, and he could drop it off the next day. He might as well put the box in the minivan while he was thinking about it.

As he picked it up, the clothing shifted and he saw a green velvet box about eight inches square. His mom's jewelry box, he remembered. He wondered if she had intended to donate it, or had put it in the box by mistake. He shook the jewelry box, and something rattled inside.

Ben opened it, and was astonished to see his father's one pair of gold cuff links, and a ring that had belonged to his grandmother. *Definitely a mistake!* There was no way his mother would have given these to the thrift store.

The ring was a rectangular amethyst in a filigreed white gold setting, dotted with tiny diamonds. It looked antique, but somehow also contemporary. He sat down on the couch and studied it in the firelight. *Annie would love this ring,* he thought. Then, he set the ring down on the coffee table. "What am I doing?" he said. "Why does everything remind me of her?"

Ben carefully put the ring and the cuff links back in the jewelry box. He reached for the next carton, and opened it.

This one was full of old photos and school yearbooks. Intrigued, Ben started to go through them, one by one. Here he was in the kindergarten class photo, wearing a shirt and tie for some reason. Annie was standing next to him, wearing a dress with a pinafore and a serious expression. Here, they were in second grade, feeding the class rabbit. And in fourth grade, the two of them showing off an elaborate model of Mission San Juan Capistrano.

Ben continued through the books, year after year, smiling now. He and Annie at a birthday party, back before they'd started having separate parties for girls and boys. The two of them roasting marshmallows at outdoor education camp. As he leafed through book after book, his smile grew bigger, and he felt something growing in his heart.

He came to his eighth grade yearbook. It fell open to the class picture, the same one he'd seen on Mrs. Martinez' wall at Thanksgiving. He was in the second row, looking like he was trying very hard to hold it together for the camera. He wasn't looking at the camera, though. He was looking at Annie, in the front row. Her hair hung down to her shoulders, and she was wearing a very pretty white sweater with a bluebird on it. And she looked, he thought with a lump in his throat, beautiful.

Ben remembered the words she'd said to him on the field trip.

"Ben Grover! I'll never kiss you—until snow falls in Macklin!"

He looked at the picture again.

"God, I'm stupid," he said. "I've been stupid for fifteen years."

He stared into space for a few minutes, thinking. Then, he picked up his phone, and started tapping the keys.

CHAPTER 37

December 23

BEN WAS WAITING IMPATIENTLY AT THE HARDWARE STORE when Dave arrived to open up the next morning. As soon as they got inside, Ben locked the door again and began talking. Dave listened warily at first, then began to smile and nod in agreement. Ben vanished into the office and began working at the computer. Dave puttered around the store, still smiling.

Jackson and Emma, on Christmas break, trundled in listlessly about an hour later. Dave pointed them toward the office. Ben pulled them inside and shut the door. In a few minutes, Dave heard squeals of delight coming through the closed door. When they came out, they were smiling and full of energy. "This is a really, really, really good day!" Emma announced.

Over at the Macklin House, Annie was having a really, really, really *bad* day.

Danielle was already at the reception desk when Annie came in, and she looked panicky. "Annie!" she exclaimed. "Something's wrong upstairs! I heard noises."

"Calm down," Annie said soothingly. "This is an old house. Lots of things creak."

"I was up on the third floor, making a room check like I do every morning. I heard a bang, and then I heard lots of little noises," Danielle explained. "Like scratching. And whooshing." She gazed uneasily at the ceiling.

"Let's go up and take a look," Annie said reasonably.

"*You* go. I'll stay here in case anything happens to you."

That seemed only fair, if slightly alarming. Annie took the elevator to the second floor, then climbed the steep staircase to the third. The third floor had been servants' quarters, and wasn't open to the public. The rooms up here were tiny, and all opened to a single hall. A few contained old chairs, but most were empty except for dust and cobwebs.

Annie walked the length of the hall, looking carefully into every room. Nothing happened until she came to the last one, which held a rusting iron bed frame and a wooden stool. She saw bits of plaster and chips of wood on the floor. Looking up, she realized there was a large crack in the ceiling. It looked new. Now, she heard faint rustling and clicking sounds. The space above the ceiling was an attic beneath the roof. As she watched, the clicking grew louder and more bits of plaster drifted down. Annie sighed. Something was living in the attic.

Back at the reception desk, she reassured Danielle as she called Ivan Renfro. "It looks like a cat or a raccoon or ... some animal ... got into the attic and can't get out. It must have knocked something down. There's a big crack in the ceiling of the room below. Can you come over?" she said into the phone.

Ivan showed up half an hour later. He had long white hair tied in a ponytail, and a large handlebar mustache. There was a western ghost town in the foothills about an hour's drive from Macklin, and Ivan liked to participate in old west re-enactments. He tended to view his contracting jobs as if he were a sheriff riding into town to save its inhabitants from the outlaws.

"No need to worry, ma'am," he said, greeting Annie. "I'll make this place safe for you again."

"I'm sure you will," Annie responded. "There's a trap door in the ceiling of the first bedroom that leads to the attic. I've never been in the attic myself."

"I went up there when I did your estimate for the county, but I don't remember seeing any animals. Mostly termite damage. But from what you tell me, something's up there now. Don't you worry, ma'am. I'll make this right," Ivan said. He headed off to the third floor with a determined look on his face. Annie and Danielle waited for him to come back. They waited. And waited. Annie finally called his cell phone.

"Ivan! Are you okay?"

"I'll be down in a minute," he said. "I'm okay, but your attic isn't."

Now what? Annie thought. *Just when I was feeling hopeful. Just when I thought we had a shot at getting the money we need.*

Ivan reappeared. He was covered in dust. He held out his phone.

"Take a look at this," he said, holding up a photo. Annie looked at it curiously. It was a small bird. An owl, to be exact, with white feathers and a brown stripe down its chest.

"Here's a video," Ivan continued. The bird skittered on the attic floor. It looked like it had two tails.

"So we have an owl in the attic," Annie said. "All you have to do is catch it."

"It's a Ludwig's double-tailed owl," Ivan said. "I looked it up on the internet. That's why I was up there so long."

"So ... you catch it," Annie said.

"It's not that simple," Ivan explained. "There's a whole lot of them. I counted fifty, but there might be more. You have a small hole in the outside wall on that side, right up under the roofline, probably from that high wind last weekend. That's how they came in. The support posts up there have a lot of termite damage, and they've knocked one of them over, flying around. That's what cracked the floor. Er, the ceiling in the third-floor bedroom."

"Okay," Annie repeated. "You catch them."

Ivan took a deep breath. "They're an endangered species," he said ominously.

Annie took a deep breath. "Which means ..."

"First, we have to get a permit from the county to catch them."

"A permit?" Annie groaned. "To take birds out of our attic?"

"I don't make the laws, ma'am," Ivan said in his most sheriff-like voice. "I just uphold them. They're an endangered species. And now that you know about them, the county says you can't just leave them there."

"Have you done this before, Ivan?" Annie asked suspiciously.

Ivan looked indignant. "This isn't my first rodeo. I had to take some foxes out of a garage, and some lizards out of a kitchen. Endangered birds are the worst." Annie looked at him dubiously. "They fly," he explained.

"So we get the permit. Then what?" she asked.

"There's a special process for removing them from wherever they are. Then they have to be transported to their native habitat. In a climate-controlled environment," Ivan explained. "A biologist has to oversee the process. I've already called someone at the Department of Fish and Wildlife. Dr. Kona Sutton. She's an ornithologist, and owls are her specialty."

"And the county pays for all this?" Annie said.

Ivan crossed his arms and leaned back against the wall. "You're not really that naïve, are you?" he asked.

Annie looked resignedly at Ivan. "All right," she said. "What's your estimate?"

"It'll run about a thousand dollars an owl."

"*A thousand dollars?*" Annie was incredulous.

"Ma'am," Ivan said. "You need a biohazard company to remove them. With hazmat suits and everything, so they can't be contaminated."

"But they're flying in and out," Annie said. "They're already contaminated."

Ivan shrugged helplessly. "I don't make the laws."

"You just uphold them," Annie and Danielle said together.

"The transport vehicle is a specially designed airtight chamber with a controlled temperature ..."

Annie cut him off. "If it's fifty thousand dollars, it's fifty thousand dollars," she said. "Go get the permit."

She buried her head in her hands. First Ben was leaving, now this. It was just one catastrophe after another.

CHAPTER 38

December 23

"THEY DON'T REALLY HAVE TWO TAILS," DANIELLE SAID cheerfully. "It just looks that way from how their feathers grow." She was reading about Ludwig's owls on her phone while she and Annie ate lunch in the conference room. Ivan had obtained the permit. They were waiting for Dr. Sutton and the biohazard team.

"It says they eat mice. And moths. They sound kind of useful. Why can't we keep a few of them?"

"We should just close off the third floor and pretend we never saw them," Annie muttered.

"But they look so cuddly. Like little white balls with a teeny brown stripe. You just want to hug them." Danielle's eyes widened. "Annie! We could find a toy company to make little stuffed Ludwig's owls for us. We could sell them in the gift shop! They could be, like, the Macklin House mascot."

"It's a thought," Annie admitted. "Could we sell enough to cover the cost of removing them?"

Ivan strolled in. "Dr. Sutton will be here in a few minutes," he reported. "The biohazard boys are right behind her."

Annie got back to business. "How much is it going to cost to repair that crack in the ceiling?"

"Probably another five thousand. I can't really tell how much damage there is up in the attic until we get the owls out. We need to fix that hole in the wall right away, though, in case it rains."

Someone yelled, "Hello?"

"That must be Dr. Sutton," said Annie. "We're in here!" she called.

Dr. Sutton had curly gray hair pushed back under an Australian bush hat. She didn't have a purse but instead wore a dark green safari jacket with a multitude of pockets. She also wore round, rimless glasses, making her look somewhat like an owl herself.

"Konie!" said Ivan.

"Vannie!" said Dr. Sutton.

"I see you two know each other," Annie observed.

"We met at the Cheyenne Frontier Days," Dr. Sutton said. Annie waited for a further explanation. None came. Dr. Sutton pulled a medium-sized camera with a telephoto lens out of one of her pockets. "This is so exciting!" she exclaimed. "I've never seen a Ludwig's owl up close."

"Can you bring one down to show us?" asked Danielle.

Dr. Sutton looked horrified. "Oh, no," she said. "They have to stay in their substitute habitat until they're transported."

"And we are here to transport!" Two young men in white hazmat suits walked in. They were both very cute and very fit. Danielle sat up straighter and smiled brightly. They smiled back.

"I'm Bryce!" the first one said. "And I'm Devon!" said the other one. "We're from Species Savior."

Annie looked at them questioningly. Bryce produced a business card. "Dr. Sutton called us. We capture and transport all kinds of endangered animals to safe, natural habitats," he recited.

"And some that aren't endangered," added Devon. "You have no idea what people have in their back yards. Lion cubs. Cobras. A lot of monkeys."

"We just have owls," Annie said. "They're in the attic. Ivan and Dr. Sutton will show you."

"Isn't there a second stairway?" asked Ivan.

Annie nodded. "There's a back stairway over on the east side of the house that goes to both the second and third floors. It was for the servants, when the house was built."

"That's perfect," said Bryce. "We'll carry them out that way. Quieter and fewer people. We need to keep them as calm as possible." They followed Ivan and Dr. Sutton out.

"I wonder how long this is going to take," Annie mused. She walked out to the porch and looked for the Species Savior vehicle. It was a three-axle truck with a gleaming white trailer. Silver ventilation pipes ran along on the top. It took up most of the visitors' parking lot.

Annie checked her watch. They had three hours until the first trolley tour. Could they possibly get the owls out before then?

She walked around to the east side of the house to see what was happening. Shading her eyes, she looked up at the hole by the roof. She caught a flash of white near the hole. Had an owl flown out? Or in? Then, she heard footsteps coming down the back stairs. A moment later, Bryce and Devon emerged onto the porch. Both were wearing hazmat hoods and gloves now. They were carrying a large birdcage covered with a blanket. One of them motioned her to come closer.

She walked over to the birdcage. They quickly looked around to see if anyone was watching, then lifted up a corner of the blanket. Annie saw that they'd captured a number of owls. They were white and feathery. She had to admit they looked adorable. One of them stared mournfully at her.

"You're going home now," she said to it, feeling idiotic. "Safe travels." Bryce and Devon quickly dropped the blanket over the cage again, and hurried off to their vehicle.

Annie felt relieved. It looked like the owls would all be safely out of the attic before the trolley tour started. She met Dr. Sutton as she was going back into the Macklin House.

"They're such interesting birds," Dr. Sutton said happily. "I got some wonderful photos."

"Where are they taking them?" Annie asked.

"They'll release them in the foothills."

"That's a long way from here," Annie observed. "I wonder how they ended up in Macklin."

"Heat and drought, probably," said Dr. Sutton. "They live in trees. You have a lot of trees here." She gestured around the Macklin House grounds and the town square. "That would attract them."

"Then why would they go in the attic?" Annie asked her.

Dr. Sutton looked at the town square. The trolley, parked at the trolley stop, was directly in her line of sight. The stage was to her left, and the craft fair across the street was starting to get busy.

"When did all this start?" Dr. Sutton asked.

"The beginning of December," Annie said. "We have trolley tours every night. To see the Christmas lights in town."

"So there's a lot of people around, every night?"

"Well, yes," Annie answered.

"That would do it," said Dr. Sutton. "With crowds of people around, they wouldn't go back to their trees. They'd look for another nesting place. They found that hole into your attic, and that was where they went."

Annie was shocked. "Our trolley tour caused them to move into the Macklin House?" she stammered.

"Yes. That's exactly what happened."

Annie shook hands with Dr. Sutton and said good-bye in a daze. It was like dominoes falling. She'd started the trolley tour with the best of intentions. But the results were disastrous. She walked slowly back to her office to meet Ivan. He had the bill for the permit, the bill from Species Savior, and an estimate for repairs to the attic.

"It's not a pretty picture, ma'am," he said, holding his hand over his heart. He held up his phone calculator, showing the total. "I wasn't too far off. Fifty thousand, six hundred forty three dollars. I'll send this to your phone."

Annie pulled herself together. Don't cry, she told herself. You're the executive director. Don't cry. "Thanks, Ivan," she said. "I don't know what we would have done without you. When can you start on the repairs?"

"How about Monday?" he said. "Right after Christmas."

"I'll see you then," Annie told him. She closed the door to her office, spread out the bills on her desk, and pulled up Ivan's total on her phone. Only then did she burst into tears.

When you're twenty-eight years old, your life is crashing around you, and you're not speaking to your almost-boyfriend, what do you do?

You call your parents.

"Dad," Annie sobbed into her phone. "Everything is awful. Everything is ruined. We can't save the Macklin House. And it's all my fault."

"Slow down, honey," her father said on the other end of the line. "We'll figure it out. Stop crying and tell me what happened."

"We found a flock of owls in the attic. We had to remove them."

"These things happen. It's not the end of the world," her dad said.

"Yes, it is." Annie continued sobbing. "They were an endangered species. Ludwig's double-tailed owls. It cost a fortune."

"You found Ludwig's double-tailed owls in your attic?" Now her father was excited. "They're practically extinct. We used to have them up in the foothills when I was a kid, but I haven't seen one in years. How many were there? Did you get a picture?"

"DAD. It was awful. It's all my fault!" Annie cried. She could hear her parents talking. Her mother came on the line.

"Annie, it's not your fault! How can you think that?"

"We had to bring in an ornithologist," Annie explained through her tears. "Dr. Sutton. She said they'd been living in the trees around the property, but the trolley tour upset them so they moved into the attic at the Macklin House."

"Well, that's what birds do," said her mother. "They fly around. You weren't responsible. It's not like they were your pet owls and you let them loose."

"If I hadn't started the trolley tour, they'd still be in the trees. We wouldn't have had to get them out of the attic. We wouldn't have the *bill* for getting them out of the attic."

Her father came back on the line. "Annie," he said. "You're an extremely resourceful person. This is just a temporary setback. You'll figure out something. You know we love you."

"I know, Dad," she said. She caught her breath. "I'll see you on Christmas. I'm going to leave early, so I should be at your house by ten or eleven." She took a box of tissues out of her desk drawer and wiped her tears as she disconnected the call. It was comforting that her parents believed in her. But they didn't fully understand her problem.

They had been on track to earn fifty thousand dollars from the trolley tour and other donations. Half of what they needed for the deferred maintenance. Half of what they needed, to keep the Macklin House open.

Now they owed fifty thousand, six hundred forty-three dollars to Ivan because of the Ludwig's owls. That was going to wipe out everything they'd earned from the trolley.

They were right back where they'd started. They still needed one hundred thousand dollars.

Someone knocked on her office door. She got up and opened it. Jackson was standing there, fidgeting. He was holding his cartoon notebook.

Annie brightened up instantly. She had a soft spot for Jackson. Emma reminded her of herself, which wasn't necessarily all good. But Jackson—she supposed, in her heart, that he reminded her of Ben. "Hey, Jackson, what's up?" she asked.

He came over to her desk and set his notebook down with a flourish. "I couldn't afford to get you a Christmas present," he began. "So I drew this for you."

He opened the notebook to reveal a drawing of the Christmas trolley. It was done in his favorite cartoon style. The trolley had eyes, a big smile, and a load of waving passengers. Strings of Christmas lights formed a border around the picture. Underneath, he had penciled in "Macklin House Christmas Trolley Tour" in a jaunty script.

"Oh, Jackson!" Annie exclaimed, completely overcome. She started to cry again. "This is—this is the best Christmas present you could ever give me!" She hugged him, and wiped her eyes again. Maybe the Christmas trolley wasn't a *complete* disaster. Lots of good things had come out of it, including this amazing cartoon.

"And you know what?" she said. "I think we just found our logo for next year's trolley tour."

"Really?" Jackson said. "You really like it? You'd really make it the logo next year?"

She nodded. "I really will. It's perfect." She just couldn't tell him there might not be a next year. "And Jackson," she added. "After the trolley tour ends, I'd like to talk with you about drawing a coloring book for the Macklin House,"

"Oh, gosh!" he said. "Wait until I tell Emma! Wait until I tell Ben! Wait until I tell my mom!"

Annie's smile grew bigger. She knew it was ridiculous, but she had hope once again.

CHAPTER 39

December 24

IT WAS DECEMBER TWENTY-FOURTH, THE LAST DAY OF THE
Christmas trolley tours. Annie arrived at the Macklin House at eight
a.m., and ate a cup of vanilla yogurt for breakfast. She was wearing
the remaining Christmas sweater from her collection. It was one of
her favorites, and she'd deliberately saved it for the twenty-fourth. The
sweater had a black background dotted with small white stars. A space-
suited astronaut was exchanging Christmas gifts with an elongated
green blob with arms, legs, and two eyeballs on stalks. They were standing on a strip of red, presumably the planet Mars. An oversized blob
of blue and green, presumably the planet Earth, hung in the sky above
them.

Annie had hoped she'd be wearing it to celebrate. Instead, the
sweater was probably going to be a reminder of her failure to keep the
Macklin House operating. The trolley tours had been exciting. They'd

brought out the best in Macklin. But it was an inescapable fact that the Macklin House was going to have to close.

It wasn't just the Macklin House, she admitted. She felt like a failure in her personal life, too. She loved Ben Grover. But their paths in life were even further away than they'd been in eighth grade, and nothing was going to bring those paths back together.

Elaine Gilpin poked her head into Annie's office around ten o'clock. Elaine looked like she was en route to brunch at a five-star hotel, instead of champagne and hors d'oeuvres at an office party. She was wearing a red blazer with subtle silver threads, over a shimmering silver tank top and gray pants. She had a red-and-silver scarf artfully tied around her neck, accented with large sterling silver earrings. Annie had admired them once, and Elaine had offhandedly confided that they were from Tiffany's in San Francisco. She'd offered to pick up a pair for Annie the next time she was in the city, but Annie had gracefully declined. Tiffany's just wasn't in her budget.

"Annie!" Elaine said in an upbeat voice. "It's time for the gift exchange!"

Every year, the docents held a gift exchange in the Macklin House's octagonal conservatory. It was one of Annie's favorite rooms. The conservatory was attached to the rear of the house by a short passageway, and its huge glass windows looked out over the gardens. They always set up another Christmas tree in the center of the room, and the lights from the tree shone brilliantly through the glass at night.

Annie welcomed its fresh pine scent as she joined her docents. There were thirty of them, both women and men. She'd brought bayberry-scented candles to give to all of them, tying bows of red-and-white striped ribbon on each candle. It was hard to find a unisex gift for a group like this, but she'd reasoned that most people liked candles, and they could always pass them on if they didn't. She'd also brought something for the gift exchange, a box of Paula's cookies. She'd applied the same logic—most people liked cookies, and if not, they could donate them to the break room. The scent of the candles mingled with the fresh pine of the tree. Annie thought the room smelled very holiday-like. She laid her candles out on an oak sideboard against one of the windows.

She expected that the gift exchange would take her mind off her problems, at least for a while. But as the docents gathered, she felt even worse. Most were retired people who loved history and shared Annie's enthusiasm for the old mansion. She looked around at the group. They were all so knowledgeable and so dedicated. And the Macklin House gave them a sense of purpose, a way to pass their knowledge on. She was going to have to take all this away, in about seven hours.

The docents were drinking champagne and mingling. Elaine had brought a silver jingle bell on a red velvet cord that matched her outfit. Annie would have bet the jingle bell was also from Tiffany's. Elaine started to ring the bell. This got everyone's attention.

"Before we start," Elaine said, "Annie—as our executive director, would you like to say a few words?"

It was the last thing Annie felt like doing, but she steeled herself.

"I think this past year," she began, "has been the best of times, and the worst of times, for us. The worst of times, because we learned that the Macklin House needs major repairs that we can't ignore. The best of times because all of you do an outstanding job of showing the Macklin House to our visitors. Day after day, you bring history alive for them. You teach them what it was like to live in the Victorian era. You make them feel like they were a part of Philip Macklin's family, living in this house and this town." At this point, she was trying not to cry. "You're the most wonderful docents any museum could possibly have, and I thank you all." Annie gestured toward the sideboard, and continued, "I have a little something for each of you, but it doesn't nearly reflect how much I appreciate and love every one of you."

Elaine started clapping, and everyone joined in. Many of them raised their champagne glasses, calling, "Here's to Annie!" Trying to keep the gift exchange on schedule, Elaine announced, "Now it's time for presents!" Annie was grateful for Elaine's timely intervention. She wasn't sure she could have said anything further at that point.

"Here's how it works," Elaine explained. She waved a sheet of paper. "I found this on the internet and it sounds great." She held out a silver bowl she'd taken from the sideboard. Annie winced—only in rare cases were the docents supposed to touch the furnishings—but kept her mouth shut. "Everybody takes a number." She started passing the bowl around. "Whoever is number one, picks a package from under the tree. Number two can take that present, or choose a new one. Number three has to pick a gift in red paper. Number four has to pick a present with a green bow. Number five can choose a present, but then has to name the first ten presidents in order or give it back." At this, two of the docents looked alarmed, conferred briefly, and then exchanged numbers. "Number six …"

Annie was totally confused by then, but the docents were nodding and looking at their numbers expectantly. She had number fifteen. She could only hope that Elaine would repeat the instructions when the time came.

The gift exchange produced socks, DVDs of holiday movies, an omelet pan, and a pair of red-and-green suspenders. It continued on through tubes of pine-scented hand cream, a bottle of Chardonnay, and Annie's box of cookies. Elaine finally called out, "Number fifteen!" Annie waved her hand in the air. "That's me!" she said. Everyone cheered. By now, they'd emptied a few bottles of champagne. "Go, Annie," she heard. "Pick a good one! No more socks!"

"What do I do?" she asked Elaine. "I forgot the instructions."

Dramatically, Elaine announced, "Number fifteen has to pick a present with a pickled purple bow!"

"A what?" Annie said.

Elaine pulled out her reading glasses and looked at the instructions again. "A *pink* and purple bow," she corrected.

"There it is!" said Grace Iwamoto, pointing to a large package under the tree. It did indeed have a pink and purple bow. Annie suspected this was a setup. She picked up the box and carried it over to a table. She pulled the ribbon off and opened her gift.

It was a Christmas sweater! It was a red pullover with a large white building on the front, flanked by two Christmas trees. It was the Macklin House.

"Oh, my God," Annie said. "This unbelievable. Who—who knitted this?"

The docents glanced at each other. Five of the women raised their hands. "We all did," they said.

Several of the men raised their hands. "We worked out the design," they said.

"I told them what size you wore," said Grace Iwamoto. "You left one of your cardigans hanging on your chair one day when you went over to the hardware store."

"And the rest of us chipped in and bought the yarn," said Elaine. "We all think you're the best executive director we've ever had. We wanted you to have something really special."

Annie clutched the sweater to her heart, and now she did start to cry, but only for a moment. She still had some champagne left. She picked up her glass and raised it high.

"Let's have a toast!" she said. All the docents raised their glasses.

"To the Macklin House!" she said.

CHAPTER 40

December 24

BY THE TIME THE GIFT EXCHANGE FINISHED UP, IT WAS almost two o'clock. Annie ate a turkey wrap at her desk for lunch. She didn't want to take a chance on running into Ben at the café. She carefully folded her new sweater and put it back in its box. She'd decided to wear it the next day, on Christmas. Her parents would love it. She put the box in the bottom drawer of her desk for safekeeping.

There were three more presents hidden in the drawer. She'd bought Jackson and Emma each a copy of the latest superhero movie. The other package was for Ben. Annie had splurged on a bottle of Benromach single malt whiskey for his collection. She'd ordered it from a wine broker after spending several nights researching Scottish distilleries online. Viewing the accompanying scenes of castles and Celtic ruins, she'd started fantasizing about a honeymoon in the highlands.

Right now, she felt like taking the bottle home and drinking it herself. Of course, she knew she would never do that. She'd give it to him and wish him well.

She was just finishing her lunch when Dave came in.

"I was going over the trolley, Annie, and I need to show you something," he said.

"Is it okay?" she asked quickly. This was the last thing she needed, a problem with the trolley.

"Oh, it's nothing that serious, but I want you to see it so you know what you're dealing with," he replied.

Annie obediently followed him out to the parking lot, where, for some reason, the trolley was parked as far away from the building as possible. It looked fine to her. What was Dave worried about?

Dave opened the engine compartment and pointed to some hoses at one side. "See those? Those are your radiator hoses for the cooling system."

"Okay," Annie said.

"And this is your valve cooling fan, and your air filter." Dave launched into an explanation of the cooling system, the brakes, and the internal wiring, none of which made any sense to Annie at all. Every few minutes, she tried to wrap up the conversation, without success. Dave seemed to find the engine endlessly fascinating, and continued to point out parts that "would need to be replaced in another five thousand miles." She had never heard Dave talk so much. Amber was right. Guys loved engines.

Annie listened patiently, but time passed, and he didn't seem any closer to a conclusion. "So what are you telling me?" she asked finally.

Dave glanced at his watch. "Well, there are several things that will need attention before next year. I'll write them down for you. Guess I'd better be getting back to the store. See you tonight, Annie." He looked quite satisfied as he headed back across the street.

"Too bad Dave doesn't know there won't *be* a next year," Annie thought as she walked back to her office.

Meanwhile, at Meyers' Hardware, unusual things had been going on all day. Most of the customers were too preoccupied with their last-minute holiday shopping to notice that Tim from the post office had delivered six large cardboard boxes since the store opened. Ben and Emma and Jackson, however, were keeping a close watch on them. Around two o'clock, Dave gave them a thumbs-up, turned the sign on the door to "Closed," and walked across the town square to the Macklin House.

Ben took a pair of binoculars out of one of the display cases. The three of them followed Dave out the door and stood on the sidewalk next to the snowman, who was currently attired in a plaid hunting jacket and a heavy cap with earmuffs. Ben trained the binoculars across the town square to the far side of the Macklin House's parking lot. He zoomed in on the trolley.

A few minutes later, Dave and Annie came out of the Macklin House. "They're out of the building," Ben reported.

"Is it time?" asked Emma.

"Not quite," said Ben, still looking through the binoculars. "Dave's opening the engine! Here we go! Remember, we've got half an hour at most!"

They ran back into the store and pulled a dolly loaded with the cardboard boxes out of the storeroom. Casually, the three of them walked across the town square and up to the front of the house. With the trolley parked at the far end of the visitors' lot, they were hidden from Annie and Dave. Ben pulled the dolly around to the side of the house, and pointed to a door opening onto the porch.

"Those are the back stairs," he explained. "They used to go to the servants' quarters. You know where these need to go. On the second floor, in front."

Each of them picked up a box and started quickly up the steep stairs. The boxes were a little unwieldy for Emma and Jackson, and Emma started to drop hers. Ben, coming up the stairs behind her, managed to catch it in time.

"It's not that heavy," she panted. "It's just awkward." Balancing his own box with one arm, Ben helped Emma maneuver her box up to the second floor. With the first three boxes safely hidden in one of the front bedrooms, they carried up their second load.

Back they went across the town square, pulling the empty dolly. Ben unlocked the store and they shoved the dolly back into the storeroom just as Dave returned.

"All clear," said Dave. "We're lucky she doesn't know anything about engines. After the first five minutes, I was making everything up."

"Okay, guys," Ben said to Emma and Jackson. "You know what you have to do."

They nodded eagerly.

"We won't let you down, Ben," Jackson said.

They high-fived all around. Then, they heard a knock on the door. Ignoring the "Closed" sign, a man was peering through one of the front windows.

Dave unlocked the door. It was Ray Martinez.

"We're out of penguins," Dave said.

"I don't want a penguin," Ray replied. "I want that deer."

Ben and Emma and Jackson looked around. There were plenty of deer—reindeer lights, reindeer mugs, reindeer ornaments, reindeer-shaped beer can holders. "Which deer?" asked Ben.

"The one on the wall," said Ray. "I made a deal with Sonia. She gets her penguins, I get a deer."

Ben looked around some more. All the walls had at least one reindeer-themed item. "Which deer?" he asked again.

"The one by the portable spa," Ray said helpfully.

"He means Rudolph," Jackson and Emma shrieked together. "He's going to buy Rudolph! We get our commission!"

Back at the Macklin House, Annie had nothing left to distract her from the dismal numbers on her spreadsheet as the day wore on. It was five o'clock, and the afternoon sky was fading into twilight. Soon, the holiday lights would be coming on all over Macklin. It was Christmas Eve, and Brent Preston had announced that the city was sponsoring a party in the town square that evening, with music and free hot dogs. She could already hear the sounds of the first partygoers arriving across the street. It would have been a fabulous celebration for the last night of the Christmas trolley, if they hadn't been so woefully short of their goal.

She heard a knock on the front door of the Macklin House. Danielle and all the docents had left, so she went to answer it. She could see Tim, in his postal uniform, through the glass inserts next to the door. Confused, Annie opened the door. Tim usually delivered the mail earlier in the day.

"Hi, Annie," he said. "Got a certified letter for you, if you'll sign here." He sounded out of breath. "It actually came in yesterday, and I brought it over to deliver it. But this guy in a hazmat suit walked out of the building and said, 'Don't come any closer.' So, I took it back to my mail truck. I've seen enough TV movies to know that if a guy in a hazmat suit says 'Don't come any closer,' you don't come any closer." He paused to catch his breath. "I wanted to get it to you earlier today, but they put me on a route on the other side of town. I couldn't get here until now." He looked around the room warily. "Is everything okay?"

"We had some endangered owls in the attic," Annie told him. "Everything's fine now. Thanks for bringing this letter."

Tim lingered by her desk. "It looks important," he said.

Annie glanced briefly at the return address on the envelope. Something called Dodge Dylan Robinson, which sounded like a law firm. "It's probably the official notice from the county that the Macklin House has to close due to code violations," she said.

"But you'll get it fixed, won't you?" Tim asked anxiously. "We're counting on you, Annie."

"I hope so," said Annie, although she really didn't have much hope. As Tim strode off toward his mail truck, she looked around at the Macklin House one more time. The Christmas lights and holly made it look festive and welcoming. Annie thought despairingly that she had never seen the house look lovelier. And it was all going to come to an end. *Along with her sort-of romance with Ben,* but she pushed those thoughts aside. It was bad enough thinking about the Macklin House.

Sighing, she steeled herself to open the envelope. She was going to have to give a speech to the crowd tonight, and she might as well deliver all the bad news at once. She opened the envelope. A formal letter fell out, along with—a check?—and a handwritten note.

The letterhead read, "Dodge Dylan Robinson LLC, Venture Capital." The letter read:

"Dear Ms. Mulvaney,

At Dodge Dylan Robinson, our mission is not only to invest in the future, but to build upon the past. We pride ourselves on partnering with non-profits who show entrepreneurship, such as you have done with your Christmas trolley. We were impressed with your initiative, and are pleased to present the Macklin House Trust with the enclosed one hundred thousand dollar donation from our charitable foundation. This is for your use in making needed repairs to the Macklin House." It was signed, "Ryan Robinson, Managing Partner."

The handwritten note read:

"Annie,

I feel like I know you even though we've never met. My Stanford roommate Ben Grover has been texting and emailing me ever since he moved back to Macklin. All he talks about is how amazing you are and all the work you're doing with that historic house, and how it's going to be a center for the whole town. I knew he'd never shut up until we made a donation. Ben really seems to have found himself in Macklin with that Christmas trolley and all his new friends. He seems pretty into you, so I hope you don't break his heart again. I want a tour when you get all the work done!" It was signed, "Ryan."

Stunned, Annie looked at the check for several minutes to make sure she was reading the amount correctly. She read the note a second time. *I hope you don't break his heart again?*

"I broke his heart?" she said aloud. "He cares about me? He broke *my* heart. Maybe we broke each other's hearts. Maybe we can—put them back together again?"

There was only one way to answer that question. She grabbed the check and both letters and ran for the door. "I've got to find Ben!" And she raced out of the Macklin House, without even stopping to turn off the lights.

CHAPTER 41

December 24

SHE DIDN'T HAVE TO GO FAR. HE WAS STANDING ON THE front walkway at the bottom of the porch steps, waiting for her. Ben felt his heart pounding. Was his plan going to work? It *had* to work.

Annie threw her arms around him, and waved the check in front of him. "Ben! You did it! You saved the Macklin House!"

Ben was smiling from ear to ear as he hugged her back. "No, Annie!" he said. "*You* saved the Macklin House! You inspired everyone with the Christmas trolley. It brought everybody together, and made us remember all the good things about Macklin."

"The trolley brought us together," said Annie. She gazed into Ben's eyes and gulped. "I love you, Ben," she said. "I know you're going to San Francisco, but I have to say it. I wish we'd never had that fight on the field trip."

"I love you, too, Annie," Ben said, stroking her hair. "I had to come back to Macklin to find that out. You're the love of my life. You always were."

"I know," Annie continued, stumbling over the words, "I know I said I'd never kiss you until snow fell in Macklin, but ..."

Ben gazed upward briefly and then looked back into Annie's eyes. "That could happen," he said, as silvery white flakes began to fall from above. It was falling into their hair. It was falling on their eyelashes. It was falling on their shoulders. It was piling up at their feet.

Annie looked around in confusion. "It's ... it's snowing?" she said. She heard giggles from above and glanced up. Emma and Jackson stood on the balcony. They were gleefully pouring a confetti-like substance over the railing onto Ben and Annie. Empty cardboard boxes were strewn around at their feet. "What *is* this stuff?"

"Artificial snow," said Ben. "You can find anything on the internet. But ... it's snowing in Macklin ... so I can kiss you." He pulled her close and they kissed. Many years of longing went into that kiss.

Annie pulled back and felt her eyes start to fill with tears. This wasn't some romantic fantasy. They had to face facts. "This can't work for us, Ben. You're going away. You've got your dream job. It's what you've always wanted. I can't take that away from you."

"I *thought* it was everything I wanted," Ben replied. "Except I realized that what I've always wanted was you. I want you in my life. Forever."

"I want *you* in my life forever. But you're going to San Francisco. I'll be here in Macklin putting the Macklin House back into shape."

"Well—about that," Ben said, grinning. He reached into his pocket and pulled out a business card. He handed it to Annie.

She read it slowly. "Ben Grover, Vice President, Business Development. Jupiter Computer Systems—Macklin Branch? 205 Birch Street, Macklin, California?"

"We're going to open an office here," he explained. "We'll have a software development hub. I sold Ed Waters on the idea. Jupiter's a tech company. What do tech companies need most?"

"Uh—programmers?" guessed Annie.

"Electricity!" Ben said enthusiastically. "And Macklin has the lowest electric rates in the state. We'll lease space in some of those empty warehouses down by the river. Then we'll put in servers and convert them into modern tech office space. I've already got authorization to hire five people for the Denton project, and more to follow as we get more business."

"You'll be bringing jobs back to Macklin!" Annie exclaimed.

"I want to start a training program at the community college," Ben continued. He was getting more exuberant by the minute. "How to code, advanced programming, how to work with clients. So we can hire people from right here in Macklin. And—internships for high school kids. We can't let our elves get too bored."

Annie was amazed. "You—you thought of all this to help the town," she said. "You really *do* want to stay in Macklin."

"With you," Ben said. He reached into his pocket again as the artificial snow crunched under his feet. "This may not be real snow, but my love for you is *completely* real."

He dropped to one knee and held out a small box covered in red velvet. Annie gasped as he opened the box. "It's my grandmother's ring. Annie, will you marry me?"

"Oh, my God, yes, yes, yes!" she cried. He stood up, and they fell into each other's arms. He put the ring on Annie's finger. "It's the most gorgeous ring I've ever seen!" she exclaimed.

They kissed again. They heard clapping. All the customers lined up for the final Christmas trolley ride had been watching them. This was far more interesting than the regular entertainment. Annie looked at the crowd and saw all their friends clapping and cheering for them—Dave and Darlene, the Martinez family with their two daughters home for Christmas, Paula and Cammie, Stacey and Adam, Brent and Natalie Preston, Allan Tolbert, Chief Mike Newton, Grace Iwamoto and her friends from the senior center, Chrissie and Charlie Belmont, and Angie Morgan, with Peanut in his basket. Even Peanut seemed happy. For once, he barked instead of growling.

"She said yes!" Ben shouted. "And I'm staying in Macklin!"

A voice cut through the cheering. "There you have it! True love triumphs in tiny Macklin, California, home of the annual Christmas Trolley Tour of Lights. And you'll see those lights for yourselves on our news roundup at ten o'clock. This is Cindy Nguyen reporting live from Macklin, where I'm standing in front of the world-famous historic Macklin House!"

Annie and Ben turned and saw Cindy and her camera crew filming from the stage. They waved. Cindy waved back. They were getting their free publicity after all.

Annie managed to climb up on the stage and grab a microphone. "And we've got wonderful news!" she shouted. "We've just received a one hundred thousand dollar grant from Dodge Dylan Robinson, a venture capital fund. Their letter says they gave us this grant because of our entrepreneurial spirit! This is because of all of you who've helped to make the trolley tour a success! We did it! The Macklin House will keep going!"

The crowd cheered again. Jackson and Emma, returned from the balcony, jumped up and down. "OH!" Ben exclaimed. "I forgot the best part about my job. I get four weeks' vacation a year!"

"Four weeks?"

"Yes! I can keep driving the Christmas trolley!"

"The Christmas trolley!" Annie gasped. "I almost forgot! It's time for the six-thirty tour to leave! We need to get everybody on board."

"Come with me!" said Ben. "It's our last chance to see the famous Macklin holiday lights!"

"Why not!" exclaimed Annie. "We're celebrating tonight!" Ben climbed into the driver's seat of the Christmas trolley, and she took a seat in the first row. The passengers started to board. They shook Ben's hand and hugged Annie.

Someone called out, "Are we invited to the wedding?" The rest of them immediately began chanting: "Invite us to your wedding! Invite us to your wedding!"

Annie and Ben both started to laugh.

"Yes, you're all invited to the wedding!" Annie cried.

THE CHRISTMAS TROLLEY

Ben rang the bell, and the Christmas trolley pulled away from the curb. Annie turned back to look at the Macklin House. White icicle lights hung from the eaves, and garlands of colored lights wrapped around the columns. Wreaths of pine and holly adorned the front door and all the windows. The old mansion looked warm, inviting, and incredibly beautiful.

"And I know *just* where we're going to hold our wedding reception!" she said.

ABOUT THE AUTHOR

Marta Mahoney was born in Detroit, but she has spent most of her life in California. From an early age, she wanted to be a writer, and graduated from Stanford with a degree in English. Life intervened, and she pursued a business career instead. Now she is fulfilling her dream. This is her first novel, and she hopes you've enjoyed it.